BOOK 1

SEA OF RED

GARY A. OSBORN

COVER BY CHARLOTTE HORLOCK

NEWMAN SPRINGS PUBLISHING
320 Broad Street
Red Bank, NJ 07701

First originally published by Newman Springs Publishing 2019

ISBN 978-1-64531-498-1 (Paperback)
ISBN 978-1-64531-565-0 (Hardcover)
ISBN 978-1-64531-499-8 (Digital)

Printed in the United States of America

Happy Birthday

Kiyah

Gary Osborn

To Linda
and to Charlotte Horlock,
who inspired me to write

CHAPTER 1

JOHN WALKED UP TO THE ticket booth. *Looks like we could have a full house.* Just what he needed to happen.

"Hey, John, should be a great game."

"Hi, Dennis. Let's hope so." He handed Dennis $5 and received the ticket. The fund-raiser table was directly ahead after passing the ticket booth. He went over and paid for some tickets for a drawing.

The band played pregame music. He acknowledged a few other people who walked by. He wanted to make sure a lot of people saw him here. Tonight could be the night.

The ramp leading to the bleachers was new. *It's about time*, he thought. He couldn't believe they finally replaced those wooden bleachers with aluminum ones. He wished he brought a seat cushion.

The cold from the bleacher didn't take long to penetrate his pants when he sat. He gazed the field and saw the Corvettes parking near the end zone nearest the entryway. They were there to transport the homecoming queen and her court. Their parents were in a separate group.

This is working out. He smiled at the thought. The band marched off the field, and the growing crowd cheered as the football team entered the field for pregame warm-ups.

Their maroon jerseys with gold pants stood out against the green grass on the field. He was always surprised at how green the grass was in late October.

The opposing team got off the school bus parked on the other side of the field, and they crowded in the bleachers. Their blue jerseys with white pants seemed out of place in comparison. The scoreboard clock started the countdown until game time. It was at twenty-eight minutes, so he dared to go to the bathroom and needed to hurry to reclaim his seat. He acknowledged a few other people along the way. The smell of the popcorn was enticing, and he gave into temptation before he returned. He was happy when the seat was still there. The clock was down to thirteen minutes. There she is. He watched the auburn-haired cheerleader, and he couldn't help but focus on her. She always had a smile on her face, and he admired her graceful moves. She seemed like a woman among the rest of the girls. She had to be at least ten years younger than him, and he wondered if she was as mature as she looked. He turned his focus to the crowd. He smiled when he saw it.

"Looks like tonight is the night," he mumbled to himself.

Ted Anderson and his wife, Marissa, were dressed in their finest. They would escort their daughter Megan to the center of the field at halftime, where she would be crowned homecoming queen. He rubbed his hands together as to warm them, but it was more from excitement than the cold. This had been in his plans for a long time. The homecoming floats started being driven around the field, and the various classes cheered. The freshmen float got the loudest ovation, and then seniors were a close second. That seemed like the usual pattern every year. The floats departed and parked behind the end zones. The kids roaming the sidelines went to investigate. The referees entered the field with five minutes to go. The crowd filled in around his seat. He acknowledged a few more people. Many knew him as he was their insurance man. Farmers Guild Insurance was his employer. His small office was in Reese, Michigan, and he dealt with many farmers. Tonight he planned on using his contacts to his advantage. It was time to move on. Ever since Evelyn left him, he felt no need to stay in the area. She had taken all his assets and ran off with another guy. He had thought things were great.

The crowd roared when the team ran through the "Rocket" banner and onto the field, taking him away from his thoughts. The cheerleaders followed and went to the front of the bleachers. They were directly in front of him, and then the PA announcer said, "Welcome to Rocket Football. Tonight we welcome the Unionville-Sebewaing Patriots for the 16th Annual Sugar Bowl."

John heard the crowd erupt from across the field in response.

The PA announcer followed up with, "I'd also like to welcome all the returning alumni for homecoming. There will be a dance in the gymnasium after the game."

John watched the band march in formation across the field.

Then he heard, "Ladies and gentlemen, please stand as the Rocket Marching Band plays our national anthem."

John stood and put his hand to his heart. He gazed at the flag and mouthed the words to the song.

The crowd cheered at the conclusion, and they all sat. He watched the band march off the field. The PA announcer then acknowledged the cheerleaders and then started calling off their name as each girl did a cheer.

He smiled when Mary Brunell was acknowledged. *I wonder if she is on Facebook*, he thought to himself.

The band marched off the field, and he watched them scurry to the section in the bleachers. The teams huddled near their respective sidelines and separated with a cheer. The kickoff teams for both teams got in formation. The kicker for Reese advanced and booted the ball. John watched the ball arc high in the sky and knew it was a good kick. The Patriots receiver fielded the ball, and after twenty yards he was tackled. John settled in and watched the game, but the thought of his plan kept into his mind. It consumed him since the day he visited the Spencer's house. They had asked him over to talk insurance and were so eager to show him their assets he could think of nothing else. They had made it tempting, as they didn't seem too concerned about security, as they led him room to room, showing off items to have insured. They had to be the richest people in the area. With his plan, after he took the items, they would be reimbursed, and he would sell off what he planned on taking. Tonight their whole family was at the game, as was most of Reese.

Reese was ahead 7–6 nearing the end of the first quarter. He got up and went to the exit steps he had sat close to. He dodged some kids as he walked behind the darkened area behind the bleachers. The concessions building came into view. The smell of popcorn popping was in the area. He entered one of the lines and gradually moved to the front.

"Hi, John, what can I get you?"

"Oh, hi, Sarah, I need a dog and a hot chocolate."

She turned and told another volunteer his order, then turned to him and said, "That will be a $1.50, John."

He handed her $2 and told her to "keep the change."

"Thanks."

He moved to the open space between the stand and the bleachers and saw the teams switch sides on the field as the first quarter was over. The hotdog tasted good, and he was tempted to get another, but instead he sipped his hot chocolate. When he finished, he headed to the men's restroom. After he relieved himself, he washed his hands and took a moment to look in the mirror. He still couldn't see the resemblance to Leonardo DiCaprio that many had commented he looked like. But he was happy with his looks. He left the restroom and stood outside in the darkened area near the exit gates.

Okay, John, this is it, he thought to himself and exited into the dark parking lot. He went toward his car parked a few rolls away. *There it is*, he thought as he walked to his car.

John searched his pockets for the car remote and unlocked the door. The red interior matched the outside color. He stepped on the brake and pushed the Start button. The push-button Start was something he had a problem getting used to. He will still reach for keys and remembered he only had the remote. The doors locked when he got out. The Nissan Altima ran great, so he just had to get used to it. There was a car approaching on the road. He watched it drive past. When the road was clear of traffic, he started to the Andersons' place. He figured it would take him around ten minutes to get there. He kept glancing in his rearview mirror and felt a surge of panic when any car lights were approaching.

"Okay, John, calm down," he said to himself.

Soon he was outside the village of Reese, and the streetlights were far and between on the country roads. He slowed down and saw the reflector lights on both sides of the driveway and drove between them. It led to the long paved driveway to the house. The woods seemed to swallow his lights.

It looks so different at night than it does in the daylight, he thought as he reduced speed with the upcoming curves. The clock in his car showed him it took eight minutes to arrive at the house. There were a few lights on in the two-story brown brick home. The windows were huge and wrapped around the home. He reached under his seat until he felt the box he was looking for and lifted it in view. It held blue surgical gloves, and he slipped them on. He grabbed a small gym bag out of his back seat and got out the car. He felt for his key remote in his pocket and shut the door. He tried the side door of the garage, and it opened. He waited inside the garage until his eyes adjusted to the darkness. He reached in and pulled out his cell phone and used it to help light the way to the entrance door to the house. He then silenced it and put it back in his pocket. He turned the doorknob and wasn't surprised that it wasn't locked. The door squeaked when he tried to open it, so he pushed it open a little bit at a time until he was able to get in and then slowly closed it. He was in the kitchen, and when he viewed the refrigerator, he felt a hunger pain as the popcorn didn't satisfy it.

"Not now," he said to himself and felt for the light switch. He searched through the drawers and pantry, and his confidence was rewarded when he found a big wad of $100 bills in a cookie jar located on a bottom shelf of the pantry. He stuffed them in his bag and moved to the dining room. He noticed a new cabinet in the corner. It was as tall as he was when he got near it. It held dishes and knickknacks, and that didn't interest him. He exited the dining room and saw the long curved stairwell to the second floor. A glance at his wristwatch. "Oh shit," he mumbled to himself.

Twenty minutes had passed, so he decided to go up to the bedrooms. He smiled at the thought of Mrs. Anderson showing him her jewelry and how much it would cost to cover their worth. He went right to her jewelry box and emptied it in his bag. He noticed there were drawers that were in one side of the bed. He almost laughed when he saw a vibrator roll toward him when he opened one of them. He hurried and went into their daughter Megan's room. He didn't find anything, but he was tempted to take her diary. He exited that room and got out on the balcony. There was another room at the end of the balcony that he hadn't been shown before. He looked at his watch and decided to do a quick check of the room. He was surprised to see a long hallway ahead of him when he opened the door. There was hesitation when he saw a light from another room shinning on the wall at the end of the hallway. There hadn't been another car in the driveway or garage, so his fear of finding someone subsided.

This isn't a good idea, entered his mind as he crept closer to the end of the hallway. He slowly looked around the end of the hallway, and fear and panic entered his thoughts. There was a bank of monitors along the wall. They were obviously for video cameras.

"What the fuck," he said as he walked closer to the monitors.

"Watch your language, pretty boy!"

His body reacted in shock at the sound of her voice. He turned to see an elderly woman who used a cane to support herself, but his eye soon focused on the gun in her hand.

"Don't move! You are in deep shit." She waited a few seconds and then said with a smile, "Excuse my language."

CHAPTER 2

JOHN COULDN'T TAKE HIS EYE off the gun. *What the hell can I say?*

She looked at him. "Drop the bag and kick it to me."

He lowered it carefully and nudged it to her.

She turned her cane upside down, and she snagged the bag with the handle. She kept her eyes on him and pulled the bag up.

"Put your hands up and turn around. I advise you to stay put. I am not going to tell you I am a good shot, but I will show you if you decide to try me."

He felt his fear rising now that he couldn't see the gun. He fought an urge to run when he heard her unzip his gym bag.

"A nice haul. Did you really need my sister's jewelry? "Now I want you to slowly drop to your knees and put your hands behind your back."

He did what he was told. He heard her open a drawer.

"Don't think about running unless you want to see the face of God."

He felt the cold steel of handcuffs being snapped around his left wrist and soon around the right. She tugged on them as a signal for him to stand up. He struggled but got up.

She moved close to his ear. "Where are your car keys?"

He nodded. "It is actually a remote to open the doors, and it is in my right pants pockets."

He heard the sound on tape being removed from a roll and felt a strip over his mouth before he could say anything.

"Walk into that bathroom. I need a few things."

She shut the door after he entered. It was a half bath with a toilet and sink and a mirror that was flat against the wall. He pulled on it, but it was anchored in the wall. He looked into the mirror.

You are a dumb son of bitch, he thought when he returned his gaze to the mirror.

The look in her eye worried him. She might be unstable, and he couldn't think of an option out of this mess.

He felt the urge to panic when she returned and covered his face with a hood. He focused on breathing slowly through his nose. She grabbed his arm and directed him slowly through the house. He felt the chill of being outside and heard the garage door open.

"That is a nice car you have. You must be a successful thief—well, you were until tonight."

She led him on the driveway then he felt the grass.

"I advise you to take a piss. It might be a while before you get another chance. Do you want to?"

It might get the handcuffs off, so he nodded yes. He then felt her grab his zipper and pull it down. He wasn't ready when she grabbed his penis and pulled it out. He felt the breeze enter his pants.

"Hurry up," she said.

He strained, and he finally started. When he was finished, she grabbed hold of him and put in back in his pants. Christ, that hurt. He tried not to show the discomfort. She zipped him and then reached in the right pocket and got his car remote. He panicked when he heard the trunk open.

"Cooperate and you might survive," she said as she led him to the back of the car. She had him sit on the open ledge of the trunk. She pushed him in, and he felt helpless when she tied his feet.

"You need to stay quiet, pretty boy, or what will happen to you won't be pretty."

The trunk was slammed shut, and his fear overwhelmed him. *Calm down*, he repeated in his thoughts.

The car was started, and he felt it move down the driveway. I need to remember everything about this drive.

The car turned right, and he started to count to try and estimate the distance between each turn. He continued, but there were many turns, and he was losing hope of any recall.

She pulled in and stopped, and he then heard the sounds of a gas pump. The gas lid open, and soon the gas started flowing. He was tempted to try and kick the hood of the trunk but decided it useless unless he heard the sounds of other people. He returned focus to his breathing. It was getting stuffy in the trunk. The breathing through a hood with his nose was becoming increasingly difficult.

So this is when I am going to die. That thought actually calmed him down. The constant jarring was killing his arms. He tried to change positions, but it caused more pain then where he was at. He was drained, and fatigue was causing him to lose focus. The steady sound and rhythm of the wheels had him in a daze. He was caught by surprise when he felt the cool breeze after the trunk was opened.

A woman's voice said, "I think you've had enough. It is time to get you out of there."

He felt a hand start to pull on his arm. He sat up and let his legs dangle outside the trunk. Fear gripped him. It was very quiet. He knew he wasn't near a city. "You sit there, and I'll be right back. There is nowhere to run."

He heard her walk away. *Yeah, like I can run*, he thought.

He turned his head in the direction of a knock on a door. He then heard voices but couldn't understand what was being said.

Maybe there is hope if someone else is involved, he couldn't help thinking.

He hoped she would return soon because after sweating in the stuffy trunk, the cool breeze was beginning to chill him.

The rustle of trees by the breeze made him realize he was in a wooded area. *I need to try and stand*, he thought as his legs were cramping. He tried to edge forward but realized it wasn't going to work without help. *I never thought I would think this, but I hope the police are looking for me. Get real*, he thought of their chances of finding him now. Kidnapped by an elderly woman during a robbery? Who would believe him, if they did rescue him? He turned to the voices as they approached. The women's voices grew louder, and he knew there was more than one. One of them gasped, then said, "What the hell did you do to him, Joyce? He looks like a packaged sausage."

"Thanks for using my name, Connie."

"You both settle down," another voice said. "Let's get him to the house."

"How do you want to do it? Let him walk or the wheelchair?" he heard Joyce say.

"The wheelchair could be hard to push on this dirt. Cut the tape of his legs and let him walk."

"We know who you are, John. Make no attempt to escape or hurt one of my friends. That understood?"

John nodded his head to acknowledge.

They grabbed both of his legs and then cut the tape. Then grabbed his arm and slowly eased him off the car and on to the ground.

He bent his left leg and then the right one to try and get some circulation in them. One held his arm and gently led him away. He almost fell after a short distance. *God, I need this hood off,* he thought. The farther he went, the more difficult it became to breathe through his nose. He tried to keep panic away and focus on staying on pace with them.

"John, we are here. You will be walking up a ramp, and there are a few turns," he heard Joyce say.

The long journey up the ramp taxed him. He was getting exhausted. A door opened, and he felt a rush of warm air. They led him in a room.

"Where do you want to put him?" asked Connie.

"In the wheelchair," responded Joyce.

He felt the chair when he brushed by it. They slowly sat him in the chair.

He panicked when he heard a voice say, "Let's get him ready."

Someone lifted the arm sleeve on his shirt, and before he could react, he felt a needle enter his arm, and soon he lost consciousness.

CHAPTER 3

THE SLOW AND STEADY SOUND of a fan entered his mind. His senses told him he was in a bed. A dull headache began to strengthen. He tried to focus his thoughts.

Where am I? he thought. The panic of that thought caused him to open his eyes. The light hurt, and he had to close them and open them gradually. He sat up quickly when he recognized he was in his bedroom. A look down and he realized he was naked.

"What the fuck?"

With effort, he sat on the edge of the bed. The headache caused him to put his head in his hands for support.

"Hello," he shouted out when he started to remember the events of the night before. He was tense as he waited for a response, but none came. He stood up and struggled to get to his chest of drawers. He got some underpants and had to return to the sit on the edge of the bed to reach down and got them over his feet. He managed to pull them up and stood up to finish the job. But the effort exhausted him, and he lay back on the bed. He reached for the television remote and turned the TV on. He was exhausted and just listened. Then it came to him, and he found the strength to sit up. The early morning show said it was Sunday. That meant he had no recall of Saturday.

"What the hell happened?" he shouted out.

He got up and knew he was functioning with adrenaline. He walked to the front room and looked out and saw his car in the driveway. It was dirtier then he remembered.

Sunday, I wonder if the police were here looking for me yesterday. Maybe I was here last night.

He started to pace back and forth, stress eliminating his fatigue.

Why did they bring me back here? How did they get me back in my bed and naked? Where in the hell are my clothes? Where are my keys and wallet? Questions came to him so fast that he didn't take time to answer.

He breathed a sigh of relief when he found his keys and wallet on top of the refrigerator. He was shocked to see dirt and blood on his clothes when he located them on top of his washing machine. He looked at them and wondered if it was his blood. He went to the kitchen and returned with a garbage bag. He put the clothes in it. He decided to have a close look in his bathroom mirror. He saw the spot on his skin where they gave him the shot to knock him out. His dark brown hair was so thick he couldn't feel anything abnormal.

He looked directly into the mirror and said, "How in the hell did you let this happen you greedy, stupid bastard?" He returned and sat on the edge of his bed.

"Think," he mumbled to himself.

The computer entered his mind, and he went down to his small but finished basement. The Lions and other Detroit sports teams' banners on the wall were totally ignored with his mind-set. He opened his laptop computer and quickly found the local news links. Relief poured over him when he saw no mention of his attempted burglary. Hunger pains got his attention and went toward the kitchen with his laptop. He got a pan he used to make spaghetti and began cooking the meal. He opened his laptop. Reese had won a close game Friday. He got up and stirred the noodles. Then went to the cupboard and got a jar of Prego spaghetti sauce. He found his noddle strainer and put it in the sink. He waited a minute and dumped the noodles in it. Put the noodles on a plate after and covered them with the sauce. Shredded cheese was next. He put the plate in the microwave for thirty seconds, and the ding from the microwave told him it was ready. He ate a plateful without thinking and went back for the rest. He started slowly on the second plateful.

My car is in the driveway, he thought. *Why haven't the police arrived? What happened? They know I can't expose them to the police. Who would believe it? And I committed a crime.*

He nearly dropped the fork when he reacted to his phone ringing. He looked at the caller ID, and it was Ted Anderson. The phone rang a number of times while he held it. Before he decided what to do, the answering machine came on. Ted's voice was saying there had been an accident in his home, and he asked him to call him to discuss it.

"Accident?" he responded after the call was over. He put the phone down and returned to his bedroom and opened the door to his walk-in closet. He reached in and felt the pull string and turned on the light. The long roll of his clothes hung on the left side, and on the shelving above the empty right side were his suitcases. He reached and got the biggest one and placed it on the bed. He unzipped it and opened it on the bed. He saw a lump in one of the inner compartments in the top half of the suitcase. He was surprised when he pulled out a black sports bra. It was Evelyn's, and he remembered her looking for it when she was moving out.

"Look at me now," he said, as he sat on the edge of the bed, holding the sports bra. Evelyn had wanted to settle down after two years of being a couple. He told her he wasn't ready and wanted to travel. He was restless and bored with his job and gave her no reason to stay. He put the bra back on top of his dresser.

If I leave now, there will never be a chance of us getting back together, entered his thoughts. But so would it if he went to jail. Ted did say he had an accident. *Why would he call me if they knew I was there?* He tried to make sense of it all.

"What to do?" he mumbled to himself. "Call Ted," he answered.

He hesitated when he heard Ted's voice on the phone.

"Ted, this is John Dwyer. You called about an accident?"

"Yeah, John, we had an accident with some equipment we have installed in the home. I am wondering if my insurance will cover the cost of getting it fixed. It would be best to show you than try an explain it."

"Okay, Ted, I am free now if that works for you."

"That would be great, John. See you in a few minutes then."

"Yes, I'll be on my way."

"Damn, John, what are you thinking?" he said to himself, as he got his briefcase containing his insurance forms. He went to his car and knew someone tall must have been driving it as his seat was slid back. He adjusted it and started the car. The oil change reminder on the windshield got his attention. He had just changed the oil and the reminder was for every three thousand miles. The car had been driven nearly eight hundred miles since the last oil change. He figured around seven hundred had been since Friday.

"The bastards could have left me some gas," he said when he noticed the low level on his gauge. The drive to the nearest gas station was nearly like being on autopilot. *This could be a dumb move*, he thought, but he wanted to see the reaction of Marissa's sister, Joyce. He knew he was in trouble, but now so was she. She also knew what happened to him. The drive to their home looked different in the daylight. Recent fallen leaves were covering the roads. The long driveway to the Andersons' seemed shorter when he arrived. There was no sight of any police car, and it gave him some relief. He felt strange walking to the front door and shook Ted's hand when Ted opened the door.

"Thanks for coming on a Sunday, John."

"Not a problem, Ted."

"Let me show you what we have."

John followed Ted through the house. When they came to the stairs, he heard giggling, and Megan and Mary Brunell came barreling from the upper hallway to the stairwell. They bumped into him and felt himself falling.

John heard someone saying, "Are you okay, Mr. Dwyer?"

He opened his eyes and was surprised to see it was Mary Brunell.

He sat up. "My tailbone hurts."

He tried to get up, and Mary came over to give him support so he could.

"Thanks, Mary?"

"Yes, my name is Mary, and you're Mr. Dwyer."

He laughed. "Sorry, but you made me feel very old then."

"Oh, I am sorry. I didn't mean to."

"No, it's fine, Mary. It's just I never felt that much older than you teens until then. High school doesn't seem that long ago."

Ted and Megan came into the room. Megan had an ice pack.

Ted looked at John. "You okay?"

"I haven't been blindsided like that since sandlot football, Ted. But I'll live."

"You want this?" she said as she held out the ice pack.

He took it and put it on his back. "Thanks, Megan."

"For a minute, I thought I would need an insurance man for my insurance man," Ted said with a smile."

John laughed and then responded with, "I hope you have coverage after that."

The startled look on Ted's face made John laugh. They all laughed when John said, "Just kidding."

Ted gestured to the table, and John followed him there. John looked at the girls. "I am okay and thanks for the help. Then he looked at Megan. "Congratulations on being elected homecoming queen."

"Thank you, Mr. Dwyer."

He rolled his eyes and said, "You're welcome."

Ted went and quietly talked to the girls. The reality of the situation returned to him while he sat at the kitchen table. *I don't think they know*, he thought to himself. Joyce must also be keeping quiet. He wondered if she was in the house and watching him on the monitors. He had a sudden urge to leave when Ted approached him. "John, you sure you are okay?"

"I will be sore tomorrow, Ted, but I will be fine. Don't worry, accidents do happen. Now what was the accident you called me about?"

"John, why don't you stay there for a few minutes? I'll get us a couple of beers. It is the least I can do for the fall and getting you out here on Sunday."

"You talked me into it, Ted."

"Good, I'll be right back. I keep it in the fridge in the garage."

John watched him leave and looked around the kitchen for the camera. He didn't locate it as he wanted to make faces just to acknowledge he knew she was watching but then decided not to.

Ted came back into view with two bottles of beer in each hand. He put two on the table and turned and put two in the refrigerator. "I hope you like Micolob, John."

"Yes, I do." He took a drink. The beer was so cold he gasped for air. "Wow, did you have them in a freezer, Ted?"

"Hehehe, I'll have to show you. It is quite the setup."

"Ted, if you don't mind, I'd rather you show me the accident. My back might start stiffing up."

"Okay, but bring your beer along."

Ted said, "Coming up," when they were on the stairwell this time. The dozen steps were uncomfortable to his back, but John didn't want to complain. Ted went past all the bedrooms and opened the door that led to the monitors. John took a swig of beer for courage and followed him in. He looked around, and no one else appeared to be in the room. The bathroom door was open, and the light for it was not on. He saw Ted pointing to a few monitors that had come off the wall and landed on some of the recording equipment. The remaining monitors on the wall were off.

"Ted, what is all this?"

"John, we got this recently. Megan thought someone may have been stalking her. She was getting weird messages on Facebook before she dropped it."

"Not good. You talk to the police or the school?"

"Yes, we did, and there isn't much they can do now since there hasn't been a direct threat."

"When did this happen, Ted?"

"It was Friday Night, when we were at the game. We all came home, and I discovered it later that night."

"So no one else was here?"

"No, we were all at the game?"

"The system was completely blank. No recordings?"

"I didn't see any. Why do you ask, John?"

John was quiet for a minute. "Ted, you think a stalker could have done it?"

Ted looked surprised, and then his face changed. "My god, that is possible."

John walked and took a closer look at the monitors. He looked at the wall.

"Ted, these monitors were installed poorly. They used an anchor that isn't made for drywall, and they didn't use the studs in the wall to anchor them securely. It was an accident waiting to happen. So they may have fallen on their own. If you said they were installed recently, the system should be under warranty. I'd call them as soon as possible and tell them about the sloppy work. If they will replace it, then you won't need to file a claim. That will be better for you in the long run."

"Okay, I will call them tomorrow."

"Ted, I need to go find a bathroom. The beer is going right through me."

Ted pointed to the bathroom. "I'll meet you in the kitchen when you are done."

"Thanks, Ted."

What was I thinking bringing up a stalker? he thought to himself. The last thing I need is for the police to get involved. He made sure he had the empty beer bottle when he left the bathroom and took his time going to the kitchen. He was hoping to see some sign of Joyce. Ted had the second beer on the table as he came to it. He was thinking it was time to go when Marissa entered from the garage area. She was carrying a hanging box of purple flowers. She looked at Ted and said, "You think you can make a hanger to hold up these flowers for Joyce?"

"I will come up with something, sweetie."

She smiled, and then she saw John and smiled at him.

"Hi, John, it is good to see you." She immediately went off to another part of the house.

"Sorry, John, she is always preoccupied this time of the year," responded Ted.

"Everything okay?"

"Yeah, the flowers are part of her yearly ritual she does for her sister Joyce's grave. She died seven years ago."

CHAPTER 4

He didn't want to follow up on that, so he turned to Ted and said, "I am sorry to hear that, Ted. I need to head out. But I'll be in the office Monday if you need anything."

He got in the car and returned the wave they all gave.

"What the fuck is going on?" he said to himself.

The drive home was a blur. His mind was trying to grasp what just happened. The monitors were down, the tapes were erased, and Joyce is dead. Ted doesn't seem to have any idea I was there. It doesn't feel right.

Something is fishy. Tapes erased. Someone did it for a reason.

I can't think of a good reason.

"I need a cold beer," he said when he arrived home and went to the refrigerator to retrieve a bottle of Guinness.

Where did I put that mug? He retrieved it from the cupboard and poured slowly to watch the dark brew fill the mug. He lifted the mug and drank nearly half of it. He could feel the alcohol entering his bloodstream and felt a light buzz. *It goes down smooth*, was his thought as he took another swig.

Joyce is dead. Wait a minute. Joyce seems too old to be Marissa's sister. Joyce looked to be near eighty, and Marissa looked to be in her mid-forties. He retrieved his laptop.

This is strange. I can't locate any information on the Andersons. Teds file is at work, so I will check that tomorrow.

A glance at the clock told him the Lions game was about to start. A trip to the refrigerator for another beer and he grabbed a bag of potato chips. *This should take my mind off things, but then again they are the Lions.* The food tray was conveniently next to his recliner,

22

and he placed his cell, beer, TV remote, and chips on it before he sat down. A tear came to his eye when he realized how thankful he was able to view the game. If only Evelyn had still been here. He picked up his cell phone and glanced at it. He knew she wouldn't contact him but couldn't break the habit of checking his cell phone in case she might. The game got his attention, and he always got riled up in a close game. He leaped out of his chair when the Lions got a game winning TD with three seconds left to beat the Dallas Cowboys. He sat back down to watch the game follow-up report.

The buzzer on his alarm started its constant blast. He tried to gain focus of where he was. He slowly got out of the recliner and grabbed his remote to turn off the television. I can't believe I zonked out and slept all night in my recliner. He stretched out and slowly moved to the bedroom to shut off the buzzer. He started his morning work routine, coffee, and a quick breakfast of cereal. He ironed his white shirt and adjusted his suit and tie. The ping informing him of the low amount of gas got his attention on the way to work. He made a mental note to fill up on the way home. Maxine's car was in the parking lot when he arrived. The building he rented from had three rooms. The secretary was located near the front door and then two rooms to the left and right. His office was to the right. The left one was vacant and currently used for a lobby.

"Good morning, John," greeted him when he walked in.

"Good morning, Maxine, how was your weekend?"

"Hectic, we had the grandkids over all weekend. Those girls can be a handful."

"Oh, does that happen often? How old are the girls now?"

"No, Russ and Christine had a high school reunion in Minnesota. I thought it would be fun to have a grandma time with them. It was for the most part, but I was ready for them to go home last night. Oh, Jennifer is twelve, Shannon is ten, and Savannah is eight. How was your weekend? Anything happen that was exciting?"

"Not really, Maxine, I went to the game Friday night. Saturday flew by, and I watched the Lions on Sunday. Oh, Ted Anderson did call Sunday about some video monitors that fell off his wall. I went over, and it was strange that they all fell at once."

"Think he's planning on putting in a claim?"

"I am not so sure. They may be under warranty. It did look like shoddy work. When you have a chance, I would like to see his file." He walked to the other room. "You want any coffee, Maxine. It looks ready."

"Yes, thanks, John."

He washed out her cup at the counter sink, added two creams, and filled it with coffee. He brought it to her with a stirring stick inside.

"Thanks, John. Here is Ted Anderson's file."

"Well, thank you, Maxine." He got his coffee and went to his office. He studied the policy they had with the company. He hadn't realized they came to Reese four years ago, just before, he arrived. He had lived in the Ann Arbor area and transferred here to be close to Evelyn. They had met online. He drove up for as few dates, and she asked him to stay overnight after one of them. A position opened in Reese when the agent retired, and he didn't hesitate to put in the transfer papers.

The phone rang.

"Yes, Maxine"

"Ted Anderson is on line 1."

"Okay, thanks."

"Hi, Ted, what can I do for you?"

"Hey, John, just calling to let you know those monitors were under warranty. They will be taking care of them."

"That is great news, Ted."

"Yeah, thanks. Are you going to the game Friday, John?"

"If nothing comes up, I probably will."

"Great, maybe I will see you there. Take care."

"Yeah, it should be a great game. Goodbye, Ted."

John hung up the phone. He wondered if he will be able to go to the game, entered his thoughts. The sound of small motors got his attention. "I can't believe they are still using them," he mumbled to himself. He glanced and counted about a dozen riders on their mopeds. For some reason, the moped became the thing to do in Reese. There were so many it even got the attention of the local news. He never had the urge, but often wondered where they went for hours at a time. Maxine notified him that he had a customer, and he settled into his work routine for the rest of the day.

The week went by without any issue, and John's stress level dropped with each day. Friday Night came, and John decided to go to the Reese game. They played Vassar, and it was a local rivalry. Reese usually had the upper hand in the rivalry, but Vassar's program was improving. The October nights were coming early, and there would be a chill in the air.

"What coat do I wear?" he mumbled to himself. The Reese hoodie would be ideal, but the last time he tried it on, it was a struggle because of his weight gain since Evelyn left. He reached for it anyway, and he was surprised on how easy it went on. Pulling it over his head was easy as well. Curiosity got the best of him, and he headed for the bathroom scale. He hadn't wanted to get on it since she left because he knew he had gained weight. He took off his clothes and stepped on the scale. He was shocked, as he had lost twenty pounds.

"What the fuck?" He went to mirror in his bedroom. *What is going on?*

He couldn't believe it, but he had a six-pack on his abdomen. *I haven't had those since high school. I have heard stress can cause weight loss, but this was well beyond that.*

He got down on the floor and started doing pushups. He was able to do about fifty when he was in high school. A few years ago he couldn't get to ten. He sat up after doing forty. Could the Saturday blackout last week have anything to do with this? That thought stuck in his mind. How could it be the reason? Then again, what other explanation is there? *I sure didn't put in the work to get this buff.*

CHAPTER 5

THE PARKING LOT FOR THE game was just starting to fill up. John found a spot so he could have an easy exit. He found an old Reese seat cushion he had purchased a few years ago. Evelyn usually claimed it when they went to a game. There was a time he considered throwing it away because of that but never got around to it. The cool night with a chance of rain had him reconsidering. Those aluminum bleacher seats were cold to sit on. He put the cushion under his arm when he got his ticket. The volunteers selling 50/50 tickets for various causes were vying for his money. He bought one for a chance to win a car. It cost $5 to have a chance of winning the car if you kicked a fifty-yard FG. No one had come close in the years since the local car dealer had offered that promotion. The money the promotion generated went to the school's athletic fund. The popcorn smell sent him to the concession stand. He acknowledged a few people who were in line ahead of him. The popcorn bag felt warm in his hands as he walked up the bleacher ramp. He found a good seat near the team's forty-yard line. He had views of the team, and he was near the cheerleaders. The teams were doing there warm up drills. He watched as the scoreboard clock ticked off the time before the game started. The popcorn was salty, but hunger made it easy to overlook. The Vassar Vulcans players ran on the field as their names were announced for the starting defensive team. John heard the cheer when the Reese Rockets ran through a stretched out Rocket banner. He saw Mary Brunell with the other cheerleaders as the followed the team. They then ran toward the sidelines and turned toward the bleachers. They formed a straight line parallel to the bleachers. He saw Mary lined up just to the left of him. They started their cheers when Vassar lined up to kick off. The ball sailed in the air, and the Reese receiver gathered it in and ran the ball back about thirty yards. John tried to focus on the game, but last week's game and events made it difficult. He occasionally glanced at Mary, and he noticed that she was looking at him.

She waved when she saw the she had his attention and he waved back. The game was a defensive struggle, and it looked like it would be a scoreless first half. The sudden strong wind was becoming a factor, and it helped caused the Vassar receiver to fumble a punt return. Reese recovered it and scored with fifteen seconds left to lead 8–0 at the half. John got up to stretch his legs. He was thinking about returning to his car to retrieve his umbrella when he felt a tap on his shoulder. He turned and saw a smiling Mary.

"Hi, John, how is your back?"

"The back is fine, Mary. Don't you have to be with the rest of the girls?"

"Oh, we have some time to socialize. Besides I was pretty rough on you so I had to know how you were doing."

John could feel the eyes of a few parents who could hear the exchange.

"Mary, it was an accident. I am fine, and thanks for the concern."

"I know, but I should have been prepared. It was so careless of me. I am just glad I didn't hurt you when I was on top of you. Megan said the same thing."

"Tell Megan everything is okay. I was just knocked on my ass. It's not the first time. I better get going to retrieve my umbrella. I hope you have rain gear here."

Mary laughed. "We are always prepared."

He was surprised when she gave him a big hug, and then she whispered in his ear, "I like your new look."

He recoiled and looked at her. She gave him a wink and ran off. He didn't dare look into the crowd. He knew that in a small town rumors had legs. The bleacher exit seemed like a mile away, and then he heard the numbers for the drawing of the weekly prizes announced over the loud speaker. A quick search though his pockets produced the tickets. He didn't win with the dollar tickets, and then he heard one of his numbers called for the chance to win the car. A volunteer came to him when he raised his arm to acknowledge that he had the ticket. She looked at his numbers and signaled the press box to confirm that John was a winner. She directed him to a place on the sidelines where there was a volunteer on the sidelines holding a football and kicking tee. The game announcer announced his name over the loudspeaker. He heard some applause. The crowd pushed to the chain-link fence surrounding the field to get a better view. He hoped he didn't embarrass myself. The wind was blowing hard into his face so he chose the goalpost at the north end of the field. He put the ball on the tee, and the crowd quickly shifted to the north end. He decided to kick it straight on and took a few steps behind the ball. The goalpost looked small from that distance. The crowd noise made him realize the ball had blown off the tee. The flag on the flagpole got his attention when he returned the ball on the tee. The wind shifted and was blowing from right to left. His focus on the ball increased until he could think of nothing else, and with the feeling of someone else walking for him, he went forward and kicked the ball. His leg felt no resistance as the ball sailed high in the air. The ball seemed to be heading to the right of the goalpost, but it was above the lights so it was difficult to see. The ball suddenly veered to the left when it was near the open end of the stadium. The wind carried it over the goalpost. A volunteer raised his arms to signal that it was good. The crowd erupted. John stuck his arms up in the air to celebrate. He didn't have time to brace himself from the group of cheerleaders bolting to him in excitement. Mary leaped on him, and he couldn't stop himself from falling on his ass. The girls surrounded them, and before he could catch his breath, Mary kissed him.

"That was for good luck."

"I think you are a little late for that, Mary," he said with a laugh. She got off him and helped him up.

"Oh, you might need it later," she whispered in his ear.

The crowd was still cheering him when he left the field. A volunteer directed him to the press box. The door flew open by the power of the wind, and it took all his strength to close it. The wooden steps led him to the second floor. Marc Peterson of the Tuscola County News walked over and shook his hand.

"That was an amazing kick, John! We got it all on video. We will need your permission to play it on the local news."

"Thanks, Marc, I would like to see it first. I am still shocked it went over."

"I'll set it up on my laptop. It will take me a few minutes."

Marc went and entered the room next to him. "Hey, Charlie, the lucky man is here."

Charlie Schultz walked up to him and gave him a firm handshake.

"John, I never thought anyone would win the car, but I am so glad you did. You caused a lot of excitement with that kick."

He reached in side his jacket and gave an envelope to John.

"Just fill this out and take it down to the Chevy dealer. I already signed it. They will be in for a surprise, and since we have a video, they will know it is legit."

"Thanks, Charlie."

"No need to thank me, John. Thank the wind," he said with a laugh.

A thunderous sound made both men jump. It was the sound of a hard rain hitting the metal side of the building.

"Whoa," Charlie yelled out. He looked at John. "You are welcome to stay up here, John, for the rest of the game. I sure don't want you to get that letter wet."

"Good point, Charlie. Thanks I will."

John moved to the furthest window from the announcers. He watched as the rain drove most of the students from their usual gathering points to under the bleachers. The older generations, opened their umbrellas or were scurrying to the vehicles. John noticed Mary had put on her cheerleader rain gear, but there weren't many fans left to cheerlead. The players were tearing up the field by sliding when they lost their footing. The game play became sloppy, as the ball was difficult to hold. Reese managed another touchdown to lead 14–0. Vassar scored in the last minute to make the game close, but it wasn't enough as Reese held on to win 14–6. The wind had tapered off, and only a light rain remained. Those in the press box were happy. Reese had clinched a playoff spot in the state tournament. Marc sought him out and gave John his laptop.

"Here is your kick, John."

John put the laptop on his lap. He watched himself kick the ball and marveled on how much leg drive he exhibited. The ball sailed high, and again he watched the wind blow the ball left through the goalposts. He was surprise by how quick the cheerleaders got to him. He looked carefully to see if Mary's kiss was visible, but with all the girls surrounding them, he couldn't see it.

Thank God, he thought to himself. The exchange in the bleachers with her might have some tongues wagging already. He closed the laptop and walked toward Marc. "Thanks, Marc, did you say it would be on the news? I would like to get a copy."

"It should be, John. Give me your email and I'll send you a copy. Oh, now that you are here, mind if I ask a few questions so I can put it in the Tuscola news?"

"Ask away, Marc."

"John, have you ever kicked before?"

"Not football. I just played soccer in high school."

"That couldn't have been too long ago. Do you play football?"

"Oh, it was nearly ten years ago since high school. The only thing I play anymore is slow pitch softball."

"What are you going to do with your new car?"

"I haven't even thought about it yet. I guess I need to see it first."

"Hope you enjoy it, John. That was a kick many will remember."

Marc turned off his video camera. "Thanks again, John. If I could, I would like to get a picture with you in the new car."

"Okay, give me your number and I'll give you my email."

John acknowledged those who were in the press box and received many congratulations in return. He went down the stairwell and stopped at the doorway. He pulled his left arm out of its sleeve on the hoodie. He put it within his hoodie and put the letter in his left hand to provide protection from the rain. He opened the door with his right hand and felt the rain hit his face. He ducked down and tightened his hood and started running to his car. The lights were still on for the field, so he could make out his car in the distance. He got to his car and reached his hand in his right pocket. He realized his remotes must be in his left. He tried to reach over with his right arm and tried to maneuver his body to make it work. Then he heard laughter. Mary came up to him. "Need some help, John?'

"I have a letter under my hoodie that I don't want to get wet. I need to switch arms to get my car remotes."

He was surprised when he felt her hand enter his pocket. She pulled out the remote and, to his surprise, quickly used it to unlock his doors.

She opened the door for him and then quickly ran behind the car and entered the passenger side door.

He stood there for a second and then entered the car.

She handed him the remote when he got in.

"Thank you."

"You're welcome. How's your back?"

"My back is fine. It's my ass the hurts. I think I might have grass stains on my pants. You hit me harder than most of your team hit tonight."

She laughed. "You do have a grass stain on your ass. I couldn't help but notice."

Car lights from a departing car blinded him for a second.

He looked at her. "You know, some might think we are having an affair if they see us here."

"People are going to think what they want. Besides, you don't have to worry. I am not jailbait. I am eighteen."

"Yeah but you are still in high school."

"And your point is? You don't think there is sex in high school. These days you can't go on a date without a guy expecting a blowjob. If you make it through a few dates, then sex is expected. That is the worst part of being eighteen. I'd rather date older men, but some are afraid of what people will say. Well, screw them. Pardon my pun."

John chuckled. "I always thought you were more mature then your age. What did you mean when you told me you liked my look?"

Mary looked at him. "Well, the hoodie of course. What else could it be?" she said with a smile.

He laughed. "Thank you for the laugh and knocking me on my ass again. I have been down for a while after my break up with my girlfriend. You have helped me forget about things."

"Glad I could help. John, my car is the red Camaro over there."

"Great-looking car," he said as they pulled up.

"Thanks," and she got out the car. She stopped before closing it and stuck her head in the door. "Have you heard from Evelyn?" and she quickly closed the door and entered her car. He sat there and watched her drive away. *How does she know about her?*

CHAPTER 6

JOHN ENTERED HIS HOUSE AND pulled his hoodie off. He hung it in his front closet. There was an ink pen on the kitchen counter, and he filled out the winning form. The letter went on top of his refrigerator next to his car remote. He grabbed a beer from the fridge and sat in his recliner.

Wait a minute. He got up and walked to his bedroom. *Well, I'll be damned. There is a grass stain on my ass.* He took them off and removed his shirt.

"Who are you?" he asked himself. *How did I get this body? I thought this was what Mary was talking about when she said, "I like your new look." How would she know if it was? I think she stays with Ted and his family. Maybe that could explain it. For a small town I am surprised I don't know her background.*

His cell phone rang.

"Hello."

"Hi, John, this is Marc Peterson. I just called to tell you TV-5 will be showing your kick on the 11:00 p.m. broadcast."

"Great, Marc, I was wondering if it was going to be on tonight. Thank you."

"Not a problem, John. Take care."

"You too."

His sweat pants seemed baggy when he slipped them on. *Looks like I might need a new wardrobe,* he thought as he returned to his recliner.

A glance at his clock informed him that he had thirty minutes before the news. He rocked in his recliner as he tried to recapture the mental images of tonight. *Oh God,* he thought when he remembered how the exchange with Mary and him must have come across to those within hearing distance in the bleachers. *I hope it doesn't hurt my business.* He sat quietly for a second, then started laughing so hard he couldn't catch his breath. *Yeah, hurt my business, I didn't give shit about that last week. I could still go to jail. Hell, I won a car, and I will be on the news. It's as "here I am, come and get me, you old ladies." At least let me remember if it was a good time. After Evelynn left, I could use the action.* He laughed harder. *Maybe I should try to hook up with Mary. What do I have to lose? Forrest Gump was right—stupid is what stupid does.*

I should pack up and leave after I win the car. I could sell it and transfer out of here while I can. I can feel that something is about to happen.

He reached for the TV remote, and the television came to life. The news came on. The lead story was his kick. He quickly turned on the DVR recorder. The kick video appeared, and he relived the kick. He laughed when he saw the tackle Mary gave him during the celebration. *No wonder I got grass stains.* He was glad he never felt it. The newscasters marveled at the kick and then started on the next story.

The buzzing of his cell phone got his attention. It was a text. He opened and it read, "Sorry about the tackle. You are okay?"

"Yes, Mary, I assume?" he texted back.

"I hope you don't have other women tackling you. But yeah."

"Ah, so you are the jealous type? How did you get my number?"

"I asked, Ted. I am not jealous, but I am competitive. I just want to be the one who knocks you on your ass."

John couldn't help but laugh before he texted. "I see, so do you know how to get the grass stains off the ass of my pants?"

"Of course I do. Do you want me to come over and show you how?"

"You want to right now?"

"I'm game if you are. It is Friday night, and it's boring here."

John hesitated. *What am I doing?* Then he remembered. *She said she is eighteen.*

"Do you know where I live?"

"I'll be there shortly."

He put down his phone and went and put his dirty dishes in the dishwasher. The grass-stained pants were on his bedroom floor. He checked all the pockets and put the pants on top of his washer.

Everything looks good, he thought as he sat down in the recliner. Mary entered his thoughts, and he became aroused. *Damn, I can't believe it happened so fast.* He got up to try to walk it off. The flash of lights on his front window signaled her arrival. He reached in his pants to push his penis down. It hurt, but at least it didn't show. The doorbell rang, and when he opened it, he was stunned. There was Mary in a classic black dress, black heels, and her auburn hair tied in a bun. A charming necklace with a heart-shaped blue sapphire over her ample cleavage.

"Well, you want me to work on your pants?" she said with a smile.

More than you know, he thought. "They are back on my washer. You sure you want to dress like that?"

"Actually I am going to tell you how to do it." She walked in. "A nice bachelor pad you have. Where is your washer?"

"Thanks." He led her to the rear of the house and opened the door to the utility room. He switched on the light. She looked around and saw his laundry cleaning supplies.

"Do you have any stain remover products?"

"What you see is what I have."

"John, you need to buy some. Anyway, for now put the detergent on the stain and rub it on that portion of the pants together like this." She showed him the motion. "Then wash them immediately."

"Well thank you, Martha Stewart. I am in your debt."

"Okay, smart-ass," she said with a smile.

"I am curious, Mary. Where does an eighteen-year-old go dressed like that on a Friday night?"

"Well, John, this eighteen-year-old goes wherever she wants. I also came over to ask if you want to accompany me. It would help if I had someone with me."

"Where might that be?"

"A surprise. I'll do the driving, and the trip is on me."

"If it doesn't involve anything illegal or some kind of prank, I'd be happy to."

"No, it doesn't, but you need to think more positive. Let's have fun."

"Okay, I need to go dress up a bit. You look too sexy for me to accompany you in my sweats."

"I didn't think you noticed. Thank you. I'll be waiting in the car."

"What am I doing?" he mumbled to himself. He found the clothes to wear, hurried, and changed. He made a quick stop to the bathroom to find his deodorant, and then he did a quick rinse with his mouthwash.

He locked the house door when he left. He saw she was in the driver's seat, so he got in the passenger side.

She looked at him. She smiled when he fastened his seatbelt. "I am so glad I didn't have to ask you to do it."

"Oh, I have read all the reports. Seat belts save lives. It is part of my job. If you need insurance, I will give you a good rate." He gave her an exaggerated grin.

She laughed, then put the car in reverse and pulled out of his driveway. He examined the red Camaro's interior. "This is really sharp. Is it yours?"

"Yes, it was the first thing I bought when I turned eighteen."

She drove toward I-75.

"You bought it? I am assuming you must have received money when you were eighteen?"

"John, I'd rather not talk about it right now. I need to know something. Have you ever kicked before?"

"Not really. I still don't believe I made it."

"That was amazing."

"What is amazing is your transformation to your look now. You will turn heads entering any establishment. By the way, where are we headed?"

"'Turn heads' and 'headed.' Are you playing with me, John? Sending a message playing word games?'

What is she talking about? Then he laughed when it dawned on him.

"Sorry, but I am not that clever."

"Oh, with you being an older man, I had to check." She smiled at him. "Have you been to the casino, John?"

"Yes, I have been there."

"That is where I want to go tonight. Would you like to go with me and show me the ropes? Just treat me as you would a woman your age. Everything is covered."

Now I wonder if she is sending me a message. "Let's do it."

CHAPTER 7

THE CASINO PARKING LOT WAS less than half full when they arrived. Mary drove to the front door where they offered valet parking. *I wonder how she knew about that*, he thought. But decided not to question. He waited for her to walk behind the car. *God, she is beautiful. It is hard to believe she is in high school.* He smiled at her and offered his arm. She obliged and grabbed hold. They entered the vast room of lights and people. A security guard looked at them and nodded as they walked past.

Yeah, she does appear older than eighteen.

"Where do you want to start?"

Mary looked around. "Can we walk around and see everything first?"

"It's your dime," he said with a smile.

"You say the sweetest things."

He chuckled and led her to the slot machine floor.

He informed her on the machines and their different costs. He told her the twenty-five-cent machines were his favorite. The next section had the blackjack tables. She said she was familiar with blackjack. He didn't ask for details. Then they came up to the roulette tables. She pulled on his arm and whispered in his ear, "Let's try this."

He noticed two empty seats at one of the tables and led her to them.

"We have to put money on the table, and it is converted to betting chips."

"Two hundred enough to start, John?"

"Yeah, that is plenty."

She reached in her purse and gave him two one-hundred-dollar bills. He put the money on the table after the latest spin and payout.

"Sir, how would you like that broken down?" asked the woman running the table.

"Four $25 dollar chips, five $10, and the rest singles."

She counted them out and spread them in front of him. He nodded in agreement and pulled them in front of him. He pointed to an electronic board over the roulette wheel. "The numbers listed are the ones that were called recently. The ones in red lights were the red numbers called, and the yellow are the black numbers called. You can bet black or red for the next spin. They are the best odds. There are to zero numbers that are green on the board. They come up and black and red lose. You can also bet on any one number. You win thirty-five dollars for each dollar bet if that number is where that ball lands. You can split two numbers by putting a chip on the border for two numbers. You can also cover four numbers if you put a chip on the corner where four numbers meet. The payout drops when you do, but you get better odds. You want to bet, Mary?"

She reached and tugged his arm. He bent down to her.

"Remember when I said you might need your luck later? Here is your chance," she whispered in his ear.

He looked at her, and she smiled in response. Treat me like any other woman, she had mentioned. *That won't be difficult, as she sure isn't acting like a girl. She had this all planned, and I was played. She knew I would accompany her.*

He looked at the board and noticed the last four numbers posted had been red. He put fifteen dollars on red. The four other players at this table placed their bets, and the ball was spun. The spinning roulette wheel went one way and the ball the other. It eventually came down and bounced around before ending up on red 29. The woman running the table quickly removed the chips for the nonwinning bets, then counted out fifteen and slid the chips to John. Mary squeezed his arm and gave him a peck on the cheek. He took the fifteen chips he won and placed them on fifteen different numbers on the board. The others finished their bets, and the ball was spun. The roulette spinner then locked down all bets before the ball stopped.

"Number 14," she announced, and John had a chip on that. He looked at Mary. "We spent fourteen, but we won thirty-five dollars."

He could tell she was getting excited, and she started putting down bets as luck was on their side. A new employee took over the table, and John gave the woman leaving a five-dollar tip. They continue to play. A server came over and asked if he wanted a drink. He told her he needed a Bud. Then she turned to Mary. "I'd like a gin and tonic."

The server left, and John just shook his head in wonder. The server returned with the drinks with no questions asked. John stopped betting a short time after and counted the chips. He figured they were around five hundred dollars ahead.

"Mary, we are about five hundred dollars ahead. Do you want to stop now? It is nearly 4:00 a.m."

"Yeah, we better quit before the luck runs out. Let's go cash out."

"You sure you never gambled before?"

"Nope, it is my first time."

"Okay, Miss Gin and Tonic."

"Hey, I never said I haven't had a drink before. Besides, I gave her a big tip before the order, when you were betting."

"Oh, and I was supposed to be showing you the ropes. I think I am being roped in."

Mary looked at him and smiled. "You are smarter than I thought."

John laughed aloud. "That was supposed to be my line."

"Are you enjoying yourself, John? Isn't this better than last weekend?"

That comment stopped him. "What do you know about last weekend?"

"Let's cash out and go up to the room I reserved at the hotel complex. We'll discuss it there."

"You reserved a room for tonight? Did that happen when I was betting also?"

She didn't answer him and continued toward the casino cashier. The stress that had eased since last weekend returned in full force.

Mary had to be hiding something. He had sensed it by her behavior. She was a woman who acted well beyond her years. He felt the urge to leave, but he didn't have many options at this time of night. He saw that Mary was standing in line at the cashiers. Maybe she would give him some of winnings, and he would try to leave. He walked up beside her. He watched as Mary collected $535 from the cashier. She divided it and gave him his share. "It is important that we talk, John."

"Can we do it tomorrow in Reese?"

"John, it would be best to do it now. If you have any ideas of leaving town, you will regret it if you try."

"What, is someone going to kill me if I try?"

"John, if they had wanted to do that, you wouldn't be here now. They actually think you could help them. Just follow me, and I'll tell you what I know."

She started down a corridor, and he followed closely. He couldn't help notice how well the dress fit her figure. The heels she was wearing highlighted the muscled legs. She seemed to walk in them as if they were second nature to her. They arrived in the hotel lobby, and he admired the décor.

This is a high-class hotel.

He observed her chatting with the lobby desk clerk, and she turned and signaled for him to meet her at the elevator. The doors opened when he arrived, and they walked in. She pushed the elevator button for the fifth floor. Another couple scurried in, and Mary asked what floor they wanted. They responded in unison, "For the third floor." The doors closed, and it was a quick ride to the third and then fifth floor. Mary led him to the door at the end of a hall. This appeared to be the only door on that wing. She opened it, and he let her enter first. She found the light switch, and he was stunned when he saw the luxurious accommodations. An iced bottle of champagne greeted them. There was a huge flat-screen television hanging on the wall. A full-size kitchen was next to the living room. Mary opened the stocked refrigerator and grabbed a few strawberries. She munched on them and motioned for John to follow her. She led him to the balcony, and he admired the view. A Jacuzzi was located in a corner of the room. There was a flat-screen television on the wall across from it. You could soak and watch it. He heard Mary gasp and followed her to the bathroom. It was enormous, with a three-sink counter, a walk-in bath, and multi-shower heads for the huge walk-in shower. Mary walked and opened its door, and she turned the shower on. The multi-shower heads sprayed the water from various directions, causing a water cloud in the middle.

"Oh, hell yes," she said, and John watched as she started to undress. She slipped off her dress and then reached back and unhooked the bra. He saw her perfectly shaped breasts set free, and he was becoming aroused. Her panties were next, and her tight buns were difficult for him to take his eyes off. She reached down to take off her heels, and he saw that she was indeed an auburn-haired woman. He couldn't stop himself from having a very hard erection. This is harder than the ones he had as a teenager. His balls were starting to hurt. She entered the shower, and before she closed the door, she gave him a signal with her finger to join her. It was tempting to try to relieve himself before he entered, but the thought of Mary possibility seeing him made him think it would be a bad idea. It was difficult to find her in the cloud of water, but eventually he felt her grab his erection. He felt her put soap on it and then slowly started stroking it. Closing his eyes didn't help his focus of trying to stop his pending explosion. The stroking became faster; his body stiffened. He exploded on the shower wall. She giggled but didn't let go of him. Her body rubbed against his when she came up and kissed him hard on the mouth. He turned to the side so he could breathe because of the water hitting him in the face. She then moved down and got on her knees. She slowly stroked him again, and he could fell another erection coming on. She put it in her mouth, and he backed to the shower wall as she became more forceful. Watching her really turned him on. He knew he needed to explode again when she stopped and shook her head no. She turned the shower off and led him out of the shower. She didn't let go of him while they gave each other a quick drying with the towels. He followed her when she led him to the round bed. She let go to turn off the lights, and he fell back on the bed when she jumped on him.

"I like knocking you on your ass. She moved quickly to mount his throbbing member. Her hands pressed against his chest for support as she started a rocking motion, and her inner muscles made it feel like she was massaging his erection. "Oh God," she said and sped up the motion. "Oh god, that is the spot," she moaned. Then she went faster and became louder. "Oh, it's been so long," she shouted as he came with her. She collapsed and then crawled up next to him. "I will be right back," she said. He could see her shadowed image walk toward the bathroom. He put his hands over his eyes to shield them from the bathroom light. Fatigue was tapping him on his shoulder, and he felt the urge to roll over and go to sleep. The damp towel on his penis regained his attention.

"Roll on your back, John. Let me clean you up."

He rolled on to his back and saw her concentrate on wiping him off. Her face was glowing, and her nipples were firm and near his face. He reached and lightly traced his finger around the edge. She smiled and leaned toward him. He gave it a light kiss and started to massage it with his tongue. Her head started to sway back and forth. Her hand surrounded his penis, and she slowly started to stoke it. He was surprised how fast he recovered. He rolled her over, and she pulled her legs up toward her chest when he entered her. He had never been with a woman like her. She didn't want to stop. He was surprised he was able to continue after the numerous times. The last time he carried her around as she rode him with her legs around him and arms around his neck. He at times had to lean against the wall for support. They collapsed from exhaustion onto the bed as the sunshine came through the balcony windows.

He tried to focus on his watch after opening his eyes. It was 2:00 p.m. He rolled over, and the bed was empty. Panic caused him to sit up.

"Mary!"

The quiet that was the response unnerved him.

He got out of bed. "Mary!"

He walked into the bathroom. He noticed a sheet of paper near the sink. He picked it up.

John, I am sorry, but I had to leave quickly. I have arranged a limo to return you to Reese. Just call down to the desk when you are ready. I paid for the room until tomorrow, and there is money by the TV. I'll explain when I see you. Thanks for last night. Mary xoxo

"I'll be damned." *This must be how a prostitute feels.*

He crinkled the paper into a ball and threw it in the trash can. "I can't believe this shit," and relieved himself at the toilet. He noticed the towels above it and went into the shower. He leaned his head against the wall and let the water cascade down his back, the water slowly getting hotter and hotter with each dial adjustment he made. The tightness in his back muscles became loose with the hot water. He couldn't see out of the shower due to the rising steam. A chill overcame him when he shut the water off.

The two hundred dollars on top of the TV stand got his attention when he walked out of the bathroom. His hunger pains were hard to ignore. The room service menu was placed near the phone. He checked the room to see he had everything. He left $10 for the housekeeper, collected the $200 Mary left for him. *I am giving that back to her when I see her.*

He grabbed the key and left the room. The casino restaurant wasn't busy, but his mind wasn't focused on the food he ordered. When and why did she leave? consumed his thoughts. He was a bit uncomfortable at the checkout with the request for the limo, but they didn't seem to think nothing of it. The limo arrived, and after a brief conversation with the driver, he settled back in the seat. He found the refrigerator where the driver had informed where it would be. He opened it and selected a bottled water. The seat was comfortable, so he lifted his legs and put them across it and leaned back. He opened the bottled and lifted it to his lips and drank nearly half of it. With the bottled closed and put on the floor, he felt a nap coming on.

CHAPTER 8

"I SEE THEM," MARY SAID when she saw the Black Escalade enter the driveway. Ted made a quick move to the garage to open the garage door. The Black Escalade entered the empty garage, and the door closed behind it. Mary heard them greeting Ted, and they entered the house to the connecting kitchen. They then opened the basement door that was in the kitchen entryway, and she heard them enter the basement. "You coming?" a voice said. It was Megan.

"Oh, you sure it is okay?"

"Yes, we have a lot to go over, and you need to know what is going on."

Mary got up and followed Megan down the steps to the basement. They walked the length of the basement and saw no sign of the others. Megan opened the door at the end of the basement, and there was the elevator door. Megan pushed the button. She glanced at Mary.

"You have circles under your eyes. You get much sleep?"

She saw a small smile on Mary's face. "Not much."

"Oh really? So how was it? Did you remember how?"

"Oh it was great, and he lasted all night long. It was like riding a bike or in this case, riding a horse. I take it he had been given the shot to make him younger? Yes, he gave me a good one too."

They both laughed.

The elevator arrived, and they stepped in.

The elevator ride down three floors was quick. They got in the electric golf carts. and Mary drove and entered a long tunnel.

I'd hate to walk this, entered Mary's thoughts.

Mary soon saw other carts parked near a door. It had an electronic locking mechanism. Megan stopped the cart, and they walked to the door. Megan punched in some numbers, and the door opened. Megan saw an elderly woman.

"Welcome, Megan, I am Joyce."

"Thank you, Joyce. I am honored to be here."

"How has your transition been? Are you happy to be part of the cause?"

"It has been amazing. I see life with a different view. Yes, I'll do anything."

Joyce asked, "What is your opinion of Mr. Dwyer?"

"He is easily manipulated. Just thinks of himself and not that intelligent."

"That is our opinion as well. He is someone we might consider. Right now we have decided to return him to his home. He is drugged, and we will leave him naked as before to really confuse him. The fact he might be known, because of the kick, does delay the process. Think you can keep him under control, Mary?"

"I have no doubt. Besides, it could be fun."

"I don't need those details," Joyce said with a smile.

She looked at both of them. "Let's go to the meeting room. Time for the monthly report."

They followed her down the hall and entered a closed door. They were greeted by the dozen people sitting around a round table. Joyce went to a seat reserved for her. Megan found two empty seats together across from Joyce. There were more people coming in, and the chairs quickly filled. When Joyce saw they were all filled, she picked up the headset that was in front of her and waved for the others to do the same. She did a sound check, and the others nodded in acknowledgment that they could hear. "This meeting is called to order." Joyce looked at one of the persons to her right. "Roll call?"

"All board members are here plus two visitors."

Joyce introduced Megan and Mary to the board.

"They have proven trustworthy, and they have blended in with the culture of today's youth. It is time they become informed with our mission."

Joyce looked to her right. "Jonathan, what is the status of the product?"

"We are filled to capacity, and the harvest should occur in two weeks."

"So do we need more storage space?"

"Looks like we might. I'd say we now have a twenty-year supply with the present population."

"Jonathan, we need to contact the others to see if they have a need."

"I will take care of it."

"Thank you, keep me posted."

She turned her direction to Phyllis. "Recruiting status?"

"We have two prospects at this time. One at Wintergreen Manor and the other at Oakwood. We are doing a background check, and if it is satisfactory, they will be presented to the board."

"Thank you."

"Brent, facility status?"

"We are scheduled to go online for the thumb area in two weeks. Everything checks out, and we should have plenty of power for our facilities despite the load the area requires. The windmills themselves have been inspected and secured. There will be no access to our underground facilities available from up top, and the video stations are being monitored."

"Do you have a plan to test the alarm status of the individuals monitoring the system?"

"Yes we have unannounced tests on a regular basis."

"Excellent, after the last breach from an unexpected source, we need to be more vigilant."

"I agree."

Joyce glanced at her clipboard. "Julie, the treasure's report?"

"We are self-sustaining, and the profits from going online will allow us to expand when needed. The others will be pleased."

"I am sure they will be. Thanks all. Next meeting will be the first Wednesday next month."

They all got up to leave. Joyce signaled for Megan to come to her. Mary saw them in a discussion and wondered if it was about her status.

Megan approached her. "Mary, follow me."

They entered the hallway, and Megan led her to a golf cart a short distance away. They got in it, and Megan started going down the long hallway. She turned to Mary. "I am giving you the complete tour."

Megan turned right on to another hallway that had blue walls.

"Remember we were on the white-walled hallway? There are also red walls, and those you avoid. I'll give you a diagram of the layout when we return."

Mary nodded in acknowledgment. The end of the hallway was near, and Mary could see an entry door on the right. They got out, and Megan reached for the phone on the wall near the door. Megan spoke in the phone, and soon the buzzer lock on the door sounded. Megan opened it, and they entered. Mary could see a table in the small room. There were goggles on it. Megan looked to her. These are night vision goggles.

"Find one that fits you."

Mary tried on a few until she found one that fit her comfortably. She could see there was another doorway at the other end of the room and followed Megan through it. It was a huge room, and at first Mary couldn't make out the end of it. The product was on long tables with pipes the dripped water over it. She leaned over to get a close look at it. They looked like a mushroom with small bumps covering it. She couldn't see what its color was wearing the night goggles. They examined the room for a few more minutes before leaving.

Back in the hallway Megan asked, "Any questions?"

"They ever explain how it was discovered?"

"That is one question that is best left unasked. Remember this is a highly secretive and secure operation. I will explain more to you later, and I am not privy to all the details. You have to prove to be highly trustworthy. Especially if you want to enjoy the benefits."

"Trust me, I do. I can't believe this is happening."

"It is hard to believe where we were a few years ago until they approached us," Megan responded.

"I will be forever grateful you recommended me for this, Megan."

"That is what friends for are," Megan said with a smile. "The lab is next on the agenda, then you can go home."

"I am ready for that."

It seemed like an endless white hallway to Mary, but Megan finally slowed down and turned left onto a green hallway. She had to use the phone near the door, and Mary couldn't hear what she said, but the buzzer to open the door was loud and clear. The door opened to another long hallway. Mary could see their many doorways on both sides of the hallway. They walked down to the end of the hallway, and Mary could see many of the rooms contained an exam table. None of the rooms were occupied until she noticed one of the rooms had its door closed. Megan knocked on the door and was told to come in. Mary gasped when she saw John on the exam table, and he was unconscious and naked. She noticed he was connected to medical equipment. He was getting a thorough exam by two medical personnel. One came over and had a discussion with Megan. Mary looked at John, and it was difficult to imagine the time she had with him hours ago. He was barely breathing. Megan nodded to the medical person and came over to Mary. "Let's go in the hallway."

"I am sure you don't remember being here, Mary, but we all were examined. Most go home fully dressed as per the agreement and are unaware of the exam. You know the situation with John. We needed some leverage while we determined his status. The exam will determine the amount of product he will need if we alter his status. He will be going back to his home in a short while. I think it is a good time for you to get some sleep. Your car is outside near one of the windmills close to your home. One of the maintenance workers will lead you to it. I will contact you tomorrow." She came over and gave Mary a hug.

They went out the door, and there was a guy in a cart waiting for her. He drove her for quite some time until he stopped at an elevator. They got out, and he said, "This is the emergency exit for this area."

"That is what this circle on the door means?"

"Yes."

They entered and went up until the second story. The door opened, and she saw a ladder. He asked if she thought she could climb it, and despite her fatigue, she signaled she could. *It is great being eighteen*, she thought, and she climbed to the top. She got off at a platform and remembered to close the door that sealed the ladder shaft. She thought for a second if she had everything because once the door was sealed, it couldn't be opened from platform. She had her car keys in her jeans pocket. She closed the door and pulled on the handle to make sure it was secure. She did the same for the door at the base of the windmill when she left. The swoosh sound of the giant windmill blades always unnerved her, and she went to her car. She opened the trunk and retrieved her purse. She got behind the wheel and started the car. Her mind was dwelling on what to say to John when she saw him. The drive home was quick, and she couldn't undress fast enough to get into bed.

CHAPTER 9

HE HEARD THE PHONE RING and reached out in the direction of the noise. He found his bed stand and patted around until he located the phone. His blurry vision made it difficult to recognize the phone ID listing. He pushed the On button.

"Hello," he managed to mumble. The dial tone greeted him when he lifted the phone to his ear. He hung up the phone and wanted to go back to the oblivious state he had been in. But slowly his mind started to grasp where he was. His blurry eyes started to clear, and he realized he was in his bedroom. It pained him, but he managed to sit up. A quick scan had him locating his clothes on top of his dresser. He pulled off his blankets. He was nude. "The bastards got me again."

He laid back down and pulled the covers over him. "Fuck it," he said and fell back to sleep.

It was dark outside when he awoke. The alarm clock read 11:45. He rolled over and sat up on the edge of the bed. *How in the hell do they manage to get me here?* entered his thoughts. *I wonder if it is Saturday or Sunday.*

He found his TV remote, and when the TV came on, he selected the weather channel. He noticed that the weather was still on for Saturday and a cool rainy Sunday was expected. He stood and stretched and went looking for his cell phone in his pants pockets, but it wasn't there. *Where is it? I think I left it in my jacket.*

He slid his pants on and went to the kitchen. He located the jacket draped over one of the kitchen chairs, and the cell phone was where he had left it. He unlocked the screen and saw a number of emails. Most were congratulating him on the kick. He scrolled and was disappointed there wasn't a contact from Mary. He went to his computer and found the same results.

It seems like the kick was a lifetime ago, he thought. *It was one of my best nights and also the worst. I don't know what the hell is going on.*

The refrigerator light came on when he swung open the door. There were still a few beers left. He noticed the pizza box and pulled out a few cold slices and put them on a paper plate. The microwave was set for two minutes, and he put the pizza in. He felt a chill and went and retrieved his shirt from the bedroom while the pizza warmed up. The ding from the microwave let him know the pizza was ready. The beer nearly choked him with the first swallow, but he quickly recovered. The recliner was welcome as he still felt a bit groggy. He started rocking it at a slow steady pace.

Last night was pretty fucking stupid. I let my penis do my thinking. It was fun, but I think I am in deeper shit than I was before. Mary set me up. There is more to it than her being in high school. The money and her sexual experience.

Her saying "It's been too long" came to the forefront. *I am sure she said it,* and not that he was too long.

"Oh shit!" *I never even asked her about birth control. She had said everything was covered. I hope it is the case, but with her being in high school, who knows? I could be in a world of shit.*

The pace of his rocking increased. He was so tempted to text her. It is late and to ask her about birth control now is beyond stupid. He needed those other beers.

Her clock read 3:45, and she knew it was Sunday morning. Mary went to the bathroom to relieve herself. She flopped back on the bed and felt her cat Midnight jump on the bed. Midnight was completely black, and only her purring attempts for attention let Mary know she was there. "Okay, I know you are hungry."

Mary went to her kitchen, and her night light was enough for her to locate the can of cat food. She emptied it in Midnight's food dish and filled up the water dish and went back to her bedroom. She looked at her cell phone that was on the table next to her bed. There was a text message from Megan but nothing from John.

Good, I need to think on this. What would the old Mary do? That was her last thought as she pulled her blankets over herself.

Megan got the outfit she planned to wear to church from the closet. She turned when she heard the knock on her bedroom door. "Come in."

Marissa's head came into view. "Joyce needs to talk with you. It's on the red phone."

"Then you and Ted better leave without me. If it isn't long, I'll drive myself to church."

Megan went to the old monitor room. They had moved them to another more secure location. The red phone was on a desk.

"Hello, Joyce."

"Yes, Megan, I just received an order from the Deciders, and they plan on expanding operation in the Michigan thumb area. We will need more recruits soon. The reason I am calling you is that they have brought one of the prospects into the holding room, and I would like you to assist with his potential signing. He is cleared from where he was and officially available."

"Okay, you do know this will be my first attempt at this task."

"Yes, I am well aware. You have had the training. I have confidence in you."

"What time do you need me?"

"As soon as you get what you need together, go to the holding room and ask for Tina. She is expecting you."

"Who is the person I will be discussing this with?"

"His name is Bradley Raymond. He was in construction when he lived in New York. He helped build bridges. He moved back here a few years ago to be with his very ill sister. She passed on, and he now lives alone. He had a stroke six months ago. He is better but not well enough to live alone. He has no family left. The more detailed report is at the holding room for you to exam."

"Can he speak?"

"Yes."

"I will be there soon."

"Call me later."

53

Megan went back to her bedroom and entered the closet. She opened a file on the floor and got the items she needed and went to the elevator entrance. *I need this to go well*, she thought during the elevator ride. She unplugged one of the charging golf carts and made her way to the holding room. The desk clerk noticed her enter and turned to gather a folder when Megan entered. "Hi, what room is he in, Tina?"

"Megan, he is in room 6, and the observation room is 7."

"Thanks, has he been there long?"

"He arrived an hour ago."

Megan nodded and gathered the report and walked to room 7. There was a table that faced the one-way mirror, and she put the report on it. She pulled out the desk chair and settled into it. She saw the name Bradley Raymond on the folder and looked up and saw him sitting in a recliner observing a television. A glance down to the open folder informed her that he was eighty-seven years old. He had been in World War II and was an engineer for the Army Corp of Engineers.

He certainly has the qualifications, she thought. *I wonder why he never married.* That is one question she could ask. She finished the report and gathered her thoughts. She added the report to her folders and got up and went to room 6. Mr. Raymond slowly stood up when she entered. She stuck her hand out. "Greetings, Mr. Raymond."

His handshake was weak, but a strong voice answered "Hello, you must be Ms. Anderson?"

"Yes, but please call me Megan."

"Okay, Megan. Please call me Brad. I heard it so much in the service it stuck."

"Please sit in the recliner, Brad," and she walked to the couch near it and faced him when she sat. He looked at her. "How old are you Megan?"

"I am seventeen at the moment, Brad."

"At the moment? I don't understand."

"Well, this is what I am about to address. What I am about to propose to you will give you a chance for a new lease at life."

He thought and grabbed his cup that was on the table next to the recliner. He took a drink. "I have no clue on how that is possible. You sound like a salesman after my money."

"Brad, I know Mike discussed this with you. But I can provide proof that what I am going to show is real. We don't want your money. We don't need it. We need what you have to offer."

"What would that be at my age?"

"We need your expertise and experience."

"What for?"

"We will inform you if you join the group."

"What if I don't?"

Megan tried to keep composed. She knew her answer was a lie. "We will send you back to the home where you were."

He sat back in the recliner. "I rather stay here. Refresh my memory on what this all means? I am not as sharp as I once was."

What a relief. "Brad, we need your knowledge in engineering to build more power plants. Plus the quarters underneath them. We are in one of them now. What we offer in exchange for this is another voyage in life. I know this is true. I am on my second. I am actually a few months younger then you."

He had a confused look on his face when he handed him her portfolio. "This is the story of my life in pictures."

He opened it up, and she felt his gaze every time he looked at a photo. "Are these real? They aren't fakes.

"No, they are real. But the one way to prove it to you is sign the form, and we will give you a glimpse of what you have in store. Make sure you read the form and understand the conditions on it. One thing you must agree on is that you can't have children or a wife. You will be sterilized but can date and have all the sex you can handle, but you must be loyal to the group. Any behavior that gives exposure to the group will not be tolerated."

He laughed. "All the sex I can handle? I can't even do that."

She thought a moment then laughed when she understood what he meant.

"We can get you to my age. Then you won't have the issue," she said, smiling.

"This is all difficult to believe. What if I change my mind afterwards?"

"After you sign, Brad, or after you transform?"

"Both."

"Brad, if we have the know-how to transform you into any age, you can be sure we have the know-how to return you to your present state."

"I bet you do. It doesn't sound like a good thing. Can I get a little sample of process? If it does what you say it does. I will be happy to become a member of the group."

"That is very reasonable, Brad. But you will have to sign first. It takes time for you to transform and some time after that to get you to the age you think works best for you."

"So is this a one-time thing?"

"Our group members can stay as long as they want if they follow the group's guidelines and don't get killed. We can't bring anyone back from the dead."

"Oh, I thought you aliens could do that."

"What makes you think we are aliens?"

"It doesn't sound possible any other way to me."

"I can't indulge you the information you need, but we aren't aliens. You will eventually learn more about it as a member of the group."

"Ah, secrets. I worked for the government, so I am aware of those. You a secret government project?"

"Like I said I can't indulge any information, but I can assure you we aren't part of the government."

"A mystery. Well, at this stage of my life I haven't much to lose. I will sign."

"Great!" She handed him a pen, and he signed the form.

"We can start the process after lunch." She stood up when he did and went to shake his hand. He opened his arm wide as to give her a hug, and she let him embrace and hugged him back. The door opened, and a food cart appeared. Two young women pushed it in, and another came in with a folding table. She quickly set it up, and the other opened the carts and started to distribute the contents on the table. Brad was stretching his neck to get a good look. Megan went to the table. "See anything you like, Brad?"

"Is there any fish?"

"Yes, we have salmon, and we also have shrimp."

He rose and went to the table. He got a plate and piled on all sorts of food. "I was never one to miss a meal," he said to Megan.

"Is that your secret to longevity?"

"Could be. I'd rather know yours."

"You are a sly one, Brad," Megan, said laughing.

"Will I see you after the transformation?"

"It's possible sometime in the future. You okay with that?"

"Well, you said all the sex I could handle," he said with a big grin.

"Oh, Brad, I don't think you could handle me. I will see you again, though." *Men never change*, she thought after she left the room.

CHAPTER 10

IT WAS CHILLY WHEN HE opened the door to retrieve the Sunday paper. He couldn't help but smile when he saw a picture of the ball going through the uprights on the front page. The caption for the article of the car-winning kick was "What Were the Odds?"

He walked to the kitchen and put the paper on the kitchen table. There was a clean bowl in the dishwasher. A box of Raisin Bran still had a good portion of cereal when he shook it. He smelled the milk that was in the fridge and decided to take a chance on it despite a sour smell. He munched on the cereal and continue to read the article. He decided to cut that out and save it, maybe for his kids if he ever had them.

Oh shit, he thought as his thoughts turned to Mary. He retrieved his cell phone from his bedroom. There were no calls or texts from her, and he was relieved to see no one else had tried to contact him. The cereal was soggy when he returned, but he finished it. *I wonder what they did to me this time.* The urge to return to bed was getting stronger. It was time for the Lions to come on, so he went and got a beer and took the paper to the recliner. The TV came to life. The game did get his attention due to a fight on the sidelines between the two teams. Penalty flags were everywhere. When the refs sorted it out, a player from the Lions and one from the Kansas City Chiefs were ejected. *This looks like a war now.*

A few beers later, he jumped in celebration as the Lions won 23–21 on another last-second field goal. *They are giving me a heart attack with these close games. What to do for dinner?*

He was not in the mood to cook. A submarine sandwich sounds good. He found his sweat pants and shirt and quickly put them on.

His running shoes were in sight, and he decided he would walk and run to the Subway in town. It was less than two miles. His wallet was on the dresser, and he made his way out the front door. He stretched in his front yard and then started a slow jog. He felt good. *They must have given me a shot of youth.* He laughed and quickened the pace. A few cars passed, and some honked their horns to acknowledge him. He was surprised when he looked at his clock and saw only thirteen minutes had passed when he arrived at the Subway store. *Where was this feeling when I was running cross-country in high school? It seemed so easy.*

The store was nearly empty. He noticed a few teenage boys sitting at a table near the front entrance window. He selected the sandwich and was in line when he heard one of the teen boys mention Mary's name. He paid for the sandwich and sat at a table that was within earshot of the boys.

"Those bitches Mary and Megan seemed to have influenced most of the girls. The others have been refusing to do put out," said one of the boys.

Another at the table said, "You ready for this? I was hunting in the woods near one of the windmills. I could swear I saw Mary's red Camaro parked near it, so I pulled out my binoculars, and I saw her come out of it and drive away. I think she is involved in something illegal."

The others looked at him. Then one said, "I think you are bull-shitting us."

"Oh yeah, then see what happens when you try to drive up to one of the windmills?"

"What do you mean?"

"Oh, try it and you will find out. I won't try it again."

"You are a trip, George. Mary may be strange, but you need to lay off the drugs."

"Fuck you guys if you don't believe me," he said as he left the store.

John saw them look at each other, and they soon followed.

So Mary and Megan are influencing the high school to wait on sex. That sure isn't what I saw the other night. He hurried up and finished his sandwich because the feeling of arousal was becoming strong, and it could become embarrassing. He left and started to jog home. The skies were starting to darken, and the "Sea of Red" was becoming clearer. The Sea of Red was what the people called the red lights on the windmills. They were on top of the windmills, and they all blinked off and on in unison. They were there to notify their location to air traffic. It looked like the windmills were endless as the lights could be seen for miles. He wondered what happened if you did drive up to one. The thought stuck with him on the journey home. The car keys on the kitchen table caught his attention when he arrived home.

Oh, what the hell, he thought, and grabbed the keys. It was nearly completely dark, and the headlights lit up his driveway. The windmill on Van Buren road was the closest one, so he drove to it and headed north. Its blinking red light made it seem close, but after a few minutes of driving, it still seemed far away. He looked at his odometer, and after three miles he finally saw the road leading to the windmill. He slowed and turned right onto the road, but stopped when his headlights exposed a sign. "No Trespassing allowed!" the sign read.

Oh fuck it! He had to turn around anyway. He drove up the road and was almost to the base of the windmill when bright lights came on, and he put on his brakes. A siren blared, and then an amplified voice said, "You must vacate the premises immediately. You are being videotaped and the local police will be here soon if you don't."

The kid was right, he thought, and made a quick U-turn and was off to Van Buren road. So if the kid was right about that, then he could be correct about Mary being there. He drove home and got in his recliner. They were videotaping me? Now he wondered if there is a windmill connection with Mary and Ted. He texted Mary. "I need to talk to you."

Mary was feeling much better after her long sleep. The brunch she made of tuna fish sandwich and vegetable soup eased her hunger pains. She checked her email and texts. The cheerleader coach wanted to have a practice tomorrow after school to get ready for basketball season. The indoor cheers were a bit different than the outdoor ones. Midnight jumped on her kitchen counter, which was a sign the cat wanted to be fed. She got a can of cat food and a small paper plate and fed her. "Maybe if we could include you in our cheers, Midnight. Have you run across the floor with your total blackness, causing the other team to have bad luck," Mary said with a chuckle. She looked back at Midnight. She wondered if the product works on animals. But who could she ask? *I'll check with Megan to see if she knows.*

She went to the bathroom and turned on the water for the Jacuzzi. She needed to soak and poured in a portion of scented bubble mix. She made sure her alarm systems for the house were activated and went to the bathroom, undressed, and walked into the Jacuzzi. She sank in the water until only her head was above water and then activated the water circulation vents. "Oh, god that feels good. Almost better than sex." She laughed at the thought.

Almost is right. She had forgotten how good sex can be. It had to be nearly forty years ago since the last time, the last time it was good anyway. *Damn menopause, I don't want to go through that again.* The buzz from her cellphone interrupted her thoughts. She saw a text from John, "I need to talk with you." *I bet he does. I hope he isn't too pissed. I would be.*

The cellphone was put down, and she closed her eyes to think while the water massaged her.

Megan looked up from her homework when she heard a knock on her bedroom door.

"Come in."

Ted came in. "We had someone drive up to one of the windmills. It was John Dwyer. He turned around and left immediately."

"Could you tell if he was alone?"

"He was."

"We need to find out what is going on with him. I will go visit Mary," Megan responded.

Megan texted Mary, and Mary responded that she was home.

She hoped Mary hasn't violated the guidelines, she thought during the drive to Mary's.

Mary opened her front door when Megan arrived.

"What's up?" Mary asked when Megan walked in.

"We just received a report that John Dwyer drove up to one of the windmills tonight."

Megan could tell by Mary's surprised look that she was unaware.

"He recently texted me that he needed to talk with me, but I have no idea why he went there. I haven't told him anything."

"I think you better find out what he is up to, Mary."

"I agree. I have been thinking on what to say to him because of the way I left him Saturday morning. I will find out."

"Good, I will be expecting your report," she said and closed the front door behind her.

Well, goodbye to you too, bitch. Thanks for the help. I better see what John has on his mind. She got her car keys and purse and was on her way.

John heard his ringtone and saw he had a text. It was from Mary. She was on her way over. He thought about it and responded with "Okay."

He got up and picked up his trash near his recliner and threw it away.

He wondered how she was going to respond to yesterday.

Her car lights shone on his driveway. He waited for her to knock on the door.

When he opened it, she gave him a hug. "I am so sorry," she whispered in his ear.

"What happened that morning?"

"John, I got called in by the group. There was an important meeting."

"Oh, you mean the group that drugged me on the way home? Are you connected with the mafia?"

"John, I wasn't aware that was in the plans, and no, I am not connected with the mafia."

"Well, what was the plan? To get me laid?"

"No, that was me being attracted to you."

"You say you are eighteen, but you act and have the experience of an older woman. So you take me to a casino, and we have fun afterwards. What eighteen-year-old does that? Who are you really, and what is your game?"

"John, you are correct. I am not eighteen. I cannot tell you what the group is. You were the one that stumbled onto it when you were robbing Ted's place. The group did use you because of that and apparently drugged you again to see the result of their efforts. I think you know what I mean. The kick was amazing, and I think you have looked in the mirror. I would imagine you were surprised at your sexual prowess last night but won't admit it. I wasn't because I expected it. That was another reason I asked you out. I can't tell you more because it would put you in jeopardy."

"Does this have anything to do with the windmills, Mary?"

"What are you talking about?"

"There was a kid at Subway who told his friends he saw you come out of one of them and get in your car and drive away. He said that when he went towards the windmill, he was scared away by their warnings."

"So you believe him?"

"Well, I drove to a windmill last night, and their warnings are very effective. I figured if he was correct about them, then he might be correct about seeing you. Plus the warning said I was being video-taped, and that made me think of Ted's video setup that I saw."

"Ted has a video setup? Is it for the windmills?"

John hesitated. "I actually didn't see what the video cameras were focused on."

"Anything else that kid said about me?"

"Well, he did say you and Megan were influencing your female classmates to cause them to not put out."

"Do you believe that after last night, John?" Mary said, trying not to laugh.

He looked at her and sat in his recliner. "I'm sorry, Mary, I guess the stress of my screwup is getting the better of me."

She took off her jacket and came over to sit in his lap. He adjusted his seat position and guided her in. She held his chin and gave him a direct gaze into his eyes. "Let me help you get through this."

Their lips touched, and she cuddled into his arms. He could feel the tension leave his body. "So how old are you really?"

"I am old enough to know better."

He laughed. "Just like a woman not to tell her age."

"John, I may be older then you think, but I have a ton of homework. I need to go. Everything okay now?"

"I have to ask one thing, and I feel like a heel for not asking before. Did you have birth control last night?"

"John, like I said before. Everything was covered," she said with a smile.

He smiled in return.

She gave him a soft lingering kiss and got her jacket. "I am pretty busy this week, John. But I'll be in touch."

"I look forward to it."

He stood and gave her hug. He watched her walk to her car. *So she is attracted to me. What have I gotten myself into?*

CHAPTER 11

CHARLIE SCHULTZ WAS SHOCKED WHEN he had seen the kick that won the car. *I have to give him credit. I didn't think it was possible.* The local news had contacted him. At least he was going to get good publicity. John Dwyer had called and felt relieved that John agreed to accept the red Chevy Cruze. It was fully loaded but had been on the lot for a while. He was looking forward to Monday morning.

Mary called Megan after leaving John's house.

"We need to talk about John."

"Oh, come on over."

"On my way."

So we are influencing the girls to not put out. Mary laughed and thought. *Damn straight. We are not just sex objects for those horny boys.* She never thought it was like this when she decided to return to her teen years. *The boys think they are entitled to do whatever they please with us and then shit on us when they are done. Nope, it has to stop.*

She followed the driveway to Megan house, but parked it outside and off to the side and away from the garage door. The yard was well lit, and she went to the front door. Megan opened it and let her in. She looked around and then to Megan. "Where are Ted and Marissa?"

"I told them that we needed to talk, so they went downstairs. So what is going on with John?" "He is on to me. He is sure I am older. I had to concede I was when he questioned me. I just told him the group will contact him in due time. He also heard one of our classmates say that he saw me exit a windmill and drive away. John went to one of them to see if the kid's warning of not to visit them because of an alarm was true. The speaker on the warning told him he was being videotaped, and he began to wonder if the video setup here was connected to the site. He claims he never did see what our videotape was observing."

"So he might be more intelligent than you thought?"

"Yes, I am sorry to say."

"Did he mention the kid's name?"

"Nope, but he also said the kid was telling his buddies that you and I were influencing the girls to not put out."

Megan let out a laugh. "Then it is working!"

"Well, John doesn't believe it after our night."

"That turned out to be good timing. So do you think you threw him off track, Mary?"

"For now. What is the plan for him?"

"Joyce and the deciders are discussing that. It will be put off for now because of the exposure he is getting with car promotion. You just keep tabs on him."

She wished she knew who the kid was that saw her come out of the windmill? She'd like to know where he was to spot her at that location.

"I think that isn't much of a concern at the moment. We now know that we can't do that anymore. Anything else you want to discuss, Mary?"

"No, I better get home to do my homework. Then I have cheerleading tomorrow night."

"Ah, the life of a teen. I already finished mine."

"Bitch."

Megan laughed.

John sat up in bed. God that dream seemed real. A windmill was chasing him, and he could feel the power of the blades get near him when he woke up. The floor felt cold as he walked to the bathroom. He relieved himself and went back and sat on the edge of his bed. A glance at the alarm clock showed it was 3:38 a.m.

Maybe that dream was telling me to get the hell away from this place. The bitch is that I can't afford to leave it all behind.

He lay back down and crossed his left leg over his bent right leg. He thought about what was said last night. *Mary is older than eighteen, but why is she in high school? Could this be a government sting? But over what? Could there be a terrorist threat involving the windmills?* He haven't been arrested, so it could to be something top secret. *They don't want any publicity.*

Damn, he needed to shut his brain off. The thought of a beer came to him. He wrapped a blanket around himself and dragged it to the kitchen and got a beer. He then went to his recliner. The TV glared at him with the press of the remote. He leaned back in the chair and adjusted the blanket until he was comfortable. He flipped the channel to SportsCenter and took a swig of beer. The new car entered his thoughts. He needed to get the sleep so he wouldn't look haggard for that publicity. He did make that kick, but did he get some performance enhancers to do it? Mary was right. He was surprised with his sexual stamina. It was never like that with Evelyn. But then she wasn't open to anything new sexually. He wondered what her new man thinks of her now that he had her. She was great in the beginning, but it seemed like he had to get a reservation once we began to live together. One reason he never was in a hurry to come home.

The beer was starting to hit. The TV became a glare. He was surprised when he heard the alarm clock in his bedroom. He went to it and hit the snooze alarm and crawled back in bed. It went off two more times before he knew he had to move. The shower felt good, and he left a message for Maxine that he would be in late. If she hasn't heard about the kick by now, he'd be shocked. The blender was noisy when he added ice cubes to a protein shake he decided to have for breakfast. He had to keep the energy up. You never know, he might corral Mary. He laughed at the thought. *She got me.*

The Reese hoodie was in his closet. It fit him great now with his weight loss and new six-pack. What will he say he will do with the car when he was asked that by the media? *Hmm, good question.* He'd prefer money, but decided to wait to sell it.

The local news van was in the car dealer parking lot when he arrived. Charlie Schultz greeted him when he walked in the lobby.

It became a five-minute blur as they rehearsed the promotion and then filmed it. Charlie asked where he wanted the car delivered, and John asked him if they could return his car home so he could drive the Cruze now.

"Not a problem," Charlie responded.

John handed him his keys and told him his address. "Would you have them drop off my keys at my office?"

"Sure thing. I hope you enjoy the car."

"I am sure I will. I hope this promotion gets you more business."

"That was the plan," Charlie responded with a smile. He gave John the keys.

The new car smell welcomed him when he got in. He looked at the controls and adjusted the mirrors. This had more room than he thought. The motor purred when he started it. He waved to Charlie and some of his staff and put it in gear. It was about a five-mile drive to his office, but he decided to make it longer to get a feel of the car. He was told it should get close to 40 mpg, so he was surprised at how much power the car seemed to have with four cylinders. He could get use to this. He arrived at the office and parked it in his usual parking spot. Maxine had his keys for his other car in her hands and gave them to him.

He gave her the keys to the Cruze. "You want to take it for a spin? I'll handle the phones."

She got up and gave him a hug. "I'll be right back," she responded.

John went into his office closet and got his spare suit he kept for emergency situations. He removed the hoodie and changed.

Maxine returned after a few minutes. "I love it, John. I could take it off your hands instead of you giving me a raise."

He looked at her with a smirk on his face. "Very clever try, Maxine, but I need the money from it or my other car."

"When you decide what you want to do, let me know."

"You really liked it?"

"Yes."

"Okay, let me think on it."

The phone rang, and Maxine answered it. "John, you going to be here for a while? A customer wants to see the car."

"Most definitely. I hope a few more will visit."

The customers did come, and John kept busy by offering a few rides. He took the opportunity to talk insurance and made a few sales.

"Another few days like this and you might get a raise, Maxine," he said at the end of the day.

"Music to me ears, John," she said with a smile. "So any plans tonight? There are rumors you have been seen with one of the cheerleaders."

"Maxine, they aren't rumors. I met one, and we had a chat, and we hit it off. She is eighteen and very mature for her age."

"Okay, John, I hope you know what you are doing."

"Don't worry. I will take it slow." *If Mary does*, he thought.

John was pleased he was able to tell Maxine the truth. *People are going to talk regardless, so let them. Mary isn't the teenager most will assume. She may not be a teen.* He decided it was best not to focus on that.

The Reese gym was filled for the first basketball game of the season. John decided to sit in the bleachers that were considered neutral. He could view Mary, and she was facing that side of the gym leading the cheers. The cheers were a bit different than the football ones. The top roll offered back support by leaning against the gym wall and was his favorite. The girls' game was first followed by the boys. The usual small turnout for the girls' game never seemed to change no matter what their record was. It was rather sad this year, because the girls' team was one of the best in the state. It was led by Reyna Frost, who was one of the best girl players in the state. She was an all-around player who wasn't afraid to mix it up to get a rebound. She was a team player and leader. Their total team effort that made it fun to watch.

The crowd would slowly file in as the boys' game got closer to its start. The games were fun, the girls' team won, but the boys lost a close game. Mary had come up and sat next to him when she had the chance, and now he was waiting for her after the game. He didn't care if anyone saw them together, and Mary had told him that being with him helped keep the boys away. He was surprised Megan didn't show for the game. Mary came walking toward him in the hallway next to the gym, and he couldn't help but smile.

She returned it and asked, "What is on your mind?"

He whispered in her ear, "I know they don't know how you have them fooled."

"Why is that?"

"You said you were older than eighteen. There must be a reason you are here," he responded.

"There is, John. But not now in the hallway. Let's go."

She gripped his arm and led him through the mass of people all jockeying for the nearest exit. The chill of the air when they exited caused Mary to start running to his car. He caught up with her, and she pointed her finger. "Look."

He turned to see what she was pointing at, and he heard her laugh as she sprinted away from him. He laughed to when he realized she had tricked him into slowing down. He ran as hard as he could in an effort to catch her, but her lead was too great.

"Here, you drive," John said to Mary when he arrived at his car.

"Okay," she said when given the keys. She unlocked the doors with the remote. Mary scanned the inside and looked at him. "It is bigger inside than I thought."

"I thought the same when I first got in. Let's see what you think of the ride."

John watched her put the car in gear and accelerate to the parking lot exit. There were snow flurries exposed by the headlights.

"You might want to slow down. There could be black ice."

John felt her stare and decided to keep quiet.

She turned left on Van Buren to go to the rural area between Reese and Munger. She got the car up to 80 mph then slowed down to 55. "It does have some power. But I'll stick to my Camaro."

"Oh, I was hoping for a trade."

"Ha, ha," she responded.

It was starting to snow harder. "I think we better get to my house," Mary said as she found a driveway to turn around in.

He watched her focus on the road. She was beautiful, and he wondered if she really liked him, or was it because of the group? "Mary, why are you hanging with me?"

"I like older men," she said and gave him a smile.

"Just how much older than you am I?"

He waited, and she didn't respond. He knew she heard him.

"John, I can't tell you. It would put us both in danger."

"We are alone. I won't tell anyone."

"John, we are never alone."

"Really? You mean we were being watched in the hotel room?"

"Okay, we weren't. If we were, you would likely be a porn star by now and have women lining up to date you."

He laughed. "So I was that good? But I still can't reason why it is dangerous to tell me your age."

"You do remember Joyce? The evening drive she took you on? Did you think it was a joy ride? Please let's drop the topic. I said too much when I told you I was older than eighteen. You said you wouldn't tell anyone. Then please don't mention that to anyone."

"I won't." But he didn't know what else to say. The way she told him convinced him there was a danger.

They entered the driveway to Ted's house. Mary's car was still parked outside with a layer of snow on it. She parked beside it. The view from the house blocked by her car. She leaned toward him, and he did the same to her, and they kissed. He felt the blast when the car shook. Steam surround the car and made it difficult to see.

"Oh my god," Mary blurted out.

"John, I need you to stay in the car!" She got out before he could respond.

He saw her disappear in the cloud of steam vapor.

"Screw this!" he said after thirty seconds and opened his door. He saw the shattered windshield of Mary's Camaro. The house was flattened on the north side of the home. There was a huge hole in the roof, and then he saw what looked like a water heater a short distance away. It was split in two when he examined it. It had exploded and gone through the house and roof. He had heard of it happening reading insurance claims.

"Mary," he yelled. *Oh god, I hope they are all okay.*

He went to the garage door and entered. "Mary!" he yelled again.

"John, get out of here. Leave before it is too late."

He pinpointed her voice and went toward her anyway. She was in the basement. She was upset when she saw him. "John, they are all okay. I need you to leave."

"What the hell is an elevator doing in the basement?"

"Shit," she responded. "Come here quickly. I smell natural gas from the hot water supply line."

He noticed it too and quickly followed her through a cement door she had opened. She closed the door behind them and sealed it with a push of a button. "Let's go!" she said and ran to the elevator. It opened when she pushed the button on the wall. They got in and heard a huge explosion as they went down. He looked at her. "What just happened?'

"We just died, John."

CHAPTER 12

A LOAD EXPLOSION IN THE distance and the house shaking scared Maxine. "Oh my god. What was that?"

"I don't know, but it didn't sound good," answered her husband, Sam.

He got up and went outside. He stayed a short time because of the cold temperatures. "I see what could be smoke to the east. I expect a call from to the fire department. I am going to get my winter gear on."

"Do you want a quick bite to eat?"

"Yeah, I have a feeling this might be a long night."

Maxine warmed up some leftover chili, and she heard the on call radio go in alarm mode. Sam answered it and said he would be there soon. He made quick work of the chili and told Maxine that it looked like there was an explosion at the Anderson house.

"Oh no, I hope everyone is okay."

"Time will tell," he said. He came over and gave Maxine a kiss and then left.

She decided to call John in case he wasn't aware. She got his voice mail and decided to try again later.

Sam arrived at the station before most of the other volunteers. A shovel was near the door, and he went out and started on the exit driveway. There was around three inches of snow, and it was the light, fluffy kind. It wasn't that heavy, but he hadn't done it in a while. *We need a snow blower*, and he was tempted to go home and get his. Soon, more volunteers arrived, and there was now enough to make a run. Sam, being the senior member of the group, called a quick meeting and explained the situation to them. They all had a feeling this could be a run where death was involved. The police were on the scene, so they decided to get there as fast as they could. They would radio for help if it was needed. The snow slowed them down, but after ten minutes they arrived on the property. The police closed the driveway access after they passed.

Where is the house? was his first thought.

The spotlight the police provided exposed smoldering debris. The house was completely leveled. The garage debris covered the cars inside it, and there were two cars parked on the left side of the driveway. Norman Frank, the Reese sheriff, came over to him.

"Sam, it looks like we had a hot water heater explode and launch itself through the roof. We found it about a hundred yards away. I am guessing there was a natural gas explosion afterwards. We have found no signs of life."

"I am not surprised, Norm. Do you have any idea who was here?"

"The cars are of the family members, Mary Brunell, and John Dwyer."

"That the car John won?"

"Yes, he isn't at home, so we expect he was here."

"Okay, Norm, I will call the fire inspectors in once we make sure it is safe."

Sam got the crew going. They started to soak the debris to cool it off. Back in his thoughts, he hoped he didn't have to tell Maxine that John may have perished with the others. The water tank for the fire truck was nearly empty, and the water on the debris was starting to freeze. Norm was nearby.

"Norm, that is all we can do tonight. We can be back tomorrow morning."

The evaluator came to a halt, and when the doors opened, John was taken aback by the long hallway in front of him. "How is this possible?" he said to Mary.

"Anything is possible, John, if you have the money and connections."

"So we are dead now?"

"That explosion was likely a fireball. Our cars are there, so it could be difficult to explain if we showed up out of nowhere."

"You said the others weren't there. So if that is true could we have been gone as well?"

"I am pretty certain they are down here. They will not be happy to see you with me. They will make the decisions. Follow me."

He got in the cart she choose to drive. She looked much older than eighteen as she drove with an intense look on her face. It seemed so strange with her still in her cheerleader's outfit. It made him tense thinking of what she said. "We just died," was stuck in his thoughts. She slowed down, and he saw a door. "John, I have to drop you off here. You will be alone while I discuss this with the others. Don't panic."

"I won't. I'll let you do that."

She glared at him and then led him in the room. He could see it was an interrogation room with a table a chairs.

She closed the door without saying anything. *Way to piss her off, John*, he thought to himself.

Mary got back in the cart. *The shit could hit the fan*, she thought. She turned down the hallway to the conference room. She cracked open the door and noticed Megan, Ted, Marissa, and others were sitting watching a person speak on a huge movie screen. She was in enough trouble, and she slowly closed the door. She didn't need them to think she was listening. She drove far enough away to see them when they exited. She did wonder who they were listening to. She hadn't seen that woman before. She looked up, and the group was exiting the door. They gave her some strange looks when they walked past her.

Yeah, I am a cheerleader, she thought.

Megan spotted her and ran up to her. "Something wrong?"

"You have no idea. Ted and Marissa coming soon?"

"They should be. What happened?"

"Your house blew up."

"What the hell happened?"

"I drove John's car to your driveway and parked next to my car. Just then there was an explosion, and the car was blanketed it in steam. I told John to stay and went inside the house. The bedroom area was flattened. I didn't think you would be home, so I started down the stairs to the basement to check the damage. The door to the elevator was not damaged. I then smelt natural gas, and John came down that instant. I opened the cement block door to the elevator and secured it. I decided to bring John down here, and it turned out, I was correct about the gas danger as there was a bigger explosion on the way down. I would guess there was a big fireball and there was nothing left. I think they will say we all vaporized."

"Any idea what caused the first explosion?"

"John was pretty sure it was due to a faulty water heater that launched itself through the house and exited via the roof."

"Where is John now?"

"He is the waiting room."

"I am going to find Ted, Marissa, and Joyce. We will meet you in the waiting room."

Looks like the kid was right, John thought to himself. *Mary could have come out of one of the windmills. Anything is possible now. One stupid move has led to a landslide of stupid moves. There seems to be no end. Except it might be the end if I am considered dead. Why is this place down here? Who knows about it? I need to have some answers.*

The door opened, and Mary entered. He could see her worried look and asked, "What's the verdict? Are we dead?"

"Too early to tell. They are meeting about it now."

"They didn't include you?"

"No, John, they didn't."

"I'd wish you could tell something on what this is all about."

"John, I can't. But to put you mind at ease, this isn't some secret government project or anything sinister."

"That doesn't help me trying to put some sense to it."

"They will inform you if they decide you need to know. I wouldn't try and make waves at the moment."

"I thought you said it wasn't sinister.

"The project isn't, but people can be."

"So there is an unknown underground project under the Reese area. I would guess the windmills are involved. It blows my mind, Mary."

John jumped when he heard a voice come through a speaker above the room. "John, I would advise you to stop thinking. It doesn't appear to be one of your strengths."

The door opened. "Hello, pretty boy, remember me?"

He looked at Joyce. She seemed younger than the last time.

"I could never forget you, Joyce."

"You do say the sweetest things, John. Come with me to my office. We need to talk." She opened the door, and he followed. She looked back in the room. "Mary, go with Megan. She will update you on our discussion. Oh and, Megan, find her something to wear."

"Will do."

John got in the passenger side of the cart. Joyce took off, and John noticed pipes at the top of the wall that ran parallel with the hallways. *That must supply the heat*, he thought. Joyce slowed down and stopped next to a door. She got out and punched in a code on the door lock, and it opened.

She held the door open for John.

"Thank you," John said in response.

"You are welcome."

There was a desk with a few chairs in front of it. She pointed to one of them, and he sat down. She sat down and opened a drawer. She had a pistol in her hand, and she was far enough away to make any attempt to get it. "John, you are being observed, and you see the weapon, so please don't think of trying to use force."

"It hadn't entered my mind. I don't know what I am dealing with to go there."

"Let's keep it that way. So you were at the house when it blew up, correct?"

"Yes, I went and saw the hot water tank when it landed. It had exploded and exited through the roof."

"Where was Mary?"

"She went in the house in the section that was left. I assumed she was looking for the family."

"What happened next?"

"I went towards the house yelling her name. There wasn't a response immediately, so I went in although she didn't want me to. She had told me to stay by the car. I smelt natural gas, so I went in to find her. She was in the basement and grabbed me. Then pulled me through a cement block door. She pushed a button, and it secured the door. We went to the elevator and heard a tremendous explosion on the way down."

"You were lucky the elevator motor was far enough away from the house and protected underground."

"Will you tell me why all this is here?"

"John, I would, but how can I can trust you. Care to explain why you were burglarizing the Anderson home?"

"I have no explanation for that, other than I was feeling sorry for myself after my breakup with my girlfriend. She ran off with everything."

"So you thought it would be easy pickings. Did you have another target next in line?"

"Yes, I thought it would be easy. No, I didn't have another. But I'll be honest in saying, if the first went well, I may have considered it."

Joyce sat back in her chair, and John could tell she was in deep thought.

"John, here is the dilemma I have. I think we could get you home by saying you gave Mary your car for the evening. She used it to go home and change and was going to return for a dinner you were preparing. The thing is, you must remain silent about what you have seen. Or you can be dead and we will relocate you."

"So those are my only options?"

"I am open to suggestions."

"So if I return, you still won't tell me what is going on?'

"Correct, there would be no need. The less you know, the better we feel."

"If I return, it would be difficult to prove. I would think you would have me monitored."

"You guess right."

"Would I see any of you again?"

"You mean Mary?"

"Yeah."

"No, we have other plans for her. Even if you stayed, you may not have contact with her."

"Okay, what are the options if I stay with the group? Would you tell me why this is all a secret? I assume I would have to relocate."

"You would no longer exist as John Dwyer. You cannot have contact with anyone you know. Yes, you will be relocated with a new identity. We will assign you to a task. There are policies you must agree to. Like, you can't get in a long-term relationship or have children. Now why would I or anyone agree to do this? If I tell you now, you have to stay dead?"

"You won't kill me if I can't decide?"

"John, if we wanted to kill you, you would already be dead. But time is a factor if we are taking you home. Has anyone tried to contact you?"

"Yes, but Mary told me not to respond and turn off my cell phone."

"Good. Keep it that way until we figure it out."

"It's okay, Joyce. I may be young, but a start over appeals to me."

"Good choice. Yes, you are young, and you have actually had a glimpse of it already. I think you have noticed a difference. We have a product that we grow here that can regenerate our bodies and keep us the age of choice. The truth is I am over a hundred years old. I stay at this age of around seventy for a number of reasons. Mary is actually over ninety."

"That is a lot to take in. So what happens now?"

"We have living quarters down here, and we will have a few meetings to get you acclimated to the group. Those meeting should answer your questions. I know it is getting late, so I will have Mary take you to your quarters. She should be able to inform you of the routine you need to follow. She will have to also."

Joyce got up, and he followed. She turned to him. "This is really an opportunity of a lifetime. Don't blow it."

He smiled at her and said, "I bet you have been wanting to say that."

She laughed.

Mary was in a cart parked behind Joyce's. He sat beside her.

"I am staying dead."

"Interesting, and I have no choice. Are you hungry? I am starving and the cafeteria is nearby."

"Oh, it's open this late?"

"Yes, the chefs are on call and live nearby."

"That is amazing. Yes, I am hungry. I had thought of us having taken out last night."

Mary started the cart down the hallway. "Hmm I don't recall that."

"Watching you drive took my mind off my stomach."

"Did I scare you, or were you admiring my driving ability?"

"I just wondered if you could get more out the four cylinder than I could. I have to say you did."

She turned to him and smiled. She slowed the cart near a door. "This is it."

He followed her in and was surprised. The interior looked more like a restaurant than a standard cafeteria setting. The tables had a cloth covering and wooden chairs. There were menus placed on top of them. Mary led him to one. He sat and picked up the menu.

"Choose anything you want, John."

"How do you order?"

"Someone will be out shortly to take it."

"So it is a restaurant."

"Yes, named cafeteria," she said and laughed.

They made their order to the waiter. When the waiter left, John said, "Are you upset with what happened?"

"If they can get my cat, I'll be in a better mood about it."

"You think your cat survived the explosion?'

"John, the truth is I didn't live there. I had my own place near Richville."

"Then you could have stayed here?"

"Well, I was supposed to be living at the Anderson home, and my car was there. The group provided it. I hope to get my cat and things."

"The group provided it. The car also?"

"Yes, you will be briefed on it."

"It all sounds too good to be true. Why the secrecy?"

"Think about it, John. What would happen if the world knew about this? How it would change everyone's view on life. If there isn't enough of the product to go around. Who gets it then?"

"I suppose the rich?"

"Yes, the very rich but under certain conditions. They have to fake their deaths. They become young and start over somewhere else."

"Wow, so that is what finances this?"

"That, the windmills and other things."

The food arrived and they ate quietly.

"Do I leave a tip?" he asked her.

"Nope, they are paid well."

They went to the cart.

"Do they live here?" he asked before she got in.

"Most do, and they are all members of the group. They work where they are willing and can help."

"So I can assume they are all much older."

"You assume correctly."

"I am taking you to your quarters. I doubt they got any of your things."

"You going to be nearby, Mary?"

"If you mean am I going to share yours, the answer is no. But I will know where you are."

"Joyce said you were over ninety. To think I was worried about robbing the cradle, and all along I was targeted by a cougar."

"Oh, I hate that term."

"Cougar?"

"Yes."

"Well, what term did you use back in the day?"

"A May-December relationship." She slowed the cart down. "We are at the living quarters."

81

He followed her in, and he saw a lobby desk to the right and a hallway to the left. He could see what looked like a hotel hallway straight ahead. She talked to the lobby clerk and got the key cards. She walked up and gave him his card key. "John, there is a schedule for tomorrow in your room. I will contact you and drive you to the first meeting. I am not feeling well and going to my room. Talk to you later."

"Okay, I hope you feel better. Good night."

"Thanks, good night."

He followed her down the hallway and found his room first. The card opened the door, and he switched on the light. The room was bigger than he expected. There was a queen-size bed and a television across from it. It felt weird not to see a window, but the lighting made the room bright. The walk-in shower was a surprise when he viewed the bathroom. *How did they get this in here? I can't believe no one knew about this whole project.*

There was a closet door next to the bed, and it had few of his clothes in the drawers. The heater/air conditioner unit was along a wall, and the seventy-two-degree setting was perfect for him. The T-shirt in a drawer was perfect for sleeping, and he undressed and slipped it on. The TV remote was on a stand next to the bed. He turned on the TV for an all-news channel. He lay in bed and turned off the lights. The news became noise when he focused on his thoughts.

What the hell did I do today? I committed to not have a wife or kids. He thought about Evelyn. *Maybe it is the right thing. I still need more answers about this place.*

Then he heard the word *explosion* broadcast on the national news. It was about a hot water heater explosion causing the deaths of five people.

I am dead!

CHAPTER 13

HER PHONE CONTINUES TO GET John's voice mail with each attempt to contact him. Maxine didn't want to believe that John may be dead. His other car was in the driveway at his house, and there were no lights on. She didn't get a response when she rang the doorbell. The office was dark when she drove in the parking lot. "There goes my raise," she said, laughing, before she started to sob.

What is going to happen, entered her thoughts. *I will need to call the home office when Norm or Sam confirms he is gone. I wonder if they will give me a chance to run the office, or will it be the "good ole boy" network again. I love John, but I know I could do his job.*

Her cell phone rang, and for a second she hoped it was John. She looked, and it was from Sam.

"Hello, Sam, how is it going?"

"We are calling it a night, Maxine, The gas was shut off to the house, and we put out what fire there was. Norm has the area secure, so we are on our way back."

"Did you want me to make you something to eat?"

"No, right now I am not in the mood. This is the first fatality in Reese for as long as I can remember."

"I know. One is difficult to accept, but five is difficult to believe."

"Where do we go to find the next of kin? Norm will need that before we can release the names."

"I'll check the office and see what is on file."

"Okay, I'll meet you over there."

"I am already there, Sam."

"Okay, be there in five minutes."

Maxine got a tissue out of her purse and dabbed her eyes. *Damn, makeup*, she thought when she looked at the tissue. She got the keys for the office and got out of the car. She had to get her cellphone out and used it as a light to unlock the door. The room lit up with the flip of the switch. She closed and locked the door behind her. She would see when Sam arrived. She took off her coat and hung it and went over to the file cabinet. She trusted the old system of filing more than having everything on a corporate computer system. She had both, but the files were filled out by hand for each customer.

She found the Anderson file and knew where John's was located. But what about the girl Mary? *The school might have her records. I'll mention it to Norm.* She opened the Anderson file when she noticed Sam had arrived in the parking lot. He hugged her when she let him in. He pulled up a lobby chair next to her. She scanned the Anderson file, and the only next of kin listed was each other. "Sad to say, but it looks like the Anderson clan may have ended tonight," Maxine said to Sam.

"I sure hope you are wrong."

"Me too!"

A ringing phone woke John up. He sat up trying to remember the dream he was having, but it soon faded away when he answered the phone.

"Hello?"

"Good morning, John. We are going for breakfast in an hour and then to a meeting to discuss our situation. That give you enough time to get ready?"

"Do I have a choice, Mary?" he said with a laugh.

"That would be a no," she replied.

"I will be ready. I assume you will be picking me up?"

"You assume correctly, sir."

He resisted the urge to lie back down after he hung up the phone. The hot water from the shower felt good. He wondered how Maxine was doing. *Will she miss me? Will the office stay open?* All entered his thoughts while he scrubbed himself.

He was dressed and ready when he got the text saying she was outside his door. He acknowledged Ted, Marisa, and Mary as he walked to the passenger side of the cart. Ted and Marisa were in the back seat of the cart facing the rear of the cart, and his seat faced the front. Mary drove to the cafeteria, and John ordered an omelet. They didn't speak during the meal. John wondered how they would react to being told they had to start over. John still marveled about the construction of this facility, the many long hallways and many rooms. It seemed like they were endless. Mary had a worried look on her face when she parked the cart near an entryway. They entered a small conference room with a round table that seated about a dozen. They seated themselves.

"John, think my insurance covers an exploding water heater?"

"I don't know, Ted. They would have to investigate to make sure you weren't building rockets in your basement."

They all laughed in response.

The door at the other end of the room opened, and John watched as three women and two men entered. He was surprised that Joyce wasn't one of them. They sat themselves on the other side of them. The woman in the middle looked at them and said, "Good morning, I am Ruth." She pointed to her left, "William and Mabel" and then to her right "Sharon and Greg."

"We have been discussing the situation you are in. We have decided to give you a few options and see if you can come into agreement with what you want to do. Megan, we consider you the leader, and, John, for this decision, you will have a chance to abide with what those three want. If you don't approve, we will offer you other options for you alone. Is that understood?"

"Yes."

Ruth turned to Megan. "Option 1 is for you return to Reese in your current setup. We believe we can justify a reason of why you weren't home. Option 2 is to have you all start over in a different location. You will be given the same freedoms you have now. Option 3 is to stay underground in a capacity you choose. Option 4 is to become an infant for an aboveground couple."

John was taken back with option 4. The thought never occurred to him.

Megan looked at both Ted and Marissa. Ted whispered in her ear. "Ruth, we need some time to discuss it."

"Of course, if you think you may need a few days, let me know."

"We'll go to the conference room now, and then we will let you know."

"Fair enough. John, you stay here."

Megan and the others left. He saw Mary give him a glance before closing the door. "John, is there an option you preferred?" asked Ruth.

"Not being familiar with the operation, I would take option 1."

"Is there an option you wouldn't want?"

"Option 4 seems a bit extreme. Do you lose all your current memories when you become an infant?"

"To be honest, John, we haven't had anyone revert that far back. There hasn't been a need or have we had any volunteers."

"You looking for volunteers?"

"Not overtly. Why you interested?" Ruth said with a smile.

John smiled back. "Not something I'd want to do. But you could do it if I was?"

"Yes, we have the technology to do that. You are actually younger than your present age. I am sure you noticed the difference."

"Yes, it is pretty amazing. But one question, would giving an aboveground couple a child violate the rule of having children?"

"No, because the child and couple would be one of us and know the rules. We don't want anyone having children or a wife. It could cause an issue by wanting them to be young also. Too much temptation to inform them of the secret. We can't take that chance."

John thought for a few seconds and said, "Is it okay then for a person to marry and have children if they are in the group?"

"You can be a couple, but any children would have to be provided by the group. Megan isn't Ted and Marissa's child. She actually older then both of them. She has been in the program longer, so she is considered the leader of that group."

"How long has there been a group?"

"John, that is something we keep classified for security reasons."

The door opened, and Megan and the others came in. They sat down. Megan looked at the group and then at Ruth. "We have decided that since we are established here, we want to do option 1."

Ruth looked at the others and then replied, "Then we will have to get the plan in motion now. She explained what was going to happen, then she looked at John. "John, you don't have much choice in this. You will have to return. The conditions you agreed to are still in effect. We will implement your move out of the area if necessary."

"I understand."

"Okay, time to get the plan in motion," Ruth said as they all stood up to leave.

Maxine didn't feel like going to church this morning. She would rather grieve in private. Sam just left to go back to the site. She sat at the kitchen table and was picking up her cup of coffee when her cell phone buzzed. It was a text from John. "Maxine, my phone didn't have a signal from where we were. I see you texted me a number of times. Is everything all right?"

She quickly dialed his number.

"Hello?" John answered.

"Oh my god, it is you!" she said through tears.

"Yes, why are you crying, Maxine?" he said and was having trouble keeping his emotions in check.

"There was an explosion at the Anderson house, and we thought you were killed. Are the Andersons with you?"

"Yes, they are with me. We have been snowmobiling all day. What explosion are you talking about?"

"Oh, thank the Lord. The water heater blew up and went through the roof at their house. The gas line was exposed, and it created a fireball that demolished the house. With all the cars there, we thought everyone was in it."

"That is hard to believe. I will go back and tell them. In the meantime, see if you can find a hotel nearby for them to stay while we sort this out. I'll let you know if they have other plans."

"Okay, John, I'll call Sam and Norm, and they can call the news. It went national."

"Really? Well, at least we aren't dead. I will call you back soon."

CHAPTER 14

RUTH AND JOYCE ENTERED A conference room in the underground facility. "This could be very unpleasant," Joyce said to Ruth,

"I know. I heard from my sources he wasn't pleased we made the decision without contacting the board."

"I have a feeling he never tried getting hold of board members on a weekend."

"I wouldn't use that as an explanation, Joyce."

"Oh, I won't. If he wants to change what we did, then it will be changed."

"The more things change, the more they can stay the same."

"Yes, but we are lucky to witness the changes."

The huge computer monitor that was in front of them powered up.

The screen flickered, and then a white wall in the background came into view. A camera moved to the left and focused on a door. Ruth recognized the young man as the second in command. He wore a mask that resembled a hawk, and that was what they called him. He came to his desk and sat down. The camera focused on him. "Greetings, ladies."

"Good morning," they both responded.

"I understand you have been dealing with some unwanted events. Please explain what has been transpired."

Ruth cleared her throat. "One of the operative homes had a water heater explode through the roof of the home. It caused a gas leak, and there was a follow-up explosion that completely demolished the home. Fortunately the three that lived there were in our underground facility, but one operative who, for security reason listed that home as her home was just arriving there. She went to investigate after the first explosion, and the person she arrived with followed her despite her request for him to stay in his vehicle. She smelled gas and entered the hidden entrance in the basement just seconds before the explosion. She pulled him in to save him."

"So that was last night?"

"Yes."

"What has happened since?"

"The media thought all had perished. The story went national. So we gave them the option of starting over elsewhere or returning. They chose to return."

"And the nonmember of the group?"

"We gave him an option to join, and he did. So he went back with them."

"Give me background information of him."

Ruth nodded to Joyce.

Joyce knew what he was about to say would not go over well, so she hesitated before she said "His name is John Dwyer. He is a twenty-seven-year-old insurance salesman. He came across our operation when I caught him in a burglary attempt at the home."

"He what?"

"He entered a monitor room. I stopped him there. Going by the directives, I didn't let the police get involved. I hooded him and put him in his car trunk. I drove him to one of our operative homes, and we knocked him out with a shot. We gave him the product for testing purposes and drove him home, where he woke up the next day naked and totally confused."

"I am confused. So how did he get to be at the house when the explosion happened? Could he have been the cause of the explosion to hide any evidence of his burglary attempt?"

"No, sir, we had a volunteer to watch him. She became very close to him. He was with her at a basketball game, and they just returned home when the explosion happened. The others had come down about five minutes earlier for a meeting."

They watched him write on a notepad. He looked up and said, "Let me see if I have this correct. You have a burglar who is now real close to one of our operatives. He is now part of your group because he was at the wrong place at the wrong time. A house has blown up, and you don't seem to know what the hell to do? Am I missing something?'

"Mr. Hawk," Ruth responded. "John Dwyer is their insurance man, and he can get the ball rolling in rebuilding the house at its current location as soon as possible. He will also have funds available through the insurance company. We have been in contact with the group's builders, and they are ready to get started once the investigation by the local authorities is conducted. John was told we have videos of him doing the break-in. That threat is still there if he tries to go out of line. He only knows the basic facts about the group."

"I see. I stand corrected. I will have to send this report to the board. They will decided if they want to take it to the Decider. Until that time, send in status reports. Good day."

The screen became black.

"What do you think, Ruth?"

"I hope we aren't the ones that get volunteered to become babies."

"Oh God, I hate to think of being a baby with our current minds."

"Yeah, that would be a nightmare, Joyce."

Jason walked up to Sam. "It was a faulty water heater, Sam. The safety value failed."

"I figured that was the problem. Thanks for responding so soon, Jason."

"I happened to be in the area. Oh, I heard the good news. Great when you can investigate knowing there weren't fatalities."

"You bet it is. Have a safe trip home."

"Thanks."

Sam watched him drive off. He walked over to Norm. "The inspection is over, Norm. It was a faulty safety valve on the water heater that caused it to explode. Any word on the Andersons' return?"

"Nope, but look in the driveway."

Parked across the front of the driveway was a huge brown RV. It was hauling a trailer with four snowmobiles behind it. "Now that is a setup I wish I had," Norm said

They watched as the Andersons, Mary, and John got out of the RV carrying suitcases. They waved to the driver as he left. Norm watched them proceed up the driveway and viewed their stunned reaction when they saw the remains of their house. "Holy shit!" was what he read off Ted's lips.

Marissa had her face cupped in her hands as if afraid to look. The two girls looked at him and pointed in the direction of the debris field. He nodded approval, and they sprinted to it. He saw John walking toward him.

"What's the verdict, Norm?"

"Hot water heater malfunction. Then an explosion followed that was caused by the ruptured gas line."

"I have read reports of that happening."

"Lucky you all weren't here. You going to make arrangements for lounging tonight."

"I know! Yes, I had Maxine start the process when I called her."

"Tell them to take their time going through the debris. Your car may be able to run, but the others look totaled. Oh, by the way, I see your keys were still in the ignition."

John reached for his pockets, and he didn't have the keys. Then he looked at Norm and said, "That's right, Mary drove. We were in such a hurry to leave when we got here, I never thought to ask for them."

I hope he believes because not asking for the keys is the truth, John thought as Norm waved in response and went to talk to Ted.

"Ted, when you get a chance to get your bearings, will you contact me on what your plan of action is? Will you rebuild and so forth?"

"I have discussed it with John on our way back. We do plan on rebuilding on this site. I am too fond of Reese to relocate."

He saw a smile on Norm's face. "Ted, we will keep the area secure while you get a new start."

"Thanks, Norm. That should be real soon. Do we have the okay to start?"

"Yes, the investigation is over. I hope you find something of value in that mess."

"Thanks, again."

Norm sat in the squad car. He watched them going through the debris. He wondered if John would go talk to Mary. He did believe him about the car keys. It just seemed strange to him that anyone would be careless with a new car. He waited for five minutes and drove off.

Megan was pretty upset that almost all her belongings were missing. It was the same for Mary. At least she had her laptop with her at the meeting. Mary had left her laptop at her house. Ted and Marissa actually seemed excited about the prospect of building a new home. They were already making designs on the way back. They knew what the insurance didn't cover with the cost, the group would. Megan looked at them all and waved them over to her. "I think it's time to go. It is nearly 2:00 p.m., and we might as well get settled. John, have you tried your car to see if it runs?"

He reached for his pockets. "Strange I can't find my keys. Oh wait, I wasn't driving last," and looked at Mary.

The surprised look on her face made him laugh. "They were in the car, Mary. Norm noticed them there."

"He mentioned them to you?" asked Megan.

"Yes, I told him that we were in such a hurry to leave she forgot them."

"Think he believed you?"

"Yes, I was actually telling the truth as far as that goes."

"Okay, he didn't make a big deal of it, so we won't either. Let's get going."

"Mary, you can have the honors." He picked up some of the luggage."

She gave him the look and then sprinted to the car.

That was brilliant, John, he thought to himself. *I am in trouble now.*

She stopped and looked at her busted windshield and her car and then went quickly to his. It started, and she backed it to their location. The trunk was popped open, and Ted and John managed to pack everything into it. Megan looked at them all. "Ted, you and Marissa need to sit in front. We will squeeze in the back. Megan, being the shortest, sat in the middle, with John on the right side and Mary on the left. Ted looked back. "You guys comfortable?"

"It beats riding in the trunk," John responded.

They all chuckled.

"Well, that was depressing," Marissa said, looking at the house site.

John's cell phone buzzed. "Maxine just texted. Norm sent the media to my office parking lot. They have been waiting."

"Just remember, the less said, the better," Megan instructed.

John was wondering what Mary was thinking. He hadn't had a chance to have a private talk with her since he joined the group. He looked at her differently knowing she was much older.

There were a few media trucks in his office parking lot when they arrived.

They got out, and the reporters focus were on Ted and Marissa.

John spotted Maxine and went to her awaiting arms. She hugged him

"I'm so happy you are alive, John."

He smiled at her. "Oh, I bet you were worried about a raise."

She swatted him lightly on his arm. "What a terrible thing to say."

He laughed. "Just kidding," and he gave her a hug again. "With all the work we need to do with this event, you will get your raise when we are done."

The interviews lasted about ten long minutes. John hugged Maxine. "I'll see you Monday morning, if not sooner."

"Okay, you get some rest."

Megan signaled John that it was time to leave. "John, we will take you home first," Megan said when he got in.

"Was it something I said?"

They responded with a laugh.

Megan looked at John. "Mary will drop us off at the hotel. We will stay there for a day or two. The group has delivered a car, and if you don't mind, Mary will use this one so she can return home. We will get in touch with a training schedule."

"Okay, no problem with Mary using the car. I will get the paperwork started for the insurance claims. I understand the group builders will be on site soon. I will make sure the operation is funded."

Ted put the car in reverse, and they went to John's house. John got out and checked his pockets for the house key. He pulled it out and signaled that he had it. Ted got out and opened the trunk. He found John's suitcases and put them on the driveway. Mary waved as they drove off and gave him a call on the phone signal and pointed to him. He smiled and looked forward to her call. The bed was still unmade when he entered his bedroom. The house just had minor changes, like open drawers. He put the suitcases on the bed and started to unload it. When he finished, he went to the kitchen. The beer was still in the refrigerator, and he grabbed one. *To think I was ready to give all this up*. He laughed as he sat in his recliner. The TV screen came on, and he scanned the cable listing for the movies. He found one he hadn't seen before and sat back to watch it. The show got his interest, but he fought the urge to nap. A touch on his shoulder caused him to wake up with a scare. Her blue eyes were the first thing he noticed. The auburn hair and smile came into focus.

She moved to the sofa next to him and sat down.

"You were snoring like a bear, John."

"I don't snore."

"Oh really." She had her cell phone in her hand and made some adjustments. Then she put a video on, and he saw and heard himself snore.

"Okay, but I don't sound like a bear. Maybe a semitruck, but I doubt a bear snores like that."

"Ha-ha, anyway you should get that looked at. It can be very dangerous if left untreated."

"So I can die? Even in the group?"

"Of course, you still have to be cautious. Tomorrow isn't guaranteed. We all could have perished in that explosion."

"So has it been worth it joining the group, Mary?"

She put her head down for a few moments and then looked up at him.

"John, there is a quote that youth is wasted on the youth. It took me awhile to agree with that, but as I got older, it is so true. Life goes by so fast, and eventually all that matters is finding out we aren't perfect. Once you learn to accept that, things seem so trivial. I have been given a second chance to view life in a different way. I have an old brain in a young body. Experience does matter, and now I can utilize that experience to do things I didn't take the time to do when I was younger."

"Does that explain the wild night in the hotel room, Mary?"

Mary laughed. "I said we aren't perfect, and I was horny. Besides you were given the shot, so I knew you would be at your best."

"Just how long was the last time you had sex?"

"Nearly fifty years, John. It is best you don't ask anyone's past or mention yours from this point on. That is one of the directives you will learn. I will tell you that I was married for a brief time, and my husband died in the war. That is all I will tell you, and we both will get in trouble if that is repeated. Oh, I can't have kids due to a medical problem."

"Looking at you, it is hard to believe you were older. I won't mention it to anyone." He had a feeling it wouldn't go well if he did. Another ride in a trunk was something he'd rather avoid. "I feel like a shit not asking about birth control before we started at the hotel."

"It is good to hear you say that, John. We have to get back into character tomorrow. We are dating, remember," she said with a smile.

"I won't forget. I was a bit surprised you guys decided to stay here."

"We had a discussion with another group member when we left you in the room. There was just too much of a threat of the doorway in the basement being discovered. They could fill it in, but then the buried elevator motor and shaft could become exposed. Just easier to build on the site, and that was a major influence."

"Influence or an order?"

"Both, but like I said, it's better with the less you know."

"So we can still date now that I am in the group?"

"For now, John, I need to borrow your car," she said with a laugh.

"Ah, I see the real story now. Use me, then throw me away."

"You are a smart one, John." She got up and reached for his hand. He gave it to her and got up from the recliner. She led him to the bedroom, and he closed the door behind him.

CHAPTER 15

JOYCE WAS EATING HER LUNCH when she got a text on her cell phone. It was from Ruth. She was to meet with her in the conference Room 4B. That usually meant a visit from the Hawk or, on rare occurrences, the Decider.

She had been expecting it. It had been a few months since the last contact. I hope they see the situation now as favorable. The house and cars had been replaced. John did a fine job, and so far his probation has gone well.

But she still felt something was about to happen. She finished her meal and drove to the conference room. Ruth was sitting alone at the table.

"Have any idea what this is about. Ruth?"

"It could be a decision about John and Mary."

"That is my thought as well."

The power to the monitor came on. The Hawk was waiting.

"Good afternoon, ladies.

"Good afternoon, Mr. Hawk."

"I need to be updated on the events after that disaster. Ruth, please start."

"Mr. Hawk, things have gone smoothly the last few months. The home was rebuilt without incident. The connection to the group entrance was restored. The cars were replaced, and most of this was led by John Dwyer. He coordinated the rebuilding of the house and replaced the cars."

"That is good to hear. He will likely be added to our plans. The Decider was not happy with the breach of the directives. They are there for a reason. He did understand your reasoning for it, but he can't let this breach be ignored. He has decided to have Mary and John enter in the Phase Z of our testing. He wants them to do it together. What is the status of their relationship?"

Ruth looked to Joyce. "Hawk, since they are both in the group, they have developed a strong relationship. I think he will do whatever she wants."

"I will be sending you faxes with the guidelines of when we want to initiate Phase Z. It will be before fall to give you time to react. Do you have any questions?"

"Isn't this the first time Phase Z will be tried?" asked Ruth.

"Yes, they are both young, so the transition should be easier."

"Mary is young due to being in the group. I think it is going to be difficult for her to accept this."

"You want to tell that to the Decider, Joyce? The plan needs to be carried out by any method you decide to use. You have a few months to complete the process that will be sent to you. We will take responsibility after you complete the beginning segments. Anything else?"

They answered, "No, sir."

"Good day, ladies."

The monitor shut off.

"I can't believe they did that," Joyce said.

"Really?" Ruth looked at her with a stare.

Joyce sat silently. "Okay, you win. I can believe it."

He watched Mary stretch on the infield of the track. She was sitting in a circle with her track teammates. They were talking while they pulled on their legs before the scheduled events.

She seems to transform herself to a teenager with ease. They all seem to like her. She doesn't get involved with petty issues. She said that comes with experience. She always wanted to run track, and now she is. "Life is too short" is her favorite statement, and she has influenced me. We both have been training, and once you start running, you warm up quickly no matter what the weather conditions.

They had run the St. Patrick's Day 5K race in Bay City, Michigan.

He was surprised when he finished under twenty-eight minutes and she beat him by twenty-nine seconds. That stoked his competitive spirit, and he started training harder. She never rubbed it in, but he knew she didn't want to lose to him.

He watched her take off her sweats. He maroon track uniform came into view. She was running three events today. The first was the 400 meter run. It was an event she hadn't run but volunteered to replace a sick teammate.

She was a distance runner, so he expected her to struggle with this grueling sprint. It was once around the track. He found a spot along the bordering chain link fence. It was near the finish line. There were bleachers close to him, but they were nearly filled by supporters of the four teams at the event.

He saw Mary find her running lane and lined up at the start with five other girl runners. She smiled when she located him after a quick scan.

He gave her a thumbs-up.

The runners were at the starting line. Mary choose to stand at the start. The gun went off, and they all broke off at a fast pace. Mary was last but close to the pace. They went around the first turn, and she started gaining on them in the long straight away. She made it to forth entering the final turn. She got into third as they ran the final stretch. The crowd and teammates cheered her on, but she didn't have enough of a kick to pass the two in front of her. She bent over with her hands on her hips. Her teammates came over to congratulate her. She responded with a few quick hugs. They announced the times and how they placed over the loudspeaker. She walked over to him, when she had time between events.

"That was a great run. Ready to make it another event to run in?"

"Oh god no. That was harder for me than the 5K."

"You have anything left for the 1,500?"

"No, if only I could get a quick dose of the product."

"Shh, I can't believe you said the word."

"You are converting to the group," she said with a snicker. "Don't worry, John, I have the power of youth. We recover fast."

"So I have noticed." He winked at her

"You will get yours later."

"I can only hope," he said and smiled.

Men, she thought to herself. *Things don't change much. Even after all these years it's like they are the same Kool-Aid but in different flavors.*

She went back to the girls and put her sweats on. John watched the other events. Then it was time for the 1,500-meter race. Mary was racing against a dozen runners, including two of her teammates. So far she had been the best runner at Reese for the 1,500 meter. It was early April, and the track season was in the early stages. The group of runners gathered at the starting lines. John wondered how much the 400 had taken out of her. The race started, and he could tell she was struggling as she didn't push for the lead early. She usually tried to be the rabbit and start off strong, hoping to tire out runners with her quick pace. The first of the four laps finished, and Mary was near being last. John could see she was concentrating on finding a rhythm, and her stride increased. She gained ground by the end of the second lap, but was still behind the pack of runners. In the middle of the third lap, he could see her easing up and grabbing the back of her right leg. She started limping and got off the track. She was bent down, rubbing her leg when her coach got to her. She put her arm on his shoulders for support as they walked back to the team area. Her teammates handed her gear, and she got a few hugs. When she started limping toward him, he knew she was in pain. He walked toward the fence gate and waited for her.

"What's the matter?"

"Oh, I got a cramp in my right calf. I must be dehydrated."

John helped her to her car. "You want some company tonight?"

"John, we have a group meeting tonight, so I will meet you there."

He looked puzzled.

"Tell me you didn't forget the meeting."

"Okay, I didn't forget the meeting, Mary," he said with a smirk.

She just shook her head and took off.

I need to remember being a smart-ass turns her off.

The match was nearly over, and he was certain Reese was going to win.

He got in his Chevy Cruze and started his trip home. The price that he was offered for his Nissan Altima was far more than anything he could get for the Cruze, so he sold it. Work had increased with his exposure from the kick and his handling of the Anderson disaster. Mary had added a purpose in his life, and he was absorbing some of her beliefs. Her words had a wisdom because of the experience value behind them. The pizza place was open, and it tempted him. He managed to keep going when he remembered the chicken and bean soup in his refrigerator. Mary had showed him how to make it. The trees over his driveway were starting to bud. *It won't be long before they are green again.*

There wasn't any mail when he checked the mailbox on his way in. He saw he had an hour before he had to leave and quickly showered. The microwave was set for three minutes for his bowl of soup. He waited and then went to the table to check his email with his laptop computer. The soup was quickly devoured, and a second bowl filled him up. He glanced at the kitchen clock and knew it was time to leave. The drive to Ted's house took about ten minutes. The Detroit Tiger pregame show was on the radio. The briefcase was on the passenger seat. He kept notes on the meetings. He knew the group was at various locations worldwide. The windmills were a good money maker, and since they required twenty feet of concrete deep bases for each mill, it had been relatively easy to construct underground facilities at the same time. Those facilities were used to grow the product. The product required a dark and moist setting. They had arranged to have their own water supply piped in from Lake Huron. It was a secret, but an expensive operation. He also found out that many choose to live in them. They stayed underground all the time. Many just enjoyed their positions, and some got lost in their video game reality after they were exposed to them.

There were directives for all the group members, and he was learning about them now. The Decider was the leader of the group. You followed his directives, or you would be banished. What that meant he didn't know or care to find out since this was a highly secretive group. The vast majority had been considered dead already.

He arrived at the Anderson driveway. The new house was now a three-story log cabin. It had a three-story winding staircase in the front lobby. It made you want to view each floor above ground. They put in an instant demand water heater for safety reasons. The house was rebuilt in two weeks. The Reese residents were amazed. The Andersons had an open house when it was finished for the village.

The Andersons gave John all the credit, and his business increased. But in truth the group had quietly been in charge. Mary's Camaro was parked off to the side of the driveway. He parked next to it. She greeted him with a kiss at the front door and escorted him in. "How's your leg?" he asked.

"Still a bit tight, but it is getting better."

"Good, are the others here?"

"No, they went down earlier. We better get going."

Mary led the way, and John was happy to watch her walk ahead of him. She was in great shape and had a figure to match. Although he looked older than her, he felt like he was her boy toy. She was a woman in every sense.

"Does the elevator have a video camera?" he asked.

"I don't think so, why?"

"I just wonder if we are being watched."

"Why do you think that?"

"Well, if I was to ravish you, I just wondered if I could get away with it?"

"Only if I let you." She laughed.

"Oh, you could stop me?"

"You would be surprised."

"Really?" He made a move to her as a joke, and his body was shocked when it landed on the floor. He felt her grip on his arm and looked up and saw her smiling.

"Surprised now, John?" She let him go and helped him up.

"I hope there isn't a video camera," he responded.

The elevator doors opened. They got on a nearby golf cart with Mary at the wheel. "So did you receive training for your fighting with the group?"

"No, John, I took judo during the war."

"What war was that?"

"John, you just studied the directive to not ask group members about their history. But I think you can do the math."

"Oh shit, I forgot."

"I wouldn't let it happen again."

"It won't."

She said do the math. She was in her nineties, so it must have been World War II she was referring to. *That is difficult to imagine.* He looked at her young teenage body. She glanced at him, and he smiled at her.

"What's on your mind?" she asked.

"I am just admiring how beautiful you are."

He could she her face become flushed. "Thank you, my darling."

He could feel himself blushing. It was the first time he heard *darling.*

They arrived at the conference room, and he got a kiss when he walked to her. They entered the room and was surprised it was empty. "I am sure this is the place," she said. They sat at the huge round table. He spotted the coffee pot on the back table near the door. "You want a cup of coffee, Mary?"

"Yes, with just cream."

He got hers first and took it to her.

"Thank you," she said with a smile.

He went and got his with cream and two sugars.

He sat back down when a group member came in and scanned the room until he saw them. He walked to them. "Mary and John?"

"Yes," Mary answered.

"I was told to tell you there is a delay of an hour before the meeting will begin. The cafeteria is open for you."

"Thank you," Mary responded.

She waited for him to leave and looked at John. "Hmm, that is strange. That has never happened before. I wonder what is going on."

"Good question. Do you want to go to the cafeteria?"

"Yes, maybe they will have the custard I like."

"That does sound good. Let's go."

One hour earlier, Joyce and Ruth asked Megan, Ted, and Marissa to meet early in a different conference room. Megan knew it was serious when she saw the faces of Joyce and Ruth. They showed no emotion. They sat down, and Ruth said, "We have a situation that we need to act on. We have just received an email from Mr. Hawk. It gives us the guidelines that the Decider directed us to implement Phase Z. The two members to be tested in Phase Z are Mary and John."

"Oh my god," Megan reacted. "Do they know yet?"

"No," responded Joyce. "We want your input. We have until late August to get them in the first stage of the program. They will be transported to a new location after it is completed."

"Do we have any recourse in the matter?"

Ruth looked at her "Megan, this decision was The Decider's. You know he rarely changes his mind. Do you have any reason that might have him reconsider?"

"No, but I would like to have time to think on it."

Joyce responded, "We don't have a lot of time. We have to get them on board, or we will have to force them."

"When do you think we should inform them?" Megan asked.

"We were going to ask you if we should."

"I don't know. What if they don't want to?"

"Then their fate will still be in the Decider's hands. You know what that could mean."

"It is difficult to forget even after all these years. If we don't tell them, then what happens if they recall the past. They could cause a number of problems."

"How so?" asked Ruth.

"They could keep that to themselves until they decide to use it against the group."

"I can understand them being upset, but they would still be group members and benefiting from the program."

"We have a meeting tonight in a few minute with them. We could discuss Phase Z as part of training to see what their reaction is."

Joyce looked at the clock and called a group member in the room.

She instructed him to tell Mary and John of the delay. When he left Joyce said, "That is a good idea, Megan. But first let's go over the email directive."

John got in Mary's Camaro after dropping his car off at his home. "Didn't you feel they were intense tonight going over Phase Z, Mary?"

"Things did seem a bit strange. That was option 4, correct?"

"Yes, I remember that. Why would they want a Phase Z, was my thought."

"John, it could be useful if someone is trying to hide."

"True, but they would be at the mercy of someone else."

"Yes, but being a baby is the complete start-over. Who would look for an infant?"

"Providing you have your memories of the past. Otherwise you have no way of being sure you can get your resources. It is a huge gamble."

"John, if the group wanted anyone's resources, wouldn't it just be easier to kill them?"

"Good point! I hope no one has to be part of that."

"I bet someone will."

Megan had a difficult time remembering her lines at the dress rehearsal for the school play. The Mary situation was entering her mind, and she had a difficult time focusing. The director told her to go home and get a good night's rest. She apparently thought Megan was nervous about the play.

Megan left the school parking lot with Mary on the mind. They had been friends during the war. Their husbands had served and died together. She recommended Mary to the group after she was established. She was like a sister to her. They had never been parted since they joined. The thought of Mary in Phase Z had her upset. *How could he do this? Mary has been a loyal member.* She could understand his concern about John. She wouldn't have any concern about him being part of it, and he shouldn't be in the group. How could anyone trust him? *But I need to find a way to be with Mary.*

Mary was returning home after she returned John back home. It had been an enjoyable night of lovemaking. Fatigue was starting to grab her. The darkness of the night made it difficult to see the unmarked country roads. She was shocked to see a deer in her headlight beams and reacted with a hard push on the brakes, but it was too late. She felt the impact, and the deer flew over the hood and came through the windshield.

The glass and deer hit her in the face and chest area. The car came to a stop in the middle of the road.

CHAPTER 16

JOHN HAS PASSED OUT ON his bed after Mary left. He was dreaming when the cell phone ring penetrated his thoughts. He rolled over toward his night stand and got his phone. It was 2:25 a.m.

"Hello?"

"John, this is Ted. Mary was in an accident. She hit a deer, and it went through the windshield."

"Oh god, how is she?"

"John, she is in grave condition. They took her to Saint Mary's Hospital. We are on our way now."

"I am on my way," he said and reached for his pants. He went to his closet and grabbed a clean shirt. He found his shoes, and it seemed like it took forever to put the shoes and shirt on. He felt the wallet still in his pants pocket and got the keys and was out the door. He tried not to go too much over the speed limit as he raced toward Saginaw on M-81. "Please let her live," he constantly repeated.

Saint Mary's Hospital was on Washington Street. M-81 converted to Washington inside the city limits.

The hospital parking lots were nearly empty when he arrived. It was 3:10 a.m. when he glanced at his watch. He spotted the Emergency Parking Lot sign and parked next to Ted's car. He quickly ran to the emergency room entrance and saw it was empty. Ted, Marissa, and Megan must be in the back. He waited at the empty admissions desk and was pacing back and forth when an employee finally returned. "Can I help you?"

"Yes, I am the boyfriend of Mary Brunell. I was told she was in an accident and is here."

She turned to her computer and typed. He watched her focus on the computer monitor. "Yes, she is here. But only family members are allowed. They can give you clearance. I will let them know you are here. Please have a seat in the lobby. Just remember, it's their decision."

"Okay, thank you." The lobby had a flat-screen television, but he wasn't interested. He was lost in thought when he heard, "John."

He looked at the entrance door and saw Megan holding it open. "Thanks, how is she?" he asked as they navigated the emergency room hallways. "Not good, John. They are going to take her to surgery as soon as they get all her test results." They turned a corner, and Megan grabbed his arm and stopped him. "John, she took the full force of the contact in the face and upper body area. She is really beat up and difficult to recognize. You still want to go in?"

"Absolutely."

Megan opened the room door and pulled the curtain open. John saw the monitors that displayed her heartbeat and oxygen levels. There were two nurses tending Mary and blocking his view of her. He glanced and saw the distraught faces of Marissa and Ted. Then he had a difficult time registering Mary's face when it came into view. It was bloated, and he couldn't locate her eyes with all the swelling. She had tubes in her mouth and a mask over what was left of her nose. Her breathing was shallow. A nurse turned to them and said, "We are taking her up to the operating room. There is an operating room waiting room on the sixth floor. Use the elevator just down the hallway to get to it. The other elevators don't have access. The doctor will meet with you there after the procedure is over."

"Thank you," was all Ted could respond.

John followed them to the elevator, and soon they arrived on the sixth floor. They saw the wall to the waiting room and entered the small hallway behind it. The room was empty because scheduled surgery was during the day. There were around forty chairs of various types. There were couches and recliners, but most were single seated chairs. There was a flat-screen TV hanging from a corner that gave it the most exposure. John followed them to the far corner where was the couch and chairs with extra padding.

They sat quietly until John asked, "Where did it happen?"

Megan answered, "Between Reese and Richville. Someone driving by saw the car in the middle of the road. They saw the deer and called 911. Norm arrived, and soon the ambulance followed. The fire department was called into action to remove Mary."

"Does the group know?"

"No, not yet. We will report when we have something. We are helpless at the current time."

John looked at Megan. "You think she'd be better off elsewhere."

"I think there may be other options that they can't provide. We will discuss it if there is a need."

"We need to pray there will be."

"Amen," they all said.

John prayed. *Dear God, let her live. She has made a difference in my life. She has had a positive influence with many young women. There is a reason she needs to be here. Amen.*

They turned the TV on to help pass the time, but Megan was lost in thought.

I wonder if this will change the Decider's decision if she lives. I would be willing to care for her. I can see that John cares for her more than I give him credit for. He isn't dealing with an eighteen-year-old.

They saw someone come in. The woman wore a blue surgical gown. She saw them and walked to them. "Are you Mr. and Mrs. Anderson?"

"Yes," Ted and Marissa answered.

"I am Dr. Blake. Your niece made it through the surgery. We reset her nose, so she should breathe easier. We have her in an induced coma to let her body heal. The next twenty-four hours are crucial. She is in acute intensive care. I am sorry to inform you that she had a miscarriage. She was in the very early stages of pregnancy."

Ted, Marissa, and Megan looked as shocked as John felt.

"Thank you, Doctor, is there a waiting room for that unit?"

"Yes, but I would advise you to go home and get some rest. It will be a long haul."

"Thanks, but we will stay."

"Okay, the staff and I will keep you updated."

"Thank you, Dr. Blake," Ted said as they followed her to the ACIU waiting room.

They closed the door after the doctor left. Mega looked at John "Did you know she was pregnant?"

"I had no idea. She told me that she couldn't get pregnant."

"That is what I have known for years. Do you think she knew?"

"She had been struggling running track recently. She thought she might have been overtraining as she wasn't having her period."

"She had a physical issue that wouldn't allow her to conceive. Now it seems that going back in time may have corrected it."

Ted spoke up, "Let's hope we can discuss it with her." He looked at Marissa. "I can stay up if you want to get some rest."

"No, I have my book in my purse. But if you want to—"

Megan got up. "I heard the cafeteria opens for breakfast soon. John, you want to come with me?"

It felt more like a demand then a question, but he said, "Sounds like a good idea. Do you two want anything?"

Ted and Marissa said, "No thanks."

He held the door open for Megan. "Thank you."

They walk the long empty hallway to the elevator. There was a nurses' station across from it. Megan asked a nurse, "Where is the cafeteria located?"

"On the second floor above the lobby."

"Thank you.

They waited for the elevator and took it down to the second floor.

John glanced at Megan. "Do you know where the lobby is?"

She smiled. "No."

They walked down another long hallway, and when it turned left, they saw a sign that pointed the way to the cafeteria. John noticed it was 6:30 a.m. "I hope it is open," he said.

"Me too."

John saw the door for the cafeteria, and the hours of operation were posted. "It's open," and he held the door for Megan.

"Thank you," she responded.

There were people behind the food stations setting up the stations.

"Get anything you want, Megan. I am buying."

She smiled in response. They both ordered omelets and sat in a corner of the near-empty dining room. They ate in quiet, and when finished, Megan asked, "Would you have wanted the baby?"

John was surprised by the question. "I haven't really thought about it, and I guess that says it all. I just want her to get well. Plus, if I am not mistaken, the group doesn't want us to have babies. How would that have been received?"

"Not well, in my opinion. This is a select group, and you are the only one that doesn't fit the criteria for joining. The baby would have been the second."

"You know I didn't seek or know about the group. I have asked for nothing from the group. I have done everything I have been asked to do. I understand I am basically on probation. I have deep feelings for Mary, and we both haven't any interest in being parents. At least she hasn't expressed that to me."

Megan sat quietly and looked at her cell phone. She picked it up. "I need to tell Ted to call the school. I assume they know, but it is better to be sure."

She finished her text and said, "John, you have done all the group has asked, and you may be asked to do more. The Decider may get involved, and we do what is directed by the Decider."

"The Decider may be involved, or has that already happened?"

"John, it involves more than you. So for now, let's just say *may*."

"I see. I have a feeling it depends on Mary. I hope we won't be in jeopardy."

"She already is. Let's pray she gets past this hurdle."

"I already have. Let's go back."

They got up and put the trays on a conveyor belt and then walked back in the hallway. The walk to the elevator seemed shorter. They got in, and John asked, "Aren't you supposed to be performing in the play tonight?"

"Unless Mary has a miracle recovery, I don't think I could focus on it. Besides it gives another girl a chance."

John noticed that Marissa and Ted weren't in the waiting room when they arrived. Then he noticed it was just after seven and visiting time. "They must be visiting."

"I hope you are right," Megan responded.

"I'll be right back. I need to call Maxine."

He found a quiet corner in a hallway and called her. She had known what happened and figured he wouldn't be in. He returned to the waiting room, and Ted and Marissa were there talking with Megan. They looked at him when he arrived. Megan said, "We are going home and rest. Ted and Marissa went in, and there is little change. You have permission to visit before the normal visiting hours at 9:00 a.m."

"Okay, I will call you if there is a change."

Megan came over and gave him a hug, and they left.

John went in the AICU door and asked at the nurses' station what room Mary was in. She had a breathing tube in her mouth, and he could hardly recognize her. The steady beep from her heart monitor was reassuring.

Her skin was cool when he tenderly touched her face. He whispered, "I am going to practice hard for the next 5K, so hurry back to me if you don't want to get beat." He kissed on the forehead and left for home.

Megan told Ted and Marissa she was going to chat with Ruth and Joyce. They were waiting for her when she arrived at the conference room.

Ruth asked, "What is the status on Mary?"

"She is in very serious condition. It is touch-and-go for now. But there was one thing that was shocking. They said she had a miscarriage."

"I don't see how that was possible."

"I don't either. Mary found out she was barren when she was married. They did a test later in life with the same result."

"Did you ask why they thought she was?"

"No, Ruth, I am so tired and shocked about the whole situation. I will follow up when I get a chance."

"It may be a good thing to find out. It makes me wonder if her going back to her teen years regenerated her body."

"It makes me wonder if that would help her now."

Joyce chimed in, "That would be a major find. Could be our chance to implement Phase Z."

"First thing is she has to survive," Megan responded.

"Yes, I am sorry. I will pray for her to recover. I will contact the Hawk and see if there could be a way to get her here if there is a way to increase her chances of recovery."

"I'll return to the hospital after I get some sleep."

John walked to his car in the emergency room parking lot. He got in and sat there. *Please, God, let her live.* The thought of the miscarriage had him saying a prayer for the baby too. He reached for a napkins he kept in his glove box and wiped his eyes as the tears started to flow. *I chose a wrong path, God. You helped me get on another. Please don't take her away.*

He started the car and started the trip home.

CHAPTER 17

He was ready for the knock on the door. "Sir, it is time."

"Evan, come on in."

The door opened, and Evan entered with the clothes in front of him.

"Good morning, sir. What outfit do you want to wear today?'

"The T-shirt, shorts, and cap will do, Evan."

Evan put the clothes on the bed.

"Evan, I'll dress myself today."

"Yes, sir, is there anything else I can do for you?"

"Not at this time."

Evan closed the door when he left. He gathered the clothes and went into the bathroom.

The walk-in shower was still steamed up from his morning shower, and then he went past the walk-in bath tub that was next to the full-length mirror.

He put the clothes on the two sink counter and then changed into the shorts and T-shirt.

He turned to the mirror and was pleased. The beard was neatly trimmed, and he had to admit the blond hair suited him. The years of working out had shaped his body better than he imaged. The six-pack abs could be seen below his tight clear T-shirt, and his arms and biceps were bulging muscles. The legs were well shaped, and he laughed at the thought of them being called unattractive when he was the Führer. He knew he looked in his early twenties, but he was well over a hundred.

I think I will play tennis today.

He walked over to the phone on the wall that was near the entry door. "Samuel, I am going to play tennis today. I am leaving in thirty minutes."

"Yes, sir."

He knew that thirty minutes was barely enough time for them to get his entourage together, but they hadn't failed yet. He always had bodyguards with him. Old habits were difficult to break. But they stayed far enough away from him so they didn't bring attention. They served as his Secret Service. The cell phone rang, and it was from his second in command.

"Yes?"

"Wolf, we have a problem. The situation with the Phase Z attempt in Reese Michigan has hit a snag. Mary, the one you decided on for Phase Z, has been in a car accident and is in serious condition."

"Was it just her?"

"Yes, she hit a deer. But there is more. Apparently the accident caused a miscarriage. The thing is before her transformation she was barren."

"Hawk, did they know she was pregnant before the accident?"

"If she knew, she didn't tell anyone, including her boyfriend, John. They are convinced he didn't know. He says he doesn't want kids."

"Is she in a local hospital or one of ours?"

"She is in a local hospital. She is in an intensive care. The next twenty-four hours are critical."

"Hawk, contact the leaders of her group and have them do whatever it costs to get her to one of our hospitals."

"Yes, I will keep you posted."

He put his phone down and walked to his study. There he found his master plan for the group. Phase Z was to start in ten years, but an opportunity to start now and to also discipline that group for violating a directive worked for him. Phase Z was to find out if the product could take a person to infant form. If it did, would it regenerate the brain cell and erase the memories of the past life. *If it does, then these people could be molded into the group.* An army of people under his control. That will be years in the future. His confidence of this happening was very strong. But he had learned from his past mistakes caused by arrogance. Now it is a thought-out process trying to be prepared for any concern. But he knew he couldn't. He decided to go to the local tennis courts. The summers were short. If he was lucky, it gave him a chance to practice his English. He was hoping for a chance to play someone other than his bodyguards. He had slowly learned the language of this part of Canada. The movies and documentaries of the war were in English. He left the room and went down his many hallways of his log cabin mansion built in the woods. The bodyguards were waiting for him in his multicar garage. He walked up to them.

"Tennis in town today."

His mind wouldn't shut off, so he sat on the edge of his bed. He saw 4:09 on his clock, and it took him a few seconds to realize it was in the afternoon. He looked at his cell phone and noticed there were no calls. No news was good news at the moment. She is still with us. He was surprised how much losing the baby meant to him. He didn't know she was pregnant, and he hadn't been interested in having kids.

He got up and got ready to go to the hospital. The drive there was in autopilot, and it was with dread he entered her room. She looked better, and he sat down to watch her. "Hello," caught him by surprise. Megan walked up to him. "Any word?"

"No, I just got here a few minutes ago. You are the first to visit."

"Okay, I'll go see what I can find out, John."

A nurse entered the room. She checked the IV and the connections to the machines and left. Megan returned and said, "She is doing better, and they think she will recover. Joyce contacted me, and she is working on a plan to move her to one of our facilities. They think the product can help her heal. Of course only group members are only to know."

"Of course, will she be close by."

"Yes, closer than here," she said with a smile.

He knew what she meant. He wondered how and where they would move her underground. They seem confident they can save her. He liked their chances. Megan left to find out what the plans were for Mary from Joyce. The TV in the room became a blur after watching for nearly two hours. He kissed Mary on the cheek and thought he saw her eyes flutter after he did.

He whispered, "Mary, I will come back later. I love you."

There was no response to his words. So he left.

The tennis match had gone well. He was improving every time out, and he knew they weren't trying to let him win or he would never play them again. The blonde woman and her friend were surprisingly good. They were a little overweight, but they could move. They were also friendly, and he got their numbers. He was surprised how easy it was, more so than when he was known to be in power. He wondered if he could still get their interest if they knew he was Adolf Hitler. The phone numbers were inserted into a small black book. The small town didn't offer many contacts with women. The sweat he worked up was burning his eyes, so a shower was next. The walk-in shower had sensors to automatically have the water at the desired temp once the water was turned on. The steady flow started, and he removed his clothes. He was pleased with his body image as he looked in the full-length mirror on the wall. *It is great to be young again. They think I am dead. I am the chosen one*, echoed in his mind. He always believed it, and now he had more proof. The world will know when the timing is right. He lost his thoughts when he walked into the shower.

The buzzer from his cell phone got his attention. It was a text from Norm. He had investigation report for Mary's accident finished. John replied with a thank you. He knew Norm would give it to Maxine, and she would call it in to the home office. If she had a question with it, she would contact him.

Megan entered the room and walked over to him. "If Mary's condition stays the same or improves, it has been arranged for her to be moved."

"How soon?"

"John, it could happen in the overnight hours."

"I hope it is. I can't see why it wouldn't help her."

"We are confident as well, John, but nothing is certain."

"John, I need you to meet me in my car. What I have to tell you has to be said privately."

He stared at her and gauged by her expression and body language she was very serious. He got up and said, "Okay let's go."

She led the way to the elevator and through the lobby. The cool evening air met him when he exited the door. Dread overwhelmed him as they got closer to the car. *I can't see any good coming out of this*, entered his thoughts. She unlocked the doors of her car, and he entered the passenger side door. Megan started the car and put on the air conditioning. She set the fan to low and turned to John. "John, when they get Mary back to our facilities, they plan in the near future to implement Phase Z on her. It was the decision of the Decider."

"Oh Christ! Was it because of the accident?"

"No, John, but it makes it easier with her. John, it was decided that you should join her in the process."

"So what you are saying? This could be a death sentence for Mary and I. We could be erased from the persons we have become."

"If you choose to look at it that way, but there is a possibility that you could be starting over with a very experienced mind. That is what they want to find out."

"It would be easier to deal with if I knew who 'they' were, Megan."

"They are the ones who have the rare bargaining chip that many will never have an opportunity to be aware of. You are one of a select few who have the opportunity to have that privilege. You don't have many options. It needs to be implemented soon. I want you to know they can find you if you decide to flee or violate the directives in any way."

John sat quietly and turned to look out the passenger window. He took some time, and then he turned toward her. "How soon does the process start?"

"We need to start and complete by September. But Mary's condition may alter that."

"Is there a plan on how I am to deal with leaving Reese?"

"We have a number of options. You can chose which one works for you, or you can do it your way."

"Megan, what happens after we get to the infant stage? Will Mary and I be together? Do you know who will be raising us? Where will we be living?"

"John, the details are being worked out. But from what I understand, you two will be together. Look, I am not privileged to be part of the planning. But I have made a request that I will be the one to raise you."

"Alone?"

"No, with the setup I have with Ted and Marissa."

"They agree with that scenario?"

"Yes, John, they do. It is only a request, so we will know more in the future."

"That would ease my concern if you were to handle the situation, Megan. I know how much you care about Mary."

"John, you are correct, but I know how much you care for her also. I respect what you have done since we first met. I will show you the same affection that I give to her. But we are ahead of ourselves. Still, thanks for the kind words." She reached over and gave him a hug.

Alexander watched the scene when the ark was opened in the *Raiders of The Lost Ark* again. He couldn't guess how many times. He laughed because it wasn't like that at all. The ark only contained the seeds for the product. The reason Methuselah and others lived for so long was discovered. Methuselah drank it as tea to maintain his age. His scientist found the secret of transforming a person to being younger by having it injected in the blood system. When he said there would be a thousand-year Reich, he had planned to be there at the anniversary. It was the one secret that wasn't exposed during the war. *I am the Chosen One*, he thought to himself. My legacy will be the greatest the world will know. The Wolf will prevail.

CHAPTER 18

JOHN WAITED FOR THE CALL for when they were to move Mary. Megan had asked if he wanted to ride with her in the ambulance. It was planned for after midnight, and he knew he wouldn't sleep, so he agreed. The microwave dinged, and he got up and took his bowl of soup out of it. It was hot, and he quickly made it to the kitchen table. He stirred the soup and blew on his spoonful. Childhood memories had come flooding back since he had found out his status with Phase Z. He hoped the next journey down this road would be better than the first. It had been a good memory until his parents died in the car crash when he was eleven. His mother's reluctant sister took him in. She lived in her own world, and he wasn't accepted in it.

When he was eighteen, he joined the air force and served for four years as a security policeman. The job experience of guarding aircraft and buildings didn't prepare him for the outside world. It didn't interest him enough to reenlist. One of his service buddies was training to be an insurance man, and he found it interesting when he was solicited to buy some insurance from him. He trained during his off time and became an insurance agent when he was discharged from the air force. He met Evelyn soon after, and here he is now.

The soup hit the spot, and he went and got some more. The cell phone he left on the kitchen table buzzed, and he saw it was a text from Megan. It read, "Meet me at my house in 30 minutes." He acknowledged and got ready and then locked the house and was on his way. He arrived ten minutes early, and Megan was sitting in her car. He parked his car next to hers. She waved for him to come to her car. He entered and looked in the back seat. "Just the both of us?"

"Yes, Ted and Marissa are helping prepare the room we will be using in the facility. I will be dropping you off, and I will follow the ambulance."

"So no one gets any sleep."

"There will plenty of time for sleeping."

"Easy for you to say, Megan."

"Sorry, John, you know I don't like the situation."

"Yes, I am just stressing you about the whole situation. Pay no attention."

Megan looked at him. "I won't."

He looked at her and smiled when she produced a big, wide grin.

"What do we tell friends who ask about her?"

"I would tell them they transferred her to a brain trauma facility that is near Detroit. You don't have the details. Remember, less is more."

"I agree."

She started the car, and they were both lost in their thoughts when they arrived at St. Mary's Hospital. They both walked toward the emergency room entrance, and Megan saw their ambulance already in the emergency room parking lot. She grabbed his arm and pointed. "This shouldn't take long, John."

There were a few people in the waiting room lobby when they arrived at the desk. They were immediately led into the emergency room. They waited for Mary to come down from the intensive care unit. The sound of the elevator doors opening got John's attention, and he looked toward the hallway. Mary's gurney passed him, and the nurses and equipment were close by. One nurse saw Megan and made a gesture to follow. Megan pointed to John, and he followed. He waited until Mary was put in the ambulance. Then he was allowed in. Her color and breathing seemed improved to him. The ambulance turned right on Washington Street and went through the downtown area without delay. He knew they were heading toward Reese. The nurses closely monitored Mary, so he just sat back and watched them.

They went on the overpass that crosses I-75, and he was surprised they turned right less than a mile after that. It was dark, and the only light in the area was provided by the headlights. He couldn't see much because of all the equipment, so he didn't know where they were. He heard a door open, and the ambulance went on an incline. Then they entered a well-lit building. A door shut behind them.

The back door of the ambulance opened, and he exited. They were in truck loading dock. Mary's gurney was removed, and they went toward a wide door on the other side of the facility. It was the entrance to a stock elevator, and they all easily fit in. John knew Megan was heading home, and he would use a cart to get back to Ted's house. The nurses and ambulance crew were all group members, and John wondered how old they were as they headed down toward the group facility. They pushed the gurney down the red hallway. John didn't remember touring here. He was asked to wait outside while they got her set up in the room. The room was number 21. He still wondered if all this was real. It seemed like he was in another world and he was being transported back and forth from reality. He couldn't help but marvel how they built this, and it seemed to run very smoothly. He had to admit it seemed like they had some great people working for them. The ambulance crew came out of the room, and he acknowledged them by shaking their hands. One of the nurses came out and signaled that he could come in. The other nurse was checking the IV flows and soon left. He went over to Mary and kissed her on the forehead.

"I am here, babe."

She didn't respond. He saw a flat scene TV hanging near the ceiling on one of the walls. "You want the TV on, Mary? I might be able to find a classic movie you love."

She did like watching movies of the forties and fifties. Mickey Rooney and Judy Garland movies were watched many times. One of her favorite scenes was the conga dance scene in their movie *Strike Up the Band.*" She had teased him that he should learn the conga. He had responded, "Where can you dance like that these days?"

She kept quiet. The TV scene lit up, and he changed to the classic channel. He saw James Cagney on screen. "Babe, James Carney is on the TV. There is Doris Day. Will you watch the movie with me?"

"Well, Mary, if you won't watch it with him, I will."

The voice had startled him. "Thanks, Megan. That didn't take long for you to get here. Ted or Marissa coming to visit?"

"Not tonight. I informed them I told you about Phase Z. They figured you needed to be with her alone. If you plan on being here for a lengthy time, I can call and get me another cart and leave the one I brought for you. Otherwise I can drive you back."

"This movie is nearly over. If you don't mind watching the end with us, I will take that ride as I am not sure I can find my way back," he said with a chuckle.

"I'd be honored to join you. But I didn't bring any popcorn."

"Hear that, Mary? Megan is a cheapskate."

"Hey, don't listen to him, Mary. He was here first."

John found a chair in the empty next room and gave it to Megan.

John reached up and held Mary's hand as they watched the movie. The nurses would come in from time to time, and John and Megan moved accordingly. The movie ended, and John decided fatigue was getting the best of him. He kissed Mary goodbye and whispered that he loved her after he had watched Megan do the same. She was waiting in the driver's seat of the cart when he arrived. "Megan, what happens now?"

"Our doctors will evaluate her case and will choose what course of action to take. The product usage is an option."

"Are the doctors in the group product doctors?"

"Yes, they are, but they all have been trained to know the current technology. Experience and knowledge can be a great combination."

John realized he was lost and would have never found his way back to Ted's. Megan had made a series of turns that had him confused. "I need to study this layout so I can get back to see Mary."

"I will give you directions, or if you want I can drive you back."

"Thanks, Megan, I think I may go it alone. I need to get a handle on the tunnels."

"Understood, but if you get lost, ask for help. There are areas that are restricted."

"Okay," he responded. But he often wondered why.

It was ten minutes before he was in his car and going home.

Instead of being reborn, he had a feeling that he was going to die. That thought had been difficult to shake when he arrived home at 4:00 a.m. He got in bed as soon as he could.

The ringing cell phone made him move, but he was to slow to respond. He saw it was a call from Maxine. He saw it was 10:45 a.m. She must be going to church. He laid back on the bed for a few minutes, and the next time he looked at his alarm clock, it was 12:25. He sat on the edge of the bed, and the urge to relieve his bladder made him move to the bathroom. He returned and sat on the edge of the bed and got his cell phone. Maxine should be home from church by now. He punched in her number.

"Hello, is that you, John?"

"Yes, can you talk, Maxine?"

"Yes, we just got home. How is Mary?"

"She is in very critical condition. So far she is holding her own."

"The pastor and the congregation said a prayer for her."

"Thank you. Let's hope the prayers will be answered."

"Will you see her tonight, John?"

"I plan on it. I should be into work tomorrow unless there is a setback."

"Then I hope to see you tomorrow. Tell her we are praying for her, John."

"I will, Maxine. Thank you."

He received a text from Megan. She said to text her and come over to the house as soon as he could.

He located his pants from last night and grabbed a new shirt from the closet. He went to the bathroom and got a quick swipe of his gel deodorant on his armpits and a quick gargle of mouthwash. He locked the house doors and got in the car. He started it and texted Megan that he was on his way. She was waiting for him in a cart when he got out of the elevator.

He tried to read her body language but couldn't. "What's going on, Megan?"

She turned and stared at him. Then she slowly started to grin. "Will you get your ass in here? It is good news."

He jumped in. "By the way, John, do you know you have two different-colored socks on?"

He looked down and saw a blue on his left foot and a brown on the right.

"Oh, well, it is okay. I have another pair just like it at home. But thanks for making me aware of it so I can think about it all night."

Megan laughed. "Anything for a friend."

The cart wasn't fast enough for John, but he did get a sense of how to get there and back. They arrived, and John quickly entered Mary's room. He was surprised when she turned her head toward him and reached out for his hand. He tenderly took her hand and bent down and kissed it. Then he gave her a soft kiss on the lips. "I am so happy you are back."

She whispered, "Where was I?"

"You had an encounter with a deer."

"A deer? I don't remember."

"I'll give you the details later. Have you eaten anything?"

"No, but I do feel hungry."

"I'll go tell the nurses," Megan said.

Mary turned toward Megan. "Wait."

Megan stopped and saw Mary wanted a hug. She quickly went to her, and they embraced.

Megan wiped a tear off her cheek and exited the room.

"How long have I been here?"

"Mary, you were at St. Mary's Hospital in Saginaw for two days, and we transferred you here this morning."

"What happened to me?"

"A deer jumped through your windshield and hit you in the face."

"Did it live?"

"No, it was in bad shape. I don't know what happened to it."

"Probably in someone's freezer, John."

He laughed. "I would not be surprised."

"What do I look like?"

"Oh, there is room for improvement."

"You are a lot of help."

"You asked," he said with a smile.

Megan came in accompanied by a nurse and doctor.

John stepped back to let the doctor advance past him. The doctor asked her a few questions on how she felt. Then he turned and went to Megan, and they left the room. The nurse had a menu and was writing down her dinner choices. When she was finished, she walked over to John and asked, "Do you want anything?"

"No, but thank you for asking."

John returned to Mary. "Mary, I am going to go home. I am exhausted, and you need your rest. I will be back after work tomorrow."

She grabbed his arm and pulled him to her. "It's okay, hon," and gave him a kiss.

Megan was talking to the doctor in the hallway. He stayed a respectful distance away until she finished. She came to him. "You ready to go home?"

"Yes, I am exhausted."

"I'll go say goodbye to Mary and then drive you back."

"Okay, I'll be in the cart."

John sat in a daze of fatigue. Megan starting the cart shook him out of his trance. "Will you need a ride home, John?"

"Why are you my designated driver?"

She looked at him and saw his grin. "Smart-ass."

"John, I found out that Mary's improvement was not caused by the product. She is healing fast on her own."

"That is great news. It must be her youth," he said with a smile.

Megan smiled back. They drove in silence for a few seconds, and then John said, "It was difficult to see her because of what is in store with the Phase Z. Megan, do you think it will hurt?"

"I don't recall anyone experiencing pain with the transition before, John."

"Okay, but it is difficult to imagine there not being pain in the process of bones shrinking to become an infant."

"It is hard to believe it can be done, John. But then again it is difficult to believe we can control aging. I am hoping there will be a change of heart because of her accident."

"Would that get me a reprieve?"

"I honestly don't know, John."

"Do you know who the Decider is, Megan?"

He grabbed hold of the handle used for support as the cart came to a sudden stop.

"John, you have been informed not to ask about the Decider. It can get you expelled, and I use that term strongly. I have been trying to help you. Please don't make me question that reasoning."

"I am sorry, Megan. I am totally at fault."

He knew expelled meant from living. He was so tired and needed to shut up.

They rode to the basement door. He could sense she was still upset, so he went to his car without saying good night.

CHAPTER 19

"THAT IS GOOD TO HEAR, Hawk. Is there anything else?"

"Alexander, there is a request from Megan Anderson. She is Mary Brunell's close friend, and they were together during the war. Mary is among her group. She has asked if she and her group can raise Mary and John Dwyer after Phase Z."

"How old is Megan after transformation?"

"She is around eighteen and graduating from high school. Her group members act as her parents. She says they could relocate and have her be a single mom living with her parents."

"My first thought would be no, but I will consider it. They must be close for her to make the request. Tell them if things go as planned in implementing Phase Z and the transformation is a success, her request will be granted. Do some research on her. There is time for me to change my mind."

"Yes Wolf, and I will start implementing plans for Phase Z, stage 2."

"Good, I will want to know what is decided by the board. Talk to you later. Good night."

"Good night."

He put his cell phone in his shirt pocket. *If we only had these phones during the war,* he thought. *The Ultra Secret wouldn't been a secret at all. The war plans were good. They just knew them. Too many of his staff convinced him that our Enigma coding machine was foolproof. My arrogance let me to believe that. Same with my doctor, who thought he had a cure for all my ills.*

He was surprised he survived because of the bogus treatments. Ah, they think he is dead. He had many look-alike doubles. The best one was there the final days. Even Eva didn't know the difference. She didn't listen because she wasn't supposed to be there. She paid the price. He was given the product earlier, and when he transformed into a young man, he was able to get out of the country. Hawk had disappeared earlier and arranged everything. Hawk was the only one he could trust. He got out of his recliner and went to his bedroom. He pushed a button on his console near his bed.

"Yes, can I be of service?"

"Evan, I need my pajamas and robe."

"I'll be right up, sir."

"Thank you."

Alexander Wolf was the name he gave himself. He admired Alexander the Great, and he still planned for his Reich to be the most powerful empire in the world's history. He planned on overseeing it all.

Should she tell Joyce about John ignoring the directives? That thought kept being repeated in her mind as she tried to sleep. She knew he was frightened and was tired, but that lapse of judgment concerns her. *Maybe it is best he goes into Phase Z, and if it clears his thoughts, we can use him in the future.* The same thing could happen to Mary, and she hated to lose that friendship. *It will be a long time before we will be on equal footing. But we have the time to get back together.*

She rolled over and heard the alarm clock. Oh, she had slept for four hours. Today was her first day she planned on going to school. There were only a few days weeks left. Graduation was in two weeks. She knew most of the questions today would be about Mary and maybe a few about missing the play. The story her and the Andersons came up with was Mary was sent to a specialist in Detroit. Ted accompanied her.

This morning they received the good news that Mary was awake and on the road to recovery. Megan turned on and entered her shower, and the issue with John crept back into her thoughts. She was still undecided after her shower when she got a text from Joyce.

The text read "Your request was approved, but there are conditions. TTYL."

Megan smiled at the text for a few seconds, letting it sink in. Breakfast was ready when she went into the kitchen.

"Are you ready to go back?" asked Marissa. "Yes, I like to get it over with. Oh, my request was approved, so are you ready to move accordingly?"

Marissa looked stunned "The Decider granted your request?"

"That is what Joyce texted me. But there are some conditions that have to be met. I will find them out later."

"Okay, we will start making plans."

"If it goes as planned, you know you will be a grandma, Marissa."

"It was fun the first time. I look forward to it."

"Good, I am not sure I can handle twins."

"Oh things are easier these days, Megan. Disposable diapers, microwaving the bottles, and baby monitors. It will be like riding a bike."

"Oh yes, the lack of sleep, the midnight feedings, the upset tummies—I remember that ride."

"Eat your breakfast before it gets cold."

"Yes, Grandma," she said and grinned.

"Good, you are here, John. Does that mean Mary is doing well?"

"Yes, Maxine, I got a call that she is awake and talking. She should be returning soon."

"Great news! Returning from where?"

"The Andersons had her flown to a hospital in Detroit. There is a doctor who is well known for dealing with head trauma. Looks like it wasn't needed."

"I am surprised you didn't go, John."

"Ted went alone. With comas, there wasn't any certainty of when and if she would respond. There is plenty to do here first before I could take a leave."

"True, you have a full agenda, John."

"Good, I need it to take my mind off things."

"Yeah, like what do you do with Mary's car?"

"I know, two wrecks in less than a year. I better get the ChapStick out. I might have to kiss a little ass to take care of it."

"Is there a flavor you prefer, John?"

He laughed. "No, which one do you prefer?"

"I prefer the Strawberry. But for your task, I recommend Gingerbread Kiss."

John laughed hard. "Thanks, Maxine I needed that."

"No trouble at all."

Mary looked better when she arrived in her room. She looked up and smiled. "Hi, Megan, they say I can get out of here."

"That is great news, Mary. When is that planned?"

"Tomorrow morning."

"What are you planning to do?"

"I'd like to go home. I look like I was in a prize fight, but I am feeling like I could manage. Is my cat home?"

"No, we have it. You better get home soon, as I think Marissa is getting attached to it."

"She can't have Midnight. So how was school?"

"Mary, that is all they talked about. We decided to tell them you were sent to a hospital in Detroit and that you are doing well."

"Okay, I will remember that. Anything else?"

"Mary, I don't know when the correct time is, but we have some issues to discuss."

"Sounds serious."

"They are."

"They? You mean there is more than one?"

"Well, one that happened and another one for the future. You sure you want to hear them now?"

"I will be thinking about them if you don't. I'd rather know."

"Mary, when the doctor at the hospital told us of your condition, she also said she was sad to report that you had a miscarriage due to the accident."

"Oh my god," Mary said as she put her hands to her face. "I had a feeling something wasn't right with my body. How could it be?"

"You must have transformed to a place that regenerated your cells. I am so sorry it happened."

"Does John know?"

"Yes, we all discussed telling you. He doesn't know I am here, so he may bring it up soon."

"It is shocking to me that after all these years, and when I shouldn't have children, it looks like I can. I'll have to learn about birth control. I don't need to get us in trouble."

"Mary, it is a bit late for that."

"I am in trouble?"

"Yes, you and John are. The Decider heard about the situation of bringing John in the group. He has decided that John and you will be the first volunteers for Phase Z."

Mary sat there and didn't say a word. She moved to the edge of the bed and got up. Megan watched her pace back and forth. "Does John know about this?" she asked Megan.

"Yes, he was recently informed. He seemed a bit unstable and has questioned the whole process."

"Oh god, I can understand that, Megan. When is the process scheduled for?"

"He wants it implemented by September. It has you out of school and time for John to make plans. There was one change that was surprising. The Decider changed his mind. I requested to your parent. Marissa and Ted, the grandparents. He approved that request."

"Oh, Megan, if I have to go through it, I am so pleased you will be there. You are a true friend," she said as she walked over and gave her an embrace.

"Can I have one of those?" Mary and Megan saw it was John, and both opened their arms to offer an embrace. He walked to them, and they had a group hug.

Megan looked at John. "She knows everything. I told her about the Phase Z situation, but there is one thing you don't know. I will be your parent if Phase Z is implemented."

"Oh wow, I don't know what to say other than thank you. Will you be a single parent?"

"That is the plan for now. Marissa and Ted will still be my parents and your grandparents."

Mary chimed in, "So do you know where you will have to move?"

"Not yet. I am assuming to location far from this area."

John asked, "Why don't they just keep us here after Phase Z?"

"John, the Decider makes the decisions, and it is what he wanted. It wouldn't be wise to question it."

"Sorry, I keep forgetting it is a dictatorship."

Mary gave him a stunned look. "John, you need to seriously sit down and think this situation out. You are in a position that so many others would trade you for."

"I just feel like I could be dead soon if I don't recall any memories after Phase Z. You don't feel the same?"

Megan said, "You both need to discuss this in private. Remember, the Decider isn't happy about how this played out with you, John. He is testing you. I will leave you to alone."

Mary came and gave her a hug. "I love you, Megan."

"Love you too." She nodded to John and left the room.

Mary waited for John to look at her. He sat with his head down looking at the floor. "John, I think you have pissed off Megan. If we do have to go through with it, befriending her might be the best option we have. Think about it and let's discuss this later."

"It's hard to think of anything else. But you are right. We need to discuss this later."

CHAPTER 20

"MEGAN, WE HAVE YOUR ORDERS for after Phase Z. You and your family are to relocate in New Zealand. There is a strong group community there. Do you have any questions?" Joyce asked.

"Where in New Zealand?"

"The small town of Martinborough."

"I assume we have the same setup there as we have here?"

"Megan, you are correct, but not as many windmills connected. So the grid underneath might be smaller."

"Do you know where we will be located in that area?"

"Nothing yet. The plans are still being worked out. What is the status of Mary and John? Have they said anything on when they will be ready for Phase Z?"

"I don't think they will ever be ready, but the last I heard, they were both thinking of getting it over with soon."

"Well, that will make The Decider happy, and let me know when you think we can tell him that."

"I will discuss it with Mary. She is with John now."

"Oh John, do you really want to do this? The business has done so well lately, and you have gotten your life on track."

"That is right, Maxine. I have gotten my life on track because of Mary. Despite her young age, Mary is very mature, and I want to be with her. I am happy, Maxine. Plus, living in France is appealing to me."

"I can't hold that against you. I am just really going to miss you."

"Oh, come here, Maxine."

He gave her a long embrace. "I will miss you too and just think, Maxine, you may get the job. I will do everything I can for you to get it."

"Will you use the Gingerbread Kiss Chapstick?"

"Why, of course, Maxine. Is there any doubt?" He laughed.

"Then I like my chances," she responded.

Megan looked at her cell phone. She received a text from Mary. It read, "John put in his notice today. The process has started. He was required to give them a month's notice."

"Perfect," Megan replied.

Perfect is correct, she thought to herself. Ted and Marissa have been preparing the house for their replacements. She went in the kitchen and told them both the news. They were all excited to live in New Zealand.

"I am going down to discuss it with Joyce. No need to wait for me at dinner."

"Okay, Megan, we won't," replied a smiling Marissa.

Joyce was sitting at her office desk when Megan found her.

"Joyce, I just talked to Mary, and the process has started. John gave his company his notice. He had to give them a month."

"Great news. A month should work out fine. I'll contact the Hawk so they can finish coordinating things on their end."

"Megan, have you had experience with babies? One is a handful, but two at once can be a difficult challenge."

"Joyce, I have had experience. We look forward to the challenge of the unknown mind-sets," she said.

Joyce laughed. "Unknown is correct. It is unknown if Phase Z will even work, unknown if the process will be painful, unknown why Phase Z will be worth the risk, and unknown what is in store if it does wipe the brain clean."

"I won't even venture a guess with that last one, Joyce."

"I know, you know, it is better to keep it that way."

Alexander's secretary buzzed him. "Sir, Mr. Hawk is on the line 2."

"Thank you."

"Hawk, do you have any good news today?"

"Well, as a matter of fact I do. The first step for Phase Z has been implemented. The plan is to have all matters settled in a month."

"That is great news. Did you see that British admiral from the war passed away? He was ninety-seven years old."

"Yes, I did, Wolf. In another few years, all those bastards will be gone."

"Yes, waiting for them to go has slowed down time. But time is now on our side. We will prevail."

"In a way, Wolf, it would be a great feeling to see their faces if we sprang back in the world."

"I know what you are talking about, Hawk. But let them go to the grave thinking they won. We have everything to lose if the timing isn't correct."

"I trust your judgment, Wolf. Looks where it's led us."

"Yes, I have learned from the past. We are the only ones that can redo our history. I have listened to input from others. We will utilize our wisdom and take over the world and make it a paradise."

"I can't wait!"

"Ah, Hawk, you have to."

They both laughed.

CHAPTER 21

MEGAN WAS EXHAUSTED. SHE HAD packed and moved everything she owned down into the underground complex. Ted and Marissa would still be at the house during the Phase Z. They wanted to make it look like Megan left with Mary. She hadn't been getting much sleep with the scheduled events to start soon. *First, the transformation has to work.* Mary could die in the process. *Then what happens?* she thought. She had planned to go to college and pursue a career in optometry. In the process she could look for clients to enroll in the group. But that can wait. That was the benefit of being in the group. She could do it all again. She went to her room in the underground complex, got a glass of wine, and sat and relaxed to some classical music.

The sun had lit up the bedroom when John opened his eyes. Today is the day entered his mind. Mary was already out of bed. The shower was on, and he went to the dresser and looked at the last of his clothes. He wondered when the next time would be that he'd need clothes as an adult. He thought, *Am I dressing for my own funeral?* Many questions entered his mind. Mary was still in the shower when he entered the bathroom.

"Hey, you going to leave me any hot water?"

"No, so you better hurry up and get in here."

The water was hot when he entered. "Damn, woman, you think it is hot enough?"

"Working on it. It keeps my mind off other things."

"How about survival?" he said as he jumped out. "You need to cool that down."

"Big baby," she said as she got out. "It's all yours."

"Thanks for the 'big baby.' Just what I need to hear today."

He adjusted the water and waited for it to cool down. He grabbed a towel and dried her back. "Sorry, what would you like for breakfast, John?"

"Whatever you are having."

"You are a brave man," she said with a smile.

She laughed when he raised eyebrows in response to her words, and he then disappeared in the shower.

The water started getting colder as the hot water was running out. He hurried to finish washing his hair. The bathroom mirror was steamed up, and he knew he had to wait for them to clear before he could shave. He dressed, and he saw his bowl at the kitchen table. Mary was smiling and eating out of hers. "What is this?" he asked.

"Oatmeal with slices of apple in it. You might want to add milk. It is hot."

"I can't remember the last time I had this."

"I use to have this regularly in my childhood," she responded.

"Did you get sick of it then?"

"No, it was just part of the routine. Eat and then walk to school."

He poured milk over his and stirred it in the oatmeal. "This isn't bad," he said after eating a spoonful of it.

"Of course not. You think I would want something lousy on this day? I wanted it, and you volunteered for it," she said, smiling.

She watched him devour it and asked if he wanted another bowl and was surprised when he said he did. He watched her wash out the dishes and put them in the dishwasher and did the same.

"It feels strange that we won't be the ones taking the dishes out of it when they are clean," she said.

"I know," he responded.

"I'll get Midnight her cage is in the back room."

"I'll get the cage, Mary."

Mary had the cat in her arms and pointed to John to approach behind her.

"Open the cage, John."

She moved quickly and turned and put the cat in the cage before it had time to react. John closed the gate door.

"Let's go," she said to him. They left, and she locked the door for the last time. He could see she had watery eyes but knew it was best to stay quiet.

She tossed him the car keys.

"You drive," and took the cat cage and got in the passenger side with the cage on her lap.

He got in and heard her talking softly to the cat. The motor came to life, and he put it in gear. The drive to the isolated former truck station was going to be a slow one.

Megan ate her breakfast in a hurry. She just got a text from Mary that they were on their way to the station. She left the cafeteria and drove her cart in the direction of the station. She arrived and saw the Camaro enter the building. The overhead door closed behind it. Mary got out carrying Midnight's cage.

"I am just glad she always liked you, Megan."

"Me too, but you will still be her love."

John walked up beside them. "Any last-minute reprieve from the governor?" he asked with a laugh.

Megan gave him a dirty look and then laughed at his shocked facial response.

"I am afraid not, John. We are all in for the duration no matter how it turns out."

He reached out to hand her the car keys. Megan reached and grabbed his arm. "John, let's do that downstairs and out of sight."

She led them to the elevator.

"Goodbye, outside world," John mumbled.

Mary looked at him. "Hello, new adventure. Another we hope can be a long list of them."

They got off the elevator, and Megan drove them down to a secluded hallway. Mary had seen it once before when she left using the emergency exit near the windmill. That wasn't allowed after that. They went past the exit door, and she stopped at the next door down the hall.

"This is where you two will be staying during the process. I know you have already been informed in general on what to expect, but the doctors will go over the process in more detail after Lunch. "Let's go to my bungalow and drop off Midnight before lunch."

It took about ten minutes to get to the Megan's living quarters. Mary hugged Midnight after letting her out of the cage. She was left to explore when they left for lunch. John ate, but his mind was on the procedure. They returned to Megan's quarters. Midnight had found the litter box and her food. "Okay, time to turn everything in."

Mary and John gave her their cell phones, keys, and wallets.

"Do I get a headstone?" John asked.

Mary swatted him on the arm. "That is not funny, John. There is only a small portion of the group that is aware of Phase Z, and they want to keep it that way."

John wanted to respond but decided not to. It was too late for smart-ass responses. There was nothing they could do. He followed them back to the cart and wondered why he never heard of an accident involving one.

"Megan, has there been any accidents with the carts?"

"No, I never told you they had an anti-collision chip in the dashboard?"

"No, you didn't."

"Oh wow, my bad. There is a high-pitched beep that is emitted if another cart is near by an intersection."

"Oh, that is what that was," John said, laughing.

Mary smiled and said, "Megan, for an insurance man, John's driving is a bit reckless."

"Hey, said the woman who hit Bambi."

"That Bambi committed suicide by jumping on my car."

"Ah, some more memories to store for after the transformation," said Megan.

"Do you really think we will remember everything?" asked John.

"I think there is a chance."

"Do you know that is what they want to hear?"

"John, honestly I don't know. Does it matter?"

"I guess not. Time to get it over with."

They arrived at the operating room. They were led to a small conference room. Dr. Kurt Thurman entered the room. His six-foot-six-inch frame seemed to fill the room. He had a slender build and very tanned. John wondered if his true age was near the forty he looked like, with the graying temples and dark black hair.

"I know you both are nervous, and my staff and I join you in that regards. We will be venturing into the unknown. We know the product works, but to what extent? The procedure will follow a slower process than the normal pace of transformation. We will go as far back as you let us. We don't want to take you to a place where you are in discomfort. You will be monitored at all times. John and Mary, you will stay here. Tonight eat a hearty meal but nothing after midnight. We will see you in the morning." He shook their hands and left the room.

John whispered to Mary, "His bedside manner needs work."

She smiled. "Agreed."

"I wish I could stay, but I won't want to get in the way. So I am off to my dungeon."

"You are almost funny, Megan," Mary responded and got up and hugged her. John hugged her next. She left the room.

"Now what?" Mary asked.

"Let's do what the man said and go eat."

CHAPTER 22

ALEXANDER WAS EXAMINING PHOTOS OF women his staff provided. They were photos of elderly women in their youth. He looked to Evan. "Tell Hawk I want this one." Hawk had people who would see if the one he chose could be convinced to become a group member. But they would be asked if they would be a mistress for an agreed amount of time before they were allowed to contribute in another way to the group. So far, he hadn't had anyone refuse him. The power of the product never surprised him. Most of the mistresses lasted a few months. But on occasion, he would keep them longer, if she was fun to be around. An heir was not in the plans now that he could stay alive. That was the difficult part of his existence, the constant concern of someone taking his life. It was one reason he wanted more women in power. He knew they are competitive, but there was no need for them to challenge him. They had more power than they have had. Most didn't know of his plans for the future. He was told that Phase Z was about to start. It was difficult to be patient when he used the old way of thinking. But for him time did stand still too often. Phase Z was a major event and being patient with it was not easy for him.

Megan was trying to keep her composure as she returned to her room. She had just left Mary and John. It was her last time seeing them as Mary and John. Phase Z was implemented. There was nothing for her to do but wait. The length of time for her to wait was uncertain. She hoped it was shorter than a month.

Norm looked at his calendar on his desktop pad. Today was the Reese 5K run. He called his two deputies to remind them. They

143

had to block the traffic for the race course. It was on the north side of Reese, and it started at the community park. The race volunteers monitored the course, so all he had to do was block off the few intersections along it. He decided to block Reese road at the Dixon intersection. Dixon was the north border of the course. He went about his normal duties until it was near race time, and he drove to the community park. He saw around seventy runners, and after a quick check with the race officials, he drove to the intersection. The daylight was fading, and he hoped the runners cleared his location before it was totally dark. He parked, blocking Reese road, and waited for radio communications. He saw it was past the starting time and waited for the first runners to appear. A car approached him from the north of Reese road. He gave them directions on which way to go to avoid waiting there. They took his detour, and he turned back to see the first group of runners approaching. He acknowledged them and started to clap and offer encouragement to the slower group as they went by. One of the runners slowed and pointed to the north. Norm turned to see why and saw one of the windmills' blades were going extremely fast. There was smoke exiting from the top of the enclosed motor casing. He received a call that the last runners were approaching him. He continued to watch the windmill and really encouraged the runners to get past his position. They did, and he called the race officials that they cleared and he had to respond to a call. He started toward the windmill.

"Holy shit," he said as the windmill blades flew off the propeller. One hit the windmill base, and the windmill was sliced in half and came tumbling down. Pieces of blade flew off in the distance. *Oh god, I hope those don't cause damage or hurt anyone.* He turned on the road to the windmill and swerved to avoid a blade blocking the road. He stopped and got out of the car. He turned on his video on his uniform. He walked and scanned the area. The blades had shattered a few hundred yards in every direction. The pieces varied in size. The closer he got to the base of the windmill, the larger it seemed. The entry door was still intact along, with about a seven-foot-tall section of it still standing. The door resisted, but he was able to pull it open. He scanned the area and was about to leave when he heard what sounded like a faint siren sound coming from beneath a floor cover plate. He bend down and put his ear to the plate. The sound was stronger. He couldn't find a way to pull the cover plate open, so he returned to his police car. He found his crowbar in the trunk and returned. He was able to get the crowbar around the cover plate but couldn't dislodge it. He noticed what looked like a sliding lock level and moved the crowbar directly over it. He was close enough to the wall to use as a back support and with his legs, pushed as hard as he could. The cover suddenly popped open, causing the crowbar to fly in his direction. It barely missed hitting his head. The siren sound was much louder, and he noticed a metal circular viral stairwell going down a level. The crowbar bounced off the wall and then went through the opening. He heard it land on the floor at the lower level. The opening exposed a lit stairwell, so he climbed down.

The elevator at that level caught him by surprise. He retrieved his crowbar and pushed the down button for the elevator. He waited for nearly a minute with no result. The stairwell looked like there were a few more levels lower, so he decided to go down.

"What the hell is this?" he mumbled to himself. Then he thought it could be for maintenance or power lines for the windmill. The siren was loud when he opened the door and saw two long hallways in each direction. He wedged the crowbar under the door so he could leave it slightly open. It would be easier to find if he got lost. He went to the left and examined that hallway. He wondered why there were steam pipes running along the top of the walls. A door came into view. It was on his left side. He slowly moved to the wall and approached the door. There was a window in the top half, and he edged to it. The lights were out in the room. He grabbed his flashlight, and he noticed an empty desk with a door behind it. The door opened when he turned the knob. The siren sound vanished when he closed the door. The room was bigger than he had thought. There was a hallway to the left that had file cabinets lined up against the wall that stopped at the end of the hallway. He approached the door behind the desk and noticed it had a card entry lock. He could see a long hallway in front of him, and to his surprise, three people from the left of the door turned toward the hallway he could see. One was an adult, and there was a boy at his right and a red-haired girl to this left. He watched them walk away from him, and he couldn't take his eyes off the boy. He knew that walk. It dawned on him it had to be John Dwyer. He tapped the window glass with his flashlight, and they all turned in his direction. The shock on boy's face convinced him he was right. The adult got on the radio, and the kids took off running. Norm tried but couldn't get the door to open. He thought about using his gun but tried instead to force it open, but it wouldn't budge. The kids and adult were out of sight.

What did I just see? he thought to himself. Darkness swallowed him when the outer hallway light went off. He followed his flashing light beam to the outer door, and silence greeted him when he returned to the hallway. He started to follow the hallway back to the wedged door. In the distance, he saw a combination of lights approaching him, and he looked in the other direction and saw the same thing. His urge to run to the wedged door was strong, but he waited as the lights were approaching at a fast pace. The whirl of a motor let him know they were electric vehicles.

"Officer, you are in a restricted area. We will take you to the exit," a voiced boomed from the left of him. The light blinded him, but he could see movement from approaching people. He felt a sharp object penetrate his neck, and soon he felt himself being lifted before he blacked out.

Ruth called Joyce with her cell phone. "We have apprehended the police office in the hallway. He wasn't near anything that could expose our secret. What do we do now?"

"Have you gone over him to make sure he doesn't have a video camera?"

"No, we haven't. They are moving him to one of the exam rooms. I will have them check."

"Okay, what is the status above ground?"

"The tower is gone, and pieces litter the immediate area. It was the tower that was isolated enough to have an emergency escape exit. The officer forced his way to enter the complex."

"The police vehicle still there?

"Yes."

"Okay, get a few available semitrailers from the group locations as soon as you can and have that vehicle loaded in one. Then get some group cement trucks fill in that exit. In the meantime, keep the officer sedated."

"I'll get the process started, and I will keep you posted."

"Fine, I'll contact Hawk with news."

"Good luck with that."

"Thanks, Ruth."

Yeah, 'good luck with that' is correct, she thought. *We are in the middle of Phase Z, and this happens. Let them decide what is next.* She picked up her phone.

Wolf paced the floor. The board was on its way. There was a time when a board wasn't needed. He had full control, and he knew the final decision was his. It still was, but he had set up a board from a variety of professions. They would offer solutions to issues. It helped him make decisions, but from a different prospective. He likened it to watching a chess game. The moves were easier to see watching from the sidelines than sitting at the board. This needed all their concentration. A tower had collapsed above an emergency exit shaft, and the tunnels were breached by a police officer. It is at the same location where Phase Z is being implemented.

The buzz of his cell phone got his attention.

"Yes, Hawk."

"Wolf, the board has arrived."

"Good, I will be there shortly."

He went to the bathroom and relieved himself. *I can't believe this happened*, entered his thoughts. In a way he was glad there would be input from the board. They were all focused on him when he entered the conference room. It always shocked him to see them looking so young when he knew they were around his actual age. The five women were anxious to hear what the issue was for them to be called so late. They were seated at the round table. Violet was at his left, then Tessa, Charlotte, Diana, Constance, and then Hawk to his right.

He turned and nodded to Hawk, who looked at them all and said, "Ladies we have had a tower go down and a breach of one of our facilities. It is in grid 49, and if that number is familiar to you, it is because that is where Phase Z is being implemented."

"How did the tower go down?" asked Violet.

"All we know was that the blades were going abnormally fast, and it spun off the tower and cut the base in half. Parts of the other blades flew in different directions, and there was no damage. But it also has an isolated emergency exit next to it."

"Is that where the facility was breached?" asked Diana.

"Yes," Hawk replied. "The local sheriff was the first to respond and found a way to enter the exit shaft. He was located by the security forces in the hallway near the Phase Z room."

"What have they done with him?" asked Tessa.

"They sedated him and in darkness removed his vehicle from the scene."

"So we have a local police Officer in our custody. Have they been looking for him at the location of the windmill?"

"They haven't reported that they have. I will get more information on him."

"What is the status of the emergency shaft?" asked Constance.

"They plan to fill it with cement. The trucks are on the way. They hope to have it done by morning."

"What is the status of Phase Z?" asked Charlotte.

"I was told it is progressing well. They have a projected completion date of a month from now."

"Was the product area breached?"

"No, the video cameras show him only in the area he was apprehended."

"Ladies, I leave you, and I will return when you have discussed the options." They nodded to Wolf as he got up and left the room.

Megan was reading when her cell phone buzzed. It was a text from Joyce. She wanted her to meet her in the medical station as soon as possible. She left her room and drove there. Joyce was waiting for her. "Megan, are you aware of what has happened today?"

"I heard the alarms and was informed of the tower collapsing."

"We were breached by a police officer. I believe he is from Reese. I want you to take a look at him."

"Oh my god. How much did he see?"

"We aren't sure, but he entered via the emergency exit. The found him near the Phase Z area. He has a video camera on him, and we are trying to find out if it recorded anything."

"Oh no, where is he?"

"In here. He is sedated, Megan."

Megan followed her through the hallways of the medical station and entered a small room where she saw the officer on a gurney. She walked up to him and turned to Joyce "That is Norm Peters, the sheriff in Reese. He isn't married. What will happen to him?"

"That decision is up to the board and the Decider. I will relay that information to the Hawk."

"He is well liked, if you want to provide them with more information, Joyce."

"I will add that. Thanks, Megan."

What a mess, Megan thought as she returned to the cart. *There hasn't been a breech anywhere before.*

Luckily the product is safe, but I wonder what will happen at this location. I wonder what is going to happen to Norm.

A local news report gave out the details of the windmill collapsing. The company spokesman explained what happened and their cleanup operation, but they said they never had contact the Reese police chief. They only dealt with the deputy. They finished the report stating Norm Peters was missing and to contact a number on the screen if anyone knows his whereabouts. Sam was worried. He had known Norm since childhood. It wasn't like him not to be in charge of any situation.

Hawk got off the phone with Joyce. He then went to the fax machine and got her latest update. He made six copies and returned to the board meeting. The women reviewed it, and he waited for any questions. When they all thanked him, he left the room. They would discuss, it but instead of coming up with one conclusion, the Wolf would rather read an opinion from each one. They buzzed the Hawk, and each gave a written suggestion to give to Wolf. He gathered them, and they left the room. Hawk buzzed the Wolf. "Alexander, they have completed their reports."

"Good, I was becoming impatient."

Hawk walked in and handed him the reports. "I will be in my office working for a few hours should you make your decision tonight."

"Thanks, that is good to know."

Hawk left the room. He never offered an opinion unless he was asked. He knew how Wolf operated. It is why he was still in his good standing with him.

It was the correct decision to add a board, Wolf thought. He was always impressed with what they presented and in quick fashion. They were usually in line with his thinking, and there were times when he was influenced by all five. This time was no different. They pointed out the police would be looking for their fellow officer, and that could put the security of the facility in jeopardy. But they also concluded that Phase Z was in its final stages, and it needed to be completed as soon as possible. He went over their reasoning and wrote down points he agreed with. He was formulating a plan, but decided he would sleep on it.

The bedroom ceiling started to lighten up as the morning light entered. Maxine just lay in bed hoping the phone would ring. She had been awake all night. It felt so strange not hearing from Norm. She had grown up with him also. He was best man at their wedding. She had a gut feeling something bad happened to him. She found out he did arrive at the downed windmill but left, heading north shortly after. That is what company spokesmen Joyce Sanders told her when she called. He hadn't been seen or heard from since. There was a chill in the air when she sat up on the edge of the bed. She went to the kitchen and started the coffee brewing and left for a quick shower. She wanted to stay home and not go to the site, but since she just got the job as the insurance agent for the area, she needed to go to the windmill site. She removed her cell phone from the charger. She ate breakfast and then drove to the site. The windmill base was about seven feet tall, and you could see where one of the blades had sliced it leaving a crooked edge. The top half lay on the ground, and pieces of the blades were scattered in every direction. An elderly woman approached her car. She lowered her window. "Hi, are you Maxine?"

"Yes."

"I am Joyce."

Maxine got out of the car. "What caused it to come down, Joyce?"

"It appears that the charging belt from the blades to the generator snapped, and it caused the blades to turn abnormally fast. That caused the propeller portion of the blades to get off balance and slice the tower."

"What is the plan now? Will you be replacing it?"

"The company hasn't decided. It might be relocated."

"I will take pictures and make a report to the insurance company, Joyce. Can you tell me any new information on Officer Norm Peters?"

"Sorry, Maxine, just what one of the maintenance crew mentioned when he drove here. There was an officer here walking the ground. He waved to him and then went to his car and drove away."

"Okay, Thanks, Joyce." *Where are you, Norm?* stuck in her mind as she drove back.

The board was waiting for Wolf when he arrived in the conference room. He passed out copies of his decision. "You know the process. If you see something that was overlooked, point it out to me by tomorrow morning."

They watched him walk out of the room, and they left the room without comment. Wolf knew they would each review the decision, hoping to find a better alternative. He was very confident they wouldn't find anything to alter his decision. He expected it in Joyce's hands tomorrow, and he expected it to be carried out. She had been with him since the beginning, and he was surprised when she said she rather be in the field than on the board. She did tell him she would do anything he asked. He let her have her preference, and she had done a remarkable job getting the facilities online. But he had been disappointed with her handling of the John Dwyer situation.

The buzz of his cell phone got his attention. It was a text from Hawk. There were no new recommendations to his decision, and he sent it to Joyce as he had commanded. He acknowledged the text.

Her fax machine activated. Joyce got up from her desk and patiently waited for the fax machine to finish printing. He gathered the sheet and took them to her desk. *I hope we can pull this off,* she thought to herself after she read the decision by the Decider. It wasn't what she expected. The board must have an influence on him. She picked up the phone. "Ruth, we need a board meeting as soon as possible. The Decider has issued orders for the current situation."

"I'll get on it right away."

Dr. Thurman was in awe of the product when he examined the MRI results. John and Mary were nearly infants. The process was slow, but not painful. He had no explanation on why it was working. Skulls sinking to infant size amazed him. *Will they retain their memories?* It was something he would also monitor. A clean slate was what he thought would happen. If physical ailments were being corrected, logic told him that would also reboot the brain. He was confident the next few days Phase Z would be completed.

Joyce contacted Hawk a few day later. She informed him that the orders by the Decider were implemented and completed.

Sam just got off her phone. The state police had found Norm's police vehicle. It was found near West Branch, Michigan. There was no sign of him. They said they had to have some powdery substances analyzed that were found in the vehicle. "Norm, what have you got yourself into?

The fog was lifting as he dreamed he was freezing and pulled his blankets over himself to block breezes penetrating his blanket fortress. His eyes opened to darkness, and he realized he was under a pile of blankets. His head pounded when he removed them and tried to sit up. It took him time to realize he was in an old wooden shack.

Norm grabbed the blankets and wrapped them around himself. He slowly got to his feet and examined the room. He walked over to a small mirror hang on the wall and gave it a quick glance. Then stopped and returned. "Who is that?"

Megan, Ted, and Marissa waited for the nurse to bring Mary and John in. They saw her arrive pushing two small carts. They hurried to them. Megan was stunned when she looked at them. "They are reborn," she said as she gently lifted Mary into her arms.

"I agree," Marisa said as tears ran down her cheek, cuddling John.

"Megan, will you be renaming then?" asked Ted.

"Yes."

Alexander just heard from the Hawk. Phase Z had been successfully completed. "So it begins."

The End

Book 2

WOLF BITE

GARY A. OSBORN

To Chris and Charlotte Horlock for their time and advice
and to Reyna Frost, who has moved on to
play college basketball at CMU.

CHAPTER 1

Norman Peters tried to focus on the image in the mirror. His blurred vision and pounding headache made it difficult. He turned toward the wood framed bed and collapsed on it. The room was spinning, and he closed his eyes for relief. But the spinning sensation was stubborn, and he began to feel nauseous.

The door to the outside was farther than he imagined when he forced himself to his feet. He opened the door and vomited in the snow. The strong cold wind helped him wake up, and the forest the shack was surrounded by slowly came into focus.

Why am I wearing an orange uniform? drifted in his thoughts.

It was a struggle to get back in bed, but the many heavy blankets offered relief from the cold. He fell into bed and managed to cover himself completely. It took a few minutes before he could stop his teeth from chattering. Fear grabbed control of him when he couldn't think of his name or how he got there. He lifted the blankets off his head and focused on the wooden shack. In was one room with a few cabinets hanging on the wall and one small window. There wasn't a second door. A wood stove was the heat source, and there was a small pile of wood next to it. He covered himself again and wondered why his orange uniform upset him. He had a feeling it wasn't a good thing to be wearing. Hunger pains were fighting the urge to stay in bed. He wrapped the blankets over his shoulders and walked to the cabinets. He found about a dozen cans of sardines and a box of saltine crackers. There was a loaf of bread, but it was moldy. A jar of peanut butter was quickly opened, and he scooped a good portion with two fingers on his right hand. The peanut butter started sticking to his mouth, causing him to look for water. He was shocked to find a few bottles of water in the other cabinet. He opened one and took a drink. He found a kitchen knife in a drawer. He used it to make a peanut butter sandwich with the crackers. When he finished eating, he put everything back in the cabinets and opened the door. The foot of snow made it difficult to see. He wrapped a blanket over his shaved bald head and scanned the area. He found what looked like an outhouse and noticed there weren't any footprints near it or the shack.

"How long have I been here?" he mumbled to himself. He looked down and realized he was wearing work boots. The outhouse door was difficult to open, and he cleared the snow away with his leg. It was an old-fashioned outhouse complete with old catalog papers to use when sitting on it. He spotted an old-fashioned hand-cranked water pump on the other side of the shack.

The woods surrounded the shack, and he could make out a few trails leading into the woods. On the back side of the shack, there was a pile of wood. He grabbed a few pieces. The blankets weren't keeping him warm, and he returned to the shack. There was some wood in the shack, and he put the wood he brought in in a pile next to it. The stove had room for three pieces, and he found some paper to throw in. He found a box of wooden matches in one of the drawers. He lit the paper, and soon flames were surrounding the wood. He closed the stove door and got back into bed. A burning smell made him uncover his head. He could feel the heat coming off the stove. A burning smell got him to sit up. The top of the stove was red hot, causing it to make a snapping sound that frightened him for a few minutes. He thought it might explode. The shack heated in a hurry. He sat up and removed the blankets. The stove was emitting a smoke smell, so he went and opened the door. He turned back and noticed a pot under the bed. He retrieved it and decided he would use it at night and dump the contents in the outhouse during the day. The cupboards contained more food. It was enough to last a week or more if he rationed them. He found six more bottled waters. He had drank one. He did find a frying pan, and he thought about melting snow with it and pouring it back into the bottle. He took the pan out and used snow to clean off the bottom. Then he filled it with snow and put it on top of the stove. The melted water filled about half of the bottle, and he went and got more snow. His head was starting to clear up. He knew he couldn't stay there long.

Alexander Wolf looked at the before and after pictures of John Dwyer and Mary Brunell. He found it hard to believe Phase Z was a success the first time. He also wondered about the status of Norman Peters. He listened to the board and let him live. They figured, with him being a police officer, they would never stop looking for him. With the mind-alternating chemicals he was given and the drugs planted in his patrol car, his chances of him recalling being in the facility were extremely thin. His credibility would be destroyed. Still, he decided it was time to relocate the product and shut down that grid in the near future. His glance at his office clock reminded him that he had a board meeting. The board members were in the conference room when he entered. They noticed his arrival and seated themselves at the table.

"I have decided that since Phase Z has been implemented, it is time to implement Phase I. We need to start accessing inhabited islands that will welcome our windmills and purchase uninhabited islands that fit our needs."

"Violet, do you have a report on the status of Phase C?"

"Yes," and she handed it to him.

"Thank you," He looked around the room, and they knew he had something to say. "I have decided to visit Grid 49. I will need one of you to work out the details. It will be a one-day visit, so I think a trip with one of our airplanes works the best."

"I will do it," Tessa responded. "Will you be taking any of your staff?"

"Yes, I will be bringing two bodyguards. I would like to leave as soon as possible."

"I will start making arrangements and getting the customs paperwork in order."

"I am sure you know the pilot I want. I can see the concern on your faces. I know I am taking a risk. I need to see the results of Phase Z for myself, and I have to have a discussion on Joyce. You know the procedures to follow should I not return."

He got up and left with the report on Phase C is his hand.

Charlotte turned to Diana. "I think someone is getting impatient."

"I have to admit that I am also," Diana responded.

Project Phoenix is what he called it despite the official title of Phase C. Martin Schmidt was pleased with its progress. It was intentionally slow, but the important thing was to get each stage of progress correct. There wasn't a deadline to complete in the near future, like in the war. Rising from the ashes, his program was reinstated by the great man. The Führer has completed one of the major accomplishments in the history of mankind. He is alive and well! He allowed most of my staff and me to return. The project that wasn't finished during the war is becoming a reality. It will alter world events when finished.

Joyce was shocked when Hawk informed her of Alexander Wolf's scheduled visit. She didn't have a good feeling about it. She understood he was excited about Phase Z being completed, but to come here and visit was a risk. There had to be more involved, and she figured it could be her.

She texted Megan and got an instant response asking why. She told Megan to meet with her as soon as she could. She waited for what seemed like a long time, but when Megan arrived, it was only six minutes after she called.

"Megan, please sit down."

"I was just notified that Alexander Wolf will be visiting."

Megan hesitated for a minute and then realized who Wolf was. "That is risky. Did they say why?"

"I believe he wants to see your babies and me."

"You? How are you taking that?"

"I don't think it is a good thing, but you never know."

"When is he supposed to arrive, Joyce?"

"Sometime in the next four days. Tessa is making the arrangements."

"I wonder if he will ask about Norm Peters. Have you heard any reports on him?"

"Yes, he is still alive and in the shack where we left him. I am a bit surprised he hasn't tried to leave it. They really must have disoriented him."

"I still see local news reports regarding his disappearance. Planting those drugs in his patrol car was a stroke of genius."

"I hope the Führer will think so."

"The Führer? Adolf Hitler?"

Joyce sat for a moment, and it dawned her on what she said. "Megan, yes the Decider, also known as Alexander Wolf, was the Führer. There are a select few who know his identity, and you are now a member of that group. Please don't inform anyone else. We both could be in severe jeopardy if it is found out you know without receiving permission.

"I am stunned. I can't believe he is with us. You can be sure I will not put us in harm's way."

"Thank you! Oh God, I hope I don't let Führer slip out again. I am likely in enough trouble and don't need to expose him."

"Let's hope that isn't the case, Joyce."

The heavy rain pounding on the shack roof woke Norm up. He sat at the edge of the bed. He got up and quickly put wood in the stove. He walked to the door and was surprised on how much snow had melted. He could make out a road that led into the woods. It was a muddy mess, but it gave him hope. It was time to leave before his supplies ran out. He walked to the mirror and stared intently, but recognition wouldn't come. The shaved head was starting to show some hair. It was mostly gray. His orange uniform wasn't made for the cold weather. He crawled back in bed, and the steady rhythm of the rain hitting the roof caused him to close his eyes and doze off. A loud crack of thunder shook the shed and got him back on his feet. The trash bags he located from an earlier search were loaded with the remaining food and supplies. A trash bag was used to make him a coat to cover him in case of rain. It also covered a good portion of the orange uniform. He brought the bags over next to his bed.

If the rain stops, I'll leave first thing tomorrow morning.

Megan texted Marissa and told her to meet her down in the nursery. She was still stunned on finding out who the Decider was. She had supported him in the war, but felt he had let them all down when he committed suicide. Now it appears that he didn't and had found a way to return. She wondered how Mary would have accepted Phase Z if she had known who the Decider was. She was very upset losing her husband during that war. Too late now to think about that. She needed to get everything in order for his visit. She wondered if he looked the same. *If he does, he will be exposing his identity to the group.*

Megan found a cart and drove toward the nursery. It was close to feeding time for the babies. She wanted to do that whenever she could. She was going to tell Marissa what she renamed Mary and John today. It might help her get comfortable with the names before the Decider arrived. She noticed Marissa hadn't arrived yet when she entered the nursery. One of the nurses came over. "Which baby first?"

"Bring me the girl," Megan responded. She sat in one of the rocking chairs.

The nurse went over and got her. She handed the baby to Megan. She returned shortly with a baby bottle. "Thank you," Megan replied.

She started feeding her and smiled when the Mary's blue eyes focused on her. She wondered if she knew her. Marissa entered the room and was soon sitting in a rocking chair next to her, feeding John.

Megan looked at her. "Marissa, you are holding Adam."

"Let me guess, you are holding Eve?"

"No, I am holding Allison."

Marissa smiled. "I like the sound of their names."

"Thank you."

"Will you be changing your name, Megan?"

"No, I have decided to remain Megan to see if they remember it. Same with your names."

"Okay, as long as they call me Grandma, I am happy."

"I am sure they will."

Megan scanned the room and didn't see anyone else. In a soft voice she said. "Marissa, I need you to keep this between you and

Ted just in case you meet him. The Decider is paying a visit to see the babies."

Marissa sat still for a few moments. "Do you know when?"

"No, but it will be soon. I doubt if it will be announced to the whole group. But since you are down here, just speak only when asked a question."

"Oh, don't worry about that, Megan. I know the process."

Norm opened the door of the shack. The rain had stopped, and most of the snow was gone. It was cold, and he was out of wood to heat the furnace. He stood and started to wrap the blankets around his shoulders and then managed to put the plastic trash bag on over the blankets. He could see well enough, and the blankets were heavy. He flung the bag that held the limited supplies he had over his shoulder. The mirror got his attention, and he decided to take it with him. His boots found an area of solid ground when he left the shed. He looked at the road he had discovered, but the closer he came, the more it looked more like a walking trail. He followed it, staying on the grassy edge as long as he could. The shed was no longer visible when he looked back. The urge to piss overcame his reluctance to do stop and do it. He had to maneuver the blankets and open his orange uniform. His cold hands made it difficult to secure his uniform, and the cold made him shiver after he was done. He tried to walk faster to heat himself up. The trail was getting smaller and the woods more dense. Then he heard running water and eventually came to a bank of a river. It was about a hundred yards wide, and he knew he couldn't cross it at that location. He was undecided on which was to go. He watched the water flow to his right, so he decided to go left. The shoreline was dense with bushes and trees. He found a sturdy wooden stick he used as a cane to help him keep his balance. He was getting tired after a few hundred yards. The stick he was using to support himself broke when he leaned on it. He lost his balance, and the weight of the blankets made him continue to fall into the water. He gasped when the cold water submerged him. He tried to surface, but the weight of the wet blankets and the restricted movement of having a trash bag made it difficult. He did manage to surface once and yelled for help. He heard a thundering noise and realized he was being swept off a waterfall. Panic set in, and he felt himself being airborne and blinded by the trash bag over his head. He died instantly when he landed.

CHAPTER 2

ALEXANDER WAS REVIEWING THE PHASE C report and was quite pleased with its status. Martin Schmidt had a breakthrough and was able to build the machine in a miniature scale. His tests on it were successful. The process now is to manufacture it at much bigger scale. It would take years and plenty of resources, both of which were not an issue anymore. The group was the richest in the world. Hiding the money took skill, and he recruited the best to do it. They also knew if any discrepancies were discovered, they would be severely punished. The cell phone ring got his attention, and he read a text from Tessa. The plans for his trip were arranged. He sat there a moment, then thanked her. He wondered if it was too soon to venture out. He had ventured out to play tennis recently in the small village he lived in. This was different with the heightened security checks going into the USA.

This be a test of my operations, he thought. He had always loved to fly and decided the time was right.

Sam Rupp heard his wife, Maxine, call for him to come from the kitchen to the living room. "Sam, there is breaking news. They found the body of Norm Peters in a river in the Upper Peninsula. He apparently fell in a river and went over a waterfalls."

Sam watched the rest of the report. It said an autopsy would be conducted, but they didn't expect foul play.

Sam looked at Maxine. "There has to be more to it."

"Why do you say that, Sam?"

"Norm leaves Reese. They find his patrol car in the Northern Michigan woods about eighty miles away. Then a few weeks later, he is found dead in a river a few hundred miles north of where the car was. How did he get to Upper Peninsula?"

"Yes, I agree. The thought of them finding drugs in his car and saying he was likely a drug addict still boggles my mind, Sam."

"I think the state police or FBI need to look into this. I will contact some of my connections with them. We know Norm wasn't into that. This has to be a setup to cover up something he came across."

"I hope we can clear his name, Sam."

"We will, Maxine."

The four-engine prop plane lifted off the ground. Alexander was surprised how nervous he was. He sat is a closed-off section in the rear of the plane. His bodyguards and staff were in the front section. It was in the early morning, and the flight should last around sixty-five minutes. He slowly became comfortable after takeoff and as was able to look out one of the windows. Lake Superior came into view, and it took fifteen minutes before he saw land in the horizon. He turned to the report on his meal tray. It notified him that they found Norm Peters dead from an apparent fall over a waterfall. That might change the timetable regarding Grid 49. He looked out the window and saw the Mackinac Bridge approaching and was impressed. He leaned back in his chair and thought about his meeting with Joyce. He had known her since his first days in power. She had been Eva's friend and visited her often when he wasn't with her. Eva needed companionship, and Joyce was a loyal and intelligent friend. She explained issues to Eva when Eva couldn't grasp them. Joyce was his last link to Eva. Sadly, he wasn't pleased with her performance and handling of recent events. He was going to discuss it with her and make his decision on her future by how she reacted. He closed his eyes and remembered Eva. She was a great mistress. *She got my double to marry her. He loved being me*, and he bet his double enjoyed the extremely short honeymoon. *My staff murdered them and burned the bodies.* He knew he couldn't let the Reds or the people find the bodies. They likely would have come to the conclusion it wasn't him.

He glanced out the window, and he smiled when he saw hundreds of power-generating windmills. They went on for as far as he could see. He had grids under select portions. The pilot contacted him and said they were near the airport. He fastened his seatbelt, and his attendant removed the tray from his desk. He watched as the plane descended and noticed the airport was in a rural area. He grabbed the arm rest when he could see the landing was soon. The squeal of the tires and the slight jolt from the wheels touching down followed. He was in America.

The plane taxied along the runway, and he noticed there was just a small gathering of airplane hangars. The doors of the biggest hangar started to open when they approached. The plane entered, but there wasn't much clearance for the wings. He noticed a convoy of vehicles waiting for them. His bodyguards went out and checked the security. He waited, and they came in and nodded to him. He gathered his briefcase and exited the plane. The Harry Browne Airport sign got his attention when they drove away. It was a quick trip to the former truck staging building, and he was met by Joyce. She hadn't aged gracefully, and he was surprised she continued to maintain her present status. Joyce, on the other hand, was stunned at his appearance. The long blond hair, the beard and the muscular built had her wondering if it was him. It wasn't until he said, "Greetings, Joyce, so happy to see you again," that she realized it was.

"Greetings, Alexander, welcome to Michigan. The elevator is to your left."

She led them to the elevator. It was his first time to an underground facility. He was used to living underground and in some ways preferred it. It gave him a stronger sense of security. There were carts with drivers waiting for the entourage when they arrived on the ground floor.

"Alexander, do you want to go to your quarters?" asked Joyce.

"No, I would like to see the infants from Phase Z. The others can go to the quarters."

Joyce gave the other drivers orders, and Alexander did the same for his entourage. Joyce went to the driver's seat and waited for Alexander to enter the cart. "This your first time away from the den, Alexander?" Joyce asked when they drove away.

"Other than a few tennis trips near the den, yes."

"How was the flight?"

"I enjoyed it. It was surprising on how many windmills there are in the area."

"You should see them at night. Their red warning lights can be seen for miles. The locals call it the Sea of Red."

"I would like to see it before I return."

"It will be arranged. Your English is very good, Alexander."

"Thank you, it has taken a lot of time," he said with a smile.

She returned the smile. They arrived at the hospital unit. She typed in the code as he strode next to her. Megan had been notified and was waiting for them when they entered the room. Alexander looked like nothing she expected. Blond hair, beard, and a tremendous built. He had really transformed himself. She found herself attracted to his look

"Megan, this is Alexander Wolf, the Decider."

Megan walked to him and said, "Hello, Mr. Wolf. Pleased to meet you."

"Please call me Alexander." He looked into her eyes. She was very pretty with her dark brown hair and blue eyes. She had a nice shape.

He continued his focus on her. "You are the one who volunteered for the mission of raising the kids?"

"Yes, thank you for allowing it."

"Thank me if you feel that way after they have grown," he said with a smile.

"I am sure we will."

"We?"

"Yes, my current parents, Ted and Marissa Anderson. She is in the next room with the infants. Do you want to meet them all?"

"I look forward to it."

Megan led them in to the nursery. Joyce continued to stay in the background. Marissa was holding Adam, and a nurse had Allison.

Megan led him to Marissa. "This is my current mom, Marissa. She is holding Adam."

He walked up to her and smiled. "Is the girl named Eve?"

"She is named Allison," responded Marissa.

He turned to Megan and said, "Thank you for the tour. Joyce and I have to leave. I hope to chat with you later."

"You are welcome. I hope that will be arranged."

Megan watched them leave. She still had a difficult time believing he was Adolf Hitler. She would have never guessed by his appearance. *Maybe that is why he visited. To see if anyone could recognize him.* Very few know who Alexander Wolf really is.

Alexander got in the cart and waited for Joyce to get in her seat. "Joyce, I need to have something to eat. Then we need to talk."

"Okay, do you want to go now, or do you want to return to your group and return with them?"

"Will you join me now?"

"Yes, of course, Alexander."

She drove to the cafeteria. "Alexander, they will cook you anything you want. A waiter will take your order."

"Interesting, I get to see how the operation is run. I need to start doing that. The reports are one thing, but seeing it in action lets me know who I can trust."

He opened the door for her and was surprised on how well the cafeteria was set up. "I hope the food matches this set up. It is amazing. Your work, Joyce?"

"My crew was responsible for it. I have never heard any complaints with the food. We have some experienced chefs."

He laughed and said, "Being group members, I am sure they are."

He pointed to a booth the most isolated. She led the way to it. When they were seated, a waitress approached. She was a brunette and with a nice figure. Joyce guessed she was around thirty. Joyce could see she was giving him a close look, and she figured it was because of his build. The waitress handed them a menu.

"You can order anything, or we will take a request. The request might take a bit longer, but we have nearly everything in stock."

Alexander looked at Joyce. "I know what I want, so order first when you are ready."

Joyce put the menu down. "I'd like fish and chips, with plenty of tartar sauce."

"Would you like something to drink?" asked the waitress.

"An ice tea with no lemon."

"Okay, and you, sir?" she said with a huge smile and inviting eyes.

"A large serving of salmon, a sweet potato, and asparagus. To drink, I will have a glass of red wine. I'll let you choose." He was smiling back at her.

She blushed and went to the kitchen with the order.

"I think you have her flustered, Alexander."

He smiled. "It has been awhile."

"Wine? I never remember you having that before, Alexander."

"It is something new. An occasional glass of wine is now part of my workout routine diet."

"When did you start that?"

"Around twenty-five years ago. After my last transformation. Speaking of transformation, Joyce, why do you still remain at this advanced age?"

"When dealing with outsiders, it can be an advantage to be perceived as a tough-minded old broad. But when I get hot flashes, I question my reasoning."

Alexander laughed out loud. "You always had a quick wit, Joyce."

Joyce signaled to him. The waitress was approaching. She was carrying a wide tray, and the meals were on it. She served Joyce first and then turned to Alexander. She gave him his meal and placed a wineglass next to his meal. He grabbed her wrist. "Care to share a glass of wine with me?"

He released her and watched her stunned face. "Sir, I am sure that is not allowed."

He turned to Joyce and smiled. He raised his eyebrows, and Joyce knew what he wanted. "It's okay for this time. Go get a glass if you care to share a drink with this gentleman."

"I will be right back." She smiled as she walked away.

Joyce waited until she was out of hearing range. "So you still have someone test your food and drink, Alexander?"

"My dear, it had worked well. But in my mansion, I don't."

"How often have you eaten elsewhere?"

"This is the first time."

"You need a taste tester for your food?" she said with a smile.

"No, I was just seeing if you remembered." He started to eat, and she was surprised on how slowly and deliberately he ate. When she watched him years ago, it was pretty disgusting. He ate real fast, and his table matter were terrible. It used to embarrass Eva. The waitress finally appeared with glass in hand.

"Sorry for the delay. I waited for my shift to be officially over. I am on my time now."

She opened and poured the wine in his glass and then hers. He stood up and said, "A toast to your shift ending," and they touched glasses and drank.

He put his arm around her and led here away from the table. Joyce watched while she ate. She figured she better eat quickly. He looked to be getting a positive response with his discussion with her. She gave him a hug and went toward the exit. Alexander went back to the table and sat down to finish his meal. He smiled at Joyce. "Her name is Martha. I told her how impressed I was of her for waiting to the end of her shift and for the choice of wine. I told her she is appreciated. She thanked me and said something about going to an Octoberfest nearby. She said she would save a dance for me."

"Yes, there is an Octoberfest this weekend. It is held in the city of Frankenmuth. They celebrate their German heritage in a number of ways."

"Sounds interesting, Joyce. But I am not ready to be that exposed. We need to go to your office and have a discussion."

They stood up and went to the exit.

CHAPTER 3

CYRUS MONTGOMERY LOOKED AT THE sea charts. There was a small island in the South Pacific he had to investigate. It was round, with steep cliffs surrounding its exterior. There has been a constant cloud ringing the top of it. The only way to enter it was to fly over the top and descend. But was there something to descend into? That is the mystery he wanted to solve. He was excited to see Phase I activated. He had been unofficially looking for locations to install it for over thirty years. Martin Schmidt must have developed a successful prototype. It would be years before the instillation, so there is no need to hurry. Not like during the war. The island was a speck in the horizon. The binocular view showed him the white clouded ring at the top. The island wasn't listed as habited and wasn't named. It could be the perfect location. But he had thought that many times before about other islands. The helicopter pilot contacted him, letting him know he thought the conditions were good for a flight. He responded by telling him that he would be right there. The copter motor started when he entered it.

"Well, James. What do you think of this one?"

"Cyrus, this could be interesting. I just hope the cloud cover isn't too thick."

"Yes, I must admit I am a bit concerned. But if this place works out, it would be the perfect natural camouflage."

"Let's see what we have," James said as they lifted off from the ship's deck.

They circled the island. Cyrus was amazed on how uniform it was. It had a steep natural wall of several hundred meters tall. There didn't look like away way to climb it. There wasn't much shoreline, so the only way you could get to the wall was by boat, but rocks surrounding edge of the shoreline would make that very difficult. "We are at seven hundred meters and above the cloud. You ready to slowly descend?"

"Yes, James, I am ready." He put the binoculars to his eyes, and just a white mist was the only thing in view as the slowly descended.

It was a bit unnerving being blind to what was below the cloud.

"Six hundred meters, Cyrus."

"Five hundred meters."

"It's starting to thin out, James. Keep going."

"Four hundred fifty meters."

"Oh wow, I don't believe this. Look, James, it is a flat service in the shape of a bowl. It will be ideal if the engineering crew can supply what the base will need. We could have found the launching pad."

"I'll set it down. Looks like plenty of room. Hard to believe it is flat with short grass."

"I sure can't explain it."

Cyrus was ready for the slight jolt to his body when they landed. He marveled at the height of the walls when he scanned them. With them and the cloud cover, it would be difficult to detect a base.

"Cyrus, there is a cave on this side. It could lead to the ocean." The helicopter motor stopped, so they exited and headed toward the cave.

James had grabbed the flashlight when he had pointed out the cave. They followed its beam when they entered the cave. Cyrus could hear the ocean waves nearby. They walked toward the sound and stopped when they saw what looked like a river going underground from the ocean.

"That could be a manmade entryway to go under the island," Cyrus stated.

"You think it might have been used in the war?"

"Anything is possible, but it will have to be investigated. It could be a natural development. It sure looks promising, though. Time to get back to the ship and let Hawk know."

Sam Rupp walked into his home. He saw his wife, Maxine, in her sewing room. "I got some information on Norm Peters."

Maxine turned to him. "What did you hear, Sam?"

"Hun, this needs to be between you and me. They did an autopsy on Norm. He died from brain trauma. He apparently fell in a river and went over a waterfall. It is believed he hit rocks at the base of it, and it killed him instantly."

"Oh my god."

"But that isn't all. He was wearing and orange jumpsuit that inmates wear. But there isn't a county jail that claims to have jailed him. He also had a recently shaved head. No county jail does that unless there is a lice issue. There was also a huge combination of drugs in his system that had to have him in an altered state."

"Sam, something isn't right. We know Norm wasn't like that. Any word on how they think he got up there?

"No, they are trying to locate where he fell in the river and how he got there. But the weather has made it difficult. The FBI might get involved. That is why we need to keep it here. I am sure they will be in Reese if that is the case. Sheriff Mason expects them to. He has been in contact with them. I told him everything I know about Norm that he may not have known."

"Sam, do you think they think something happened other than an officer going off the deep end?"

"Not sure what they think, but if he didn't they want to find out what happened."

Alexander Wolf finished his evening meal. He had toured the facility. He visited with Dr. Kurt Thurman. His next visit was to be with Megan Anderson. He arranged to meet her at the house they lived in. Megan arrived in a cart, and he left the cafeteria when he saw her.

"How was your dinner, Alexander?"

"It was excellent. Have you had yours?"

"Yes, after the babies were fed."

"They are growing quickly."

"Yes, but nothing abnormal."

She stopped the cart near an elevator door. She got out and pushed the up button. They waited for the elevator to arrive. They got in, and it was a short ride to the Anderson basement.

"So this is where Mary Brunell escaped the gas fire blast, Megan?"

"Yes, she pulled John Dwyer in when they smelled the gas."

Megan pushed a button on the wall, and the basement wall moved out and created an opening to enter the interior. When they went in, she pushed another button to close it.

"You have a manual way of opening that door?"

"Yes, in case of power failures. Plus, there is a winding stairwell next to the elevator shaft."

They entered the living room. Megan switched the lights on. They were the only ones there. Alexander went to the picture window. The darkness was penetrated by the blinking red lights from the windmills. He could see they blinked in unison, and it seemed to go on forever.

"The Sea of Red is impressive. I can see why they call it that, Megan."

"It can almost hypnotize you if you stare at it long enough, Alexander."

He smiled at her and then pointed toward the couch. He went and sat at one end and she at the other.

"Megan, tell me about your relationship with Mary. Why did you decide to volunteer to care for her as an infant?"

Megan was taken back. She waited a few seconds then responded, "Mary and I knew each other prior to the war. We both were in each other's weddings, and both our husbands were killed fighting for the cause. I figured it would be best for me to find out if she remembered anything about her being my friend and past life."

"Were you upset when she was ordered into Phase Z?"

Megan thought for a second. "It was your decision, so what I think isn't important."

He sat their quietly for an extended time. "Megan, do you know who I really am?"

She hesitated briefly. "I only know you as Alexander Wolf, the Decider."

He looked at her with an intense stare. "I am not sure I believe you. If you do know who I am, then I need you to think about your answer to this question: are those two babies Mary Brunell and John Dwyer?"

"Who else would they be? The procedure was videotaped from the beginning. DNA samples were taken. Why do you think anyone would risk being out of the group?"

"Human emotions can cause errors in judgment. Perhaps like I am doing now. But now that I have met you and realize your commitment, my mind is at ease. They are in good hands. It will be interesting to see how this evolves. Could you please drive me to Joyce's office?"

"Yes, Alexander. I believe she is waiting for you."

Alexander didn't say a word on the drive to the office. Megan could tell he was in deep thought. They arrived at Joyce's office. She dropped him off and left. *I wonder how that will go. He isn't in a good mood.*

Joyce got up from behind her desk when he walked in.

She pointed to a cushioned chair directly in front of her desk. He closed the door and sat.

"The facility is in fine shape. It is too bad we will have to close it, Joyce. I think you know why."

"Yes, the death of Officer Peters."

"It could bring attention to the facility. We will secure and flood the facility after we relocate everyone and everything. Joyce, you will not be in charge of completing it."

Joyce was taken back. "I am a bit surprised, Alexander. Are you disappointed in my performance?"

"Joyce, were you the one who dealt with police and insurance company at the downed Tower site?"

"Yes."

"Don't you think you are a bit old to be representing a US corporation? How many seventy-plus-year-old women do that?"

She thought about it and said, "Of course, you are correct. You have plans to on how to resolve the situation if they pursue it?"

"Yes, the board has a plan. No need to go over it now."

"Anything else to discuss, Alexander?"

"Yes, tell me why you didn't remove John Dwyer from this earth when you had the opportunity? He was robbing the house, and he ends up in the group. What was your line of thinking?"

"Alexander, I took him to my group leaders. Yes, I could have put him down and hid his vehicle, and you and the board would likely never have known. Is that what you want? A group member bypassing the chain of command and doing their own plans? So we came up with a solution where we could use his skills by potentially blackmailing him. Those plans did benefit the group. He was willing to also be the first for Phase Z when you decided to volunteer him."

He sat there in thought. "Eva always said you were a bit of a rebel. I wondered if this was the case. You are correct. I don't want a rogue area leader. But you and your brain trust weren't following directives. I want you to return with me to Canada. We will discuss your future then."

Violet Richard arrived at the board meeting room first. It was her routine to arrive very early. She liked to get the coffee made and always brought instant oatmeal. She was eating it when she found out that Joyce Sanders was relieved of her duties in Grid 49. Alexander had asked her if she was interested in being her temporary replacement. She was shocked about Joyce being removed. Alexander told her that grid would be closed and sealed. It was her job to move the people to another grid and secured all entries to Grid 49 prior to it being sealed. The microwave in the next room pinged that it had finished its setting. She walked to it and got her oatmeal. She closed the door on her way back and started her breakfast. There wasn't a meeting scheduled, so she could focus on the grid information. She decided she would do it. It would only add to her kiss-ass reputation, but she didn't care. She wanted to learn as much about the group leadership as possible. She had her own secret plans for the future.

Joyce never liked flying. The trip back to Canada was an ordeal. She stayed away from the windows and tried to keep focus on a magazine she brought on board. But her mind would focus on her future—if she had one. She knew from the past that Alexander didn't keep people alive if they failed him. *What are his future plans?* He wasn't like the man she knew before. Maybe because he has more time. Well, if the plane doesn't crash.

Maxine saw the sad expression on Sam's face when he arrived home from work.

"Everything okay, Sam?"

Maxine, I just found out they closed the case on Norm. I guess it wasn't a high enough priority to utilize resources to investigate."

"That's terrible. What now?"

"Good question. I am starting to think maybe we don't want to know. It could have been a drug deal gone badly. I don't know where to go from here."

CHAPTER 4

Eighteen years later

MEGAN LOOKED OUT THE WINDOW and saw the snow was coming down hard. It would take the huge snow blower they had on the facility to clear the path to the road. Allison and Adam were let out of the high school early because of the blizzard warning that was posted an hour ago. It took a blizzard to close the schools. They were so adept at handling snow during the long winter along the Canadian shore on Lake Superior. The move from New Zealand was ten years ago. Alexander Wolf wanted them closer so he could visit. He was leaving his lair more often. A lot had changed in eighteen years. Megan could see the changes in her face every time she looked in a mirror. But she was pleased to see the mature woman that matched her feelings. It was strange watching Allison become a teenager. She had to stop herself from calling her Mary many times. She did once to see if she would get a response from her, but a puzzled look from Allison was all she got. Adam was a typical teenager. She didn't know John at that age, so it was like she never knew what to expect from him. Adam made her forget John. It was like he was a new person or her son from the beginning. *Mom* had been a word she grew to love. Marissa and Ted were great in their roles of grandparents. Megan knew Alexander was closely checking the kids' status and decided to let whatever happened to their memory happen naturally. She would be in peril if he found out she had withheld any information from him. But she couldn't help wonder about their future. What did Alexander have in mind for them? She closed the window curtains and left the room. The wooden log mansion still amazed her. It had over a hundred rooms and many fireplaces to help keep it heated. There was a boiler room in a separate building that supplied the steam to the heating systems to all adjacent buildings. The barn was the largest one in the area, if not the province. It held snow removal equipment, cars, plows, a helicopter, an airplane, and assorted other equipment. There was space for more. Many preferred to live in the grid under the number of windmills. They supplied power to the immediate area. Winters were long and with plenty of snow.

Alexander entered the conference room. He could feel the intensity from those in the room. This was a status meeting on the progress on all phases to the ultimate conclusion of his plan—the plan to control the world. The room was full with the board and the other developmental leaders.

The group became quiet when they saw him enter. He sat down and glanced to Hawk. Hawk moved to the podium. Behind him was a large white video screen.

"Greetings, we have a video that shows the status of our project." He walked off, and the video was projected on the screen. Alexander watched his staff view the video. He had seen it. He was pleased at their reaction. They stood and applauded when it was over. Alexander waited for it to end and slowly walked to the podium. He paused and said nothing. Some of his staff smiled because they knew it was his custom to do so. Violet was one of them. He may look different, but old habits will eventually resurface. He scanned the room.

"The wait is nearly over. Our patience will soon be rewarded. We must all remember there the challenges will face not only once our plan is motion but for time after. We still need time for testing components of the plan. I expect that time needed to be minimal. It is time to be on alert and ready for action. The time for us to lead the world is near." He left the podium to applause.

Joyce watched him leave the podium. He had glanced her way. She had been his constant companion since she returned with him from Reese. Her transformation to early twenties was something Alexander demanded. The face in the mirror was a welcome change for her ego, but it took a beating being his sex partner. There was no emotion involvement, and he wasn't good in bed. He preferred kinky to satisfy his needs. She never had an orgasm with him. He also kept her out of the loop information wise. *What had Eva seen in him?* was often her thought. Violet had quietly befriended her. She knew Violet wanted information about Alexander, but she in turn used that situation for her own benefit. Alexander let her accompany him whenever he visited Megan and the kids. She knew that Megan didn't betray her trust when she had exposed Alexander to her. But she felt Alexander was trying to detect a breach in her trust. For some reason, he appeared suspicious. She managed to tell Megan to contact Violet if she needed to contact her. Alexander had increased his focus on the plan to rule the world. It was getting closer to the day of implementation. She knew she would be pushed out of his mind-set. He couldn't wait to tell the world of his return, and she saw him practice his moment of triumph speech in the mirror many times. She wondered if he would return to his Hitler look. If the plan works, she couldn't think of a reason why he wouldn't.

Allison stared at Adam while he was eating his breakfast. She had a feeling that something was different. He dream last night of living another life seemed so real. Megan had been her friend and not her mother in the dream. "Adam, I had a weird dream last night. Megan was my friend and not our mother."

He looked at her. "Was there anything else?"

She hesitated and said, "I lived another life."

"Were you Mary?"

"Oh my god, yes!"

"Then it wasn't a dream. I was scared to say anything. We aren't brother and sister, are we?"

"I don't think so, John. We were a couple."

"That is putting it nicely. Then what we went through was real. We have to tell Megan."

"I agree, John, but it sure could change our future."

"Well, we'll still be Allison and Adam, and we have to get to school."

"Yes, but now it seems different to me."

"Let's talk about it later, Mary."

She gave him a stare and went out the door.

Adam waived to Megan as he approached his home. Allison was a short distance behind him, and he waited for her. Her auburn hair was nearly covered by a knitted hat as she came near him.

"Look, Megan is watching us. Think today would be a good day to tell her?"

He felt a snowball hit his shoulder. He turned and saw her smile.

"We could show her, John. We could suck face."

John smiled. "I am game if you are, Mary."

"We better tell her in private. You never know if there are other eyes watching us."

"True, I don't want to take that chance," John said with a smile.

"Yeah, it could make the local news, and we would be branded perverts for life."

"Oh, I am sure Alexander would find a way to retrieve us."

"Really, he could let us grow old and die, Mary."

"We can die anytime, John, if Alexander decides we aren't needed."

"We better get in before Megan decides to do the job," John said, looking up at Megan.

"She doesn't look pleased. You think she can read lips?"

"I think it is time to tell her so we won't have to worry about it."

"It might not be the last of our worries," John said as he opened the back door.

The test was complete. The major hurdle he had faced was conquered. Alexander will be pleased. The network of electrical rays was complete, in sync and totally operational. He turned when he heard on a knock on office door.

"Come in."

He was surprised to see Hawk enter.

"Mr. Hawk, what a pleasant surprise. Your timing is perfect. The equipment test was a success, and it is fully operational."

"Martin, that is great news. We would be surprised if it wasn't, knowing your history."

"You mean the history where most of my projects were blackballed?"

"There are stupid and greedy people in the world. Alexander knew your value."

"I am thankful he did, Hawk. He barely got there in time to save me. I am still amazed he was able to pull it off."

"Yes, it was a huge gamble getting you out of New York City, but for you, Martin, it was worth it."

"I was and am still humbled by it. The day will come soon when we will show the world what it could have had nearly a hundred years ago."

"Yes, the world will have to acknowledge you as the greatest inventor of all time."

"That is not important to me. Being able to have full support of my projects is."

"Understood. Alexander will be pleased to know the status of your project. The plan appears ready to be implemented in the near future. Good day, Martin."

He watched Hawk depart. He shook his head. *It will be nice to use my real name again. I understand the secrecy, but soon there will be no reason for it. It was not my plan to use the power in the way they want to, but maybe their way of one unified government is the answer to save the world from itself.*

Cyrus Montgomery walked around the launching pad. *The future of the world is about to be in our hands. War will be a thing of the past. We can then focus on exploring space. With the product, traveling years to other worlds will be possible. We can actually have a real Star Trek experience.*

He then focused on the duties at hand. The launch of the super weapon was ready when they want it. Everything had been reviewed many times. He was confident, but there was a backup plan in case of an unexpected failure. He awaited the call from Alexander.

Hawk returned to the secured headquarters for the overall operations. It was located underground of an isolated airport in Northern Ontario. They had taken many security measure to keep it undetectable. A cart awaited him when he arrived at the entrance hallway. He proceeded to a huge underground theater and stage. It seated nearly four thousand. He opened a door and glanced in. It looked to be filled to capacity by group members. He closed the door and drove to the stage entrance. The door was guarded by one of Alexander's bodyguards, so Hawk knew he was there. The guard contacted someone backstage and opened the door for the Hawk.

"Sir, he is in dressing room 1."

"Thank you," and Hawk walked in that direction.

Another bodyguard was at the door, and Hawk saw him knock and told Alexander that he had arrived. He opened the door and shut it after Hawk entered.

Hawk was stunned when he saw Alexander.

Alexander laughed at his reaction. "So do I look like the real me, Hawk?"

"It will take me a moment to grasp the change. Your body is so different. You look like yourself but on steroids."

"Now you know I never use those. My old doctor may have given them to me in your past, with all the other bullshit he was giving me."

"Well, anyway, it is good to see the Führer in all his glory return."

"I hope my former troops will feel the same way. They don't know that each of them had served in the war for us in various ways. It is time to reestablish ties. They will be the first of the group members to know as we start the countdown to our domination. So what is the status of our operation?"

"Everything is ready awaiting the approval from you."

"That will be soon. First, I need to focus on this. Please tell Violet to start the proceedings."

Hawk left the room, and Alexander stood and looked in the mirror. "The makeup team had done a great job. His black hair was neatly trimmed in his old style. He was surprised with how uncomfortable his mustache felt. But then again it wasn't real. He entered the room adjacent to his and saw the surprised look on Joyce's face. "Think Eva would have approved, Joyce?" Without a doubt, Adolf." *Eva had rose-colored glasses for you*, she thought.

He was slightly taken aback upon hearing his name.

"It has been a long time since I heard my name," he said with a smile and left the room to head backstage.

The lights in the auditorium dimmed, and the group members in the crowd quieted and watched the stage go dark. A bright light then focused on the podium in the center of the stage. A young woman approached it. She adjusted the microphone. "Hello, my name is Violet. I am on the board for the Decider. I need your full attention as you are the first to learn that I am. There is a reason you were all selected to join the group over the years. We did research on every one of you. That same reason is what brings you here tonight. In your youth, each and every one of us joined a cause to change the world. I was a member of that cause. We almost succeeded, but as we now know, the cause was sabotaged by the enemy's intelligence forces. You all went on with your lives, and the cause faded away. But did it? Could it be in hibernation slowly growly stronger with each year? You have all been given the gift of extended life by this same cause. The cause that still believes the world needs one central government to eliminate all wars and live in peace. I want to introduce to you the man who has believed in this cause and has always believed in you. Here is the Decider." She made her exit and the crowd awaited the Decider. He slowly walked to the podium, and the crowd was quiet until they recognized him and then stood in unison and started a "Heil Hitler" chant.

He stood nearly overcome with emotion as they continued to salute him.

They quieted when he gave the stop signal with his arm. He stood there scanning the crowd. "We have a directive that states not to ask a group member about the past. I will invoke that now because what happened in the past is not important. But what is important is what we learned from it. I have learned a lot from the mistakes I made. Many of you experienced the time in the homeland before the war. It was a time of prosperity and peace. The war to spread that prosperity to the deserving was a failure. We are about to gather our resources and unleash a power the world has never seen. There hasn't been a need to hurry our advanced technology, and we have tested it every step of the way. I ask you to rejoin the cause, not as troops going to war but as a group that will oversee the aftermath that will happen after we cleanse the world of weapons and governments that suppress the people. We will be the new world order. We will finally meet our destiny. You will be part of the thousand-year Reich," he said with his voice getting louder as he ended.

The crowd again stood in unison, chanting "Heil Hitler" and giving him the Nazi salute. He stood there for a few seconds, and he then returned the salute, and they responded with cheers. He gave a nod to Violet let her know that he was about to leave. She walked to the podium, and he gave her hug and left the stage. The crowd continues to cheer until she held her arms up as a gesture to become quiet. She waited until they settled down and said, "You are the first group that has seen him in seventy years. The plan we have has been implemented, and you are in the first stage of that plan. Let me emphasize this. You must not discuss this with anyone outside this group. If there is anyone not interested in continuing in the group, you must state that before we start the training. You will be responsible for your actions. Same for those who violate a directive. Training will start in forty-eight hours. If you need to make arrangements for any material goods, let the group members know, and they will assist you when you leave this auditorium. Good day, gentlemen."

They gave her applause when she left, and they were met by group members at the doors.

Joyce saw Alexander strut into her dressing room. She knew he would fall back into his Führer mode. "Very impressive, Adolf. It is difficult to believe it was about seventy years ago since your last speech before a crowd."

He turned to her. "Yes, it did feel like it was yesterday since the last one."

Charlotte shut off the feed from the auditorium. She turned to the other four board members sitting at the private conference room table.

"He inspired me."

"Doesn't he always, Charlotte?" responded Connie.

Charlotte frowned at Connie. "As a matter of fact he does."

"So, ladies, just thought of something. How do we address him now?" Diana asked.

"Maybe we should wait until Violet returns. She seems to have the answer for everything," Tessa responded with a touch a sarcasm.

"Okay, ladies, let's recover our focus. We don't have time for this petty stuff," Diana said, getting their attention.

"Who has the list of targets for the Southeast Asia area?"

"I do," responded Charlotte.

"I believe we have some new reports that add targets to the list. We have new information for all the areas. We need to get them out to the field as soon as possible."

Diana watched as the other went over the reports.

"By the way, I will address him as whoever he shows up as."

The others looked at her and then nodded in agreement.

CHAPTER 5

"You two are quiet. Anything happen at school today to cause you just to pick at your dinner?" Megan asked Adam and Allison.

John looked at Mary and nodded. "Megan, we need to have a chat with you in private," Mary whispered.

Megan sat back in her chair and put her fork down. "I don't think that is needed. When you called me Megan, I knew what you meant. Let's finish the meal first as I need time to think."

They ate quietly, and when they were finished, they knew the kitchen staff would be there shortly to clear the table. Megan gave a signal for them to follow her, and they went to her bedroom. She closed the door and turned to them. "I scan this room often. I am confident there are no listening devices in here."

Mary had a worried look on her face. "Why would there be listening devices?"

"Phase Z is very important part of the group's future plans. How long ago was it when regained your memory?"

"About a week ago," Mary replied.

"The same for me," responded John.

Megan sat on her bed and gestured to them to do the same. "You must not tell anyone or give anyone a reason to think there is something between you two. If word gets out that you remember, your future could be in jeopardy. You must remain Adam and Allison until I tell you different, and with things in motion that I can't divulge, that could be a long time from now." Mary could tell by the serious look on Megan's face that she was scared. "Mom, we will do as you say," and she turned to John, who nodded in agreement. "I do love you two" and gave them a hug.

Violet sat in her living room and couldn't help but relive the moment the Führer came on the stage. The power he possessed with just his appearance was amazing. She felt honored to present him and thought it had gone well, but she was no match with his speech. *At least they know I am on the board. That is a major accomplishment.* She had earned his trust with her hard work and willingness to do any task. It had drained her a number of times, but she never complained. She had befriended Joyce and knew she could be a powerful ally in the future. Joyce didn't deserve her current fate. She got up and went to the kitchen and poured herself a class of wine. The cheese was in the refrigerator, and she cut off a number of slices. She nibbled on them as she went to her bedroom. She placed the wine and the cheese on her bed stand. She gave into the urge to fall into bed and lay on top of the covers. She felt the room spin slightly before her focus stopped it. She smiled when she thought of the applause she received when she left the stage. Then she hugged herself for a job well done.

Adolf paced back and forth in his study located in the new headquarters. Joyce went to her room as he had requested. Today made him feel like he was about to have a do-over of the life he had before. He felt he was about to fulfill his destiny. The speech wasn't prepared, and he just let his feeling flow. It had always been more effective using that approach. He was certain the people knew he was the chosen one, and their response today confirmed it. He walked to the bathroom and stared at his image in the mirror. He smiled and reached to take of his fake mustache because it was causing an itch. It peeled off slowly, and he wasn't sure if he would put in on again. *Time for the real thing*, he thought. *There isn't a hurry.* There was plenty to do before he would address the world. The world is in turmoil right now, and it would be an ideal time to strike. It would cause worldwide chaos, and his plan to control it wasn't ready for implementation. He went back to his living room and sat in his leather recliner. He rocked and let his mind relax. Maybe some chaos wouldn't be a bad thing. *If the plan works to perfection, they may never know what hit them. Maybe they would think it is aliens attacking from outer space, because the electrical fireworks that is planned will seem out of this world.*

He then just rocked and rocked.

Megan didn't sleep well. Her decision about John and Mary replayed in her mind. Knowing who the Decider was had influenced her decision. He was never one to take disappointment well. The way he took an interest in the kids was a cause for concern.

Phase Z was important to him. To her knowledge, it was the last phase to be implemented and wondered if there was an alternative if it wasn't successful. She was afraid to ask. Contacting Joyce entered her thoughts, but she knew she wasn't in a position of power and doubted if it was worth the gamble to see if she could help. The school year was coming to the end, and she dreaded it. She had a feeling that John and Mary will become part of the take-over-the-world plan if they are known to be Allison and Adam.

The thought of them leaving was difficult for her to accept. But she knew if the opportunity came, she would do it again.

The ball landed on the green about five feet from the pin.

"Nice shot, Mr. President."

"Thank you, George. It helps when I have a great caddie," he said, looking at him.

George smiled in response.

President Maurice Connelly handed the club to George and strolled to the golf cart. The Secret Service had two carts, and one went forward toward the green, and the other waited and followed the president's cart. This was a rare time the president played solo. There was often someone from Congress or a campaign donor with him. He parked the cart next to the green and got out and stretched his six-foot-five-inch body. He waited for George to give him his putter, and he approached the green. Putting was something he never got a feel for. It was difficult to kneel because of his arthritic left knee. He knew he needed a knee replacement but was determined to wait until his term was over in ten months. It didn't bother his golf swing, but that was never that great anyway. He walked around the hole and got a feeling this putt was a straight in line. He bent over the ball and without a practice swing, sank the ball into the hole.

"That gives you a par. Mr. President."

"Thanks, George, how many on the round so far?"

"Four pars with two holes to go on the front nine."

"Nice, I need to play solo more often," he said with a smile.

He needed to be alone and try not to think about events that were happening. The opposition party would howl if they found out he was golfing. But they were too busy dealing with the upcoming election. His vice president, David Foster, was going to be his party's nominee. He would campaign for him if he was asked. But he knew David wanted to run on his own merits. He didn't have an issue with that. Besides he was happy to fade away from the spotlight. The nearly eight years had aged him more than he wanted to acknowledge. The war in Korea was a bloodbath that involved the US and China trying to stay out of it. It was finally settled with the North accepting defeat. His wife was ready for a normal life—normal as it allowed with Secret Service nearby.

"What do we have next, George?"

"A par five with a dog leg to the left. With trees on both sides."

"What do you suggest?"

"The three wood."

He nodded approval and took a few swings with it. He teed the ball up and lined up for the shot. His long swing generated power, and the ball sailed to the middle of the fairway a few hundred yards before it landed, and the ball continue to roll. He was pleased. He hadn't had a shot feel that good in a long time. The ball continued to roll, and out of the woods came an animal. It was a black Lab who started chasing the ball. The dog ran a circle around the ball once it stopped. Then he lunged and picked up the ball. A nearby Secret Service agent approached the dog, and the dog ran a circle around him. When he veered to intercept the dog, the dog responded and was quick to move out of arm's reach. Then another Secret Service agent approached from a different direction, and the game was on. The dog was quicker to counter their moves. The president laughed as he watched. He turned to his head Secret Service agent who was close by and in a cart. "Wayne, make sure the agents don't harm that dog."

"Yes, sir," and he contacted the other agents with his two-way radio.

Another agent joined the fray, and the dog put the ball down and ran into the woods.

The president smiled at George. "Any other doglegs on the course?"

Hawk watched the video of the Führer's appearance last night before the group members. Watching the Führer address a crowd was something he could never get enough of. It always inspired him. The Führer's voice was different when addressing a crowd. It would raise to whatever level he pushed it. It was so different from his normal talking voice. He always said he got the energy from the crowd. He had seen nearly all the Führer's speeches. He was there at the beginning. He knew the Führer trusted him because he never asked for anything in return for doing a favor for the Führer. He also was content being a follower. The one thing he was uncomfortable about was his looks, and he preferred wearing a mask when dealing with people. He liked the advantage of them not being able to read any of his facial expressions. The Führer, understanding his situation, never had an issue with it. He closed the laptop and returned the focus on the work on his desk. The updates on the phase statuses were complete. They were ready for the board meeting in the morning. He grabbed his coffee cup and got up to his desk. He went over to the coffee maker in the adjoining lobby and scanned to see it was vacant. He rinsed the cup out at the sink and poured himself another cup of coffee. He added two creams and went back to his office and closed the door behind him. He took off his mask and leaned back in his chair. The coffee was hot and he sipped it slowly. His slurping sounds made him remember his mother yelling at him for doing it. It was difficult to think of her, knowing there hadn't been any way to let her know why he had disappeared during the war. He had been an only child, and his father had died during the First World War. He was working when he met the Adolf. He slowly became drawn to him. He knew he wasn't like most men, and he liked men more than women. It was something he kept a secret, but he had hunch that Adolf knew. It was this secret that also kept him from pursuing power. The laptop came on when he opened it. He clicked on the video of the Führer in action last night.

Mary had thoroughly gone over her room looking for listening devices and cameras. The feeling of confidence that there weren't any removed her fear. She went down the hallway and knocked on John's door. When he stuck his head out, she signaled for him to follow her. He shrugged his shoulder and closed his door and followed her to her room. She shut the door after he entered. "John, I have gone over this room, and I am confident it is secure."

"Why? Are you worried someone might be?"

"Did you see Megan's face when we told her? I have never seen her that scared, John."

"You have an opinion on why that could be?"

"I have a feeling we could be in jeopardy if the Decider finds out."

"Will you talk to her later, Mary? Give her some time to think on it?"

"Yes, of course. She obviously knows more than we do."

"Okay, but do we want to know?"

"I do. I'd like to know what is going on."

CHAPTER 6

HE KNOCKED ON THE BEDROOM door. "Joyce."

She opened the door wearing a robe. "Yes, Adolf?"

"I need to talk to you," and entered her room. She closed the door behind him and asked, "Would you like something to drink? Coffee? Tea?"

"No, thank you. I will be having a major announcement at the board meeting, and I want you to be there."

"Whatever for, Adolf?"

"I have decided to offer you a different post in our chain of command. I need someone to be in charge of the security of the group headquarters."

"That and my current duties?"

He stared at her and gradually smiled. "Current duties included if you care to continue them. Otherwise you will be replaced."

"I thank you for considering me for the new position, and I think it best that I use all my focus on that."

"I can understand that, and you have earned my trust. Get ready, the conference is in an hour. Any other questions?"

"Can I have Megan on my staff? I would also like someone I can trust."

"Yes, and find positions for Adam and Allison."

He gave her a hug and departed the room.

Oh my god, I'm getting a second chance, she thought to herself. She didn't have to be a mindless bimbo anymore. She took a quick shower and got ready. *What to wear at a conference?* entered her thoughts. She picked out a pantsuit. *Where am I supposed to go?* It caused her to panic, and she called Adolf and was told he would

196

take her and for her to be ready in five minutes. *I wonder what the big announcement will be. Could it be my appointment?* Her senses told her that wasn't it. The knock on her door gave her a startle. It was Adolf, and he was dressed in the old uniform he wore when he addressed the masses. He led her down the hallway to the elevator. Once inside she asked, "You going to grow your mustache?"

He had a puzzled look on his face. "Yes, but I forgot to put the fake one on."

They both laughed as they rode down to the tenth level. There was a cart waiting for them, and one of his bodyguards was at the wheel. She sat in the back and was surprised when Adolf sat next to her. She looked at the bodyguard and wondered if she will have any control over them. As if he was reading her mind, Adolf looked at her. "Hawk will be informing you of your duties."

"I look forward to the opportunity,"

"Make sure you get people you trust!"

"Oh, no doubt."

They arrived at the conference room. Joyce stepped out and waited for Adolf, who was having a discussion with his bodyguard.

He led her to the door, and she entered first. When they saw him in uniform, they were about to get to their feet, but he quickly signaled them to remain seated. "No need, we have business to take care of."

Joyce could see the board sitting at the table with Hawk off to the side organizing some paperwork. He directed her to a seat next to Violet.

He walked up to the podium in front of the table and looked directly at the board.

"Joyce will now be in charge of security of this facility and will have access to our meetings." He scanned the room until he located Mr. Hawk.

Joyce smiled at the board members as they nodded acknowledgment. Violet gave her a quick smile.

"Hawk, do you have the reports from your trips?"

"Yes, Führer, you want me to start?"

"Yes, and if anyone is more comfortable addressing me as Alexander, feel free. I have been Alexander longer than my real name."

Hawk walked up to the podium, and Adolf sat on the nearest chair to the left.

"Martin Schmidt and Cyrus Montgomery have tested their systems many times and have said they are ready to be implemented. Their staffs are ready and waiting for the countdown." Hawk left the podium, and Adolf returned. He looked at Tessa. "How are the supplies for the facilities?"

Tessa stood and said, "We have well over a year in food supplies at all the facilities, and water isn't an issue."

Violet then stood without being asked and stated, "We have enough product to convert around one million new group members."

He glared at her and responded with a, "Thank you, Violet. Just how soon do you think we could accomplish that?"

"Probably two years if the conditions work out like we plan."

"Charlotte, is everything targeted?"

"The primary targets have been identified and should be eliminated as planned. There are some secondary targets that will be ready for your decisions."

"So Phase M is our main drawback in implementing Operation Wolf Bite. The question I have for you board members is, give me a synopsis of what happens if we do implement it in less than a month. Because unless you give me a synopsis where it isn't beneficial to do that, the countdown will begin. I know it will cause chaos, but I am not certain that is a bad thing. Please get your reports in twenty-four hours." He left the podium and exited the room. Violet was surprised by his attitude. He was back to Führer mode.

Hawk came over to Joyce. "Congrats on the new position. We need to go to my office to discuss what is involved."

"Okay, lead the way."

Megan didn't get much sleep, and her mind kept going over options. She wandered down to the kitchen. It was too early for the kitchen staff to be there. She opened the refrigerator freezer and spotted the Death by Chocolate ice cream. *That is perfect*, and reached in and got the half gallon of it. She found a bowl in the cupboard and filled it over the brim. She put what remained in the freezer and went back into her room. She sat in her living room recliner and turned on the TV for noise. The cell phone in her bedroom got her attention when it signaled she had a contact. It was a text, and it was from Joyce, and it read, "I need to talk with you as soon as possible."

That is strange, for her to contact me this early. She picked up the phone and texted her back: "I am up. Do you want to call me or text?"

She held her cell phone, and a few seconds later it rang.

"Hello, Joyce."

"Good morning, Megan. I hope I didn't wake you."

"No, I am just sitting here eating a big bowl of Death by Chocolate ice cream."

Joyce laughed. "So I hope I am stopping a suicide attempt. I need you to join my team. I am now in charge of security at the operations headquarters."

"Interesting. When did that happen?"

"Yesterday, I also want you to bring Allison and Adam should you decide to join the team. Things are in motion."

Megan sat there and understood what Joyce meant. "How soon do you need us?"

"As soon as possible. Contact me when you are ready, and I will make arrangements to have you brought here. Ted and Marissa and the rest of the staff will be given instructions in the future."

"Okay, I will tell the kids. I don't expect them to be thrilled leaving so close to the end of the school year. But they both have enough credits to graduate."

"Okay, do want you must. Talk to you later."

"Goodbye, Joyce."

She put the phone on the stand next to the chair and looked down at her melting ice cream. She slowly ate the rest and savored every spoonful.

Hawk delivered the board responses to Adolf. "Thank you, Hawk."

He choose one and read it. The only objection was the possibility of chaos getting out of control. He had his own solution to that if the death ray worked as desired. The world was already overly populated. The other reports were basically the same. He leaned back in his chair. He wondered if he was being impatient. The timing was good as the USA was in an election year, and the president's term was nearing an end. China had to spend less on Defense because of their market crash, the Middle East was always in turmoil even after Syria was divided. The countdown would begin at midnight. He contacted Hawk.

"Yes, Führer."

"Inform the board that the seventy-two-hour countdown starts at midnight tonight. Make sure all the notifications are implemented. Contract me when they have been."

"Yes, Führer."

He hung up his phone and got up. He had difficulty containing his excitement. He did a few fist pumps in the air and danced a quick jig.

Megan couldn't go back to sleep and watched television until it was ready for Mary and John to get ready for school. She took her bowl down to the kitchen and saw the staff chef. "Good morning, Morgan."

"Good morning, Megan," she replied. "What would you like for breakfast?"

"Morgan, a cheese omelet is all I need. I also have to tell you that Allison, Adam, and I will be leaving soon. I have been reassigned."

"Sorry to see you go," and she came over and gave her a hug.

"Don't say anything to Allison and Adam. I haven't had a chance to tell them."

"I understand and won't."

She left the kitchen and was lost in thought when Mary and Adam tried to maneuver past her in the hallway. "Wait, I need to talk to you two."

"Did we do something wrong?" asked John.

"No, but things are about to change. Follow me."

John looked at Mary, who shrugged as if to say she didn't know what it was about, and they followed Megan to her bedroom. Megan shut the door.

"I actually happy you are Mary and John. Otherwise, this could have been a difficult conversation. Joyce has a new position and wants me to join her team. She wants you to also be there. She said things are in motion, and I believe if you remember what that means."

"How soon are we needed?" asked Mary.

"As soon as we can."

"No time like the present as far as I am concerned," said Mary.

"I agree," said John. "Besides I have a test today that I am not ready for."

Megan gave a fake glare. "Good thing this happened today," she said, smiling.

"But did you want to go and say goodbye to your friends."

"I'll pass on that. I don't have that many, and besides they would ask too many questions," replied John. Mary thought about it for a few seconds and said, "He's right. No need for me."

"Okay, I will contact the school. You both start packing. I want to remind you both that you will be treated as Allison and Adam. You both will be expected to be disappointed about leaving, and act like you both don't have a clue what is going on. You both are intelligent enough to figure it out for yourselves as we go along. Try and stay out of the way."

"Point taken," responded Mary.

Martin Schmidt stared at the fax that was sent by Hawk. It stated that in twelve hours the official countdown for Operation Wolf Bite will commence. He felt relieved in the sense that all the hard work by his staff and himself would finally be utilized. But he also knew for the operation to be a success, his inventions and equipment needed to function as designed. He was confident, but there could be an unknown factor that could cause havoc. It was time to contact the network he had created. There were stations at various locations around the world. When he activated the network, it was designed to form an electrical curtain the blanketed the world. As the power increased, it would then pinpoint satellites circling the globe and destroy them. That was the primary objective one by one. Then it could be used to pinpoint aircraft or missiles to destroy.

Cyrus Montgomery was told by a staff member that Mr. Hawk was trying to contact him. He just finished a 5K run on his treadmill. He preferred to run outside, but the island was too small to have a 5K course. There was plenty of room to launch the rocket carrying the death ray. That and launching their own satellite were his primary objectives. He had to wait for the window to launch was open. The plan was for all satellites to have been destroyed before he launched. It was done to try to avoid launch detection.

He decided to shower after he called Hawk. The secure phone was on his office desk. He punched in his code and heard the tone for the secure line.

"Hello, Hawk, I understand you called."

"Yes, Cyrus, I am informing you that at 1200 hours your time, the countdown begins."

"So that day is finally here. Let the countdown begin. Thank you, Hawk."

"Yes, it has. It will be a glorious day. Talk to you later."

Cyrus sat back in his chair and put his phone on the desk. *It will be the day the world changes.* He contacted Byron at the other launch site on an island in the South Atlantic. Bryon has been a trusted ally since they were together in World War II. Byron was to launch the other death ray when the one here launched from the Pacific Island location. Once in orbit, headquarters would have total control over them, and they were capable of maneuvering to any location. He wasn't concerned about the politics of the situation. It had taken years of refinement, and he was confident in the success of the mission.

"How was your trip, Megan?"

"Tiring but we got here without too much hassle."

"Where are Allison and Adam?"

"We are here, Aunt Joyce," Mary said as she walked from the back of the car.

"Aunt Joyce?"

"Mom has said you were like a sister to her."

"Oh, I did, Allison?"

"Of course, why else would you move us just before the prom?"

Megan glared at Mary. "Allison, we will discuss this later."

"Sorry, Joyce, we are all tired."

"I understand." She looked at Mary and smiled "Allison, calling me Aunt Joyce is very sweet. You can call me that if you like."

"Aunt Joyce, where do we take the luggage?" She turned and laughed when she saw Adam trying to carry five bags.

"Okay, goofball, put them down because transportation should be here any minute." She turned to Megan. "I recommend getting settled and eating before we have a quick meeting."

"You don't need to tell me twice."

"Okay, I need to leave. I see your transportation arriving. They will take you to your quarters and answer any questions you have."

Megan wasn't sure she could make it to the cafeteria as fatigue overpowered her when she sat down and watched the others bring the luggage into her quarters. It was a four-bedroom complex and one of the finest she had seen for an underground facility. It had a living room, dining room, kitchen, and a bathroom in each of the bedrooms. She thanked the facility staff for their help when the unloading was done.

She signaled Mary and John over to them. She whispered, "I have to have a meeting with Joyce after we eat. I want you two to give this place a though going-over when you are finished eating."

Mary had a confused look on her face. John looked around the room. "Okay," he replied. "Let's go eat."

Hawk entered his office. Adolf looked up from his target plans for the death ray. "Führer, the countdown is close to starting. Do you want to view it?"

"Certainly." He reached in the top desk drawer and found the large flat-screen television's remote. He aimed for the television that was on the wall, and it came on after a few seconds' wait. The control room was filled, and in the lower right corner of the screen, there was the seventy-two-hour digital readout. "How much longer, Hawk?"

Hawk glanced at his watch. "Anytime now."

There was a very loud cheer in the control room when the digital readout started counting down. Adolf stood and walked around the desk to Hawk. He gave him a hug. "If you weren't for you, this wouldn't be happening."

"You give me too much credit, my Führer. I just got you out of the homeland. The rest has been due to your brilliant plans."

Adolf smiled and nodded and went back to the desk. "Speaking of plans, I have been going over the target plans for the death rays. The board did an excellent job with their selections. But I have a feeling some might be added without their direct involvement. There are some old scores I would like to settle. Any you might want to add?"

"No, my Führer, I trust your judgment."

Joyce opened the door to her office, and Megan entered. "I know you are tired, Megan, so I'll make this quick. I am in charge of this facilities Security. I got the position because I earned his trust, and you know who I am referring to. I need someone I can trust, and I know I can trust you. I also wanted to get all of you here. The countdown has started."

Megan was stunned. "How long before it ends?"

"Just over two days."

"You know I have very little experience in security."

"Where we are located, we shouldn't be in much danger. If the phases function as well as we expect, there will be little need to be concerned. Our defensive weapons are all high tech, and our facility force is well trained. We will be dealing with policy. Any other questions?"

"What is expected of Allison and Adam?"

"For now, just have them keep a low profile. We'll discuss this later. I will contact you tomorrow, so go get some sleep."

Megan walked up to Joyce and gave her an embrace. "Thank you, Joyce," she whispered in her ear. She turned and left the room.

Martin Schmidt had a difficult time doing anything but watching the digital screen that displayed the locations of earth's orbiting satellites. It was located on the wall in his control room. There was another below it that gave him a view from the main control room. It showed the countdown: "71 hours and 22 minutes." His primary network station have double-checked their systems and appeared ready for implementation. There were a number of alternate sites available if there was a malfunction or an attack on one of the primary sites. This was important to him to insure success of his mission. He continued to watch the satellite screen as if he was hypnotized.

Megan entered her quarters. Mary looked up and saw she was in thought. "Find out anything, Mother?"

"Yes, I assume you both did want I asked?"

"Of course, Mother, we made sure the mess was cleaned up."

"Mary, the use of *mother* makes me feel old."

"Maybe you need a little bit of product."

"In due time. Where is John?"

"He is taking a shower. He said if there is a camera in the shower head, he was going to give them a show."

"Oh really. I wonder if that includes men who might be watching."

Mary laughed. "I bet he didn't think of that."

"Before you return to Allison mode, the countdown for the operation has started. That was one reason Joyce wanted us here."

"Wow, was there another reason?"

"She wants me to be part of her team overseeing the facility security."

"I didn't know you and Joyce knew much about security."

"We don't, Mary, I think she earned her trust with the Decider. Joyce trusts me."

"Would she if she found out about us?"

"Doubt it, unless the time is right. The time isn't now for all those involved. I hate to think it, but I feel your safety is best if no one knows."

"No one knows what?" Megan turned to see Adam.

"That you need to remember who you are, Adam. The countdown has started, and in nearly three days, the operation will commence. Remember that Adam has no clue to any of that. I think this isn't the time for disclosing that."

"Yes, I remember our discussion earlier. Not to worry."

"Good, you are also to keep a low profile until it is a good time."

"Not understanding what you mean by 'low profile.'"

"Don't venture out unless it is necessary. I am sure we will find something you both can contribute in. I can't stay awake any longer. Talk to you in the morning."

Adolf kept waking up. His dreams of controlling the world kept robbing his sleep. He rolled to the edge of the bed, and his feet touched the cold floor. The darkness made it difficult to find his slippers with his feet, but he eventually slipped them on. He got up and took a step to his right and found the light switch on his table lamp. He made his way to the bathroom and relieved himself. He saw his television remote on his return, and the flat screen on the wall lit up. The countdown was down to 44:40. He shut off everything and returned to bed.

CHAPTER 7

MEGAN WAS SURPRISED THAT THE defensive weapons at the facility are operated and maintained by women. "Why just women, Joyce?"

"The Decider's orders. The indoor security group consists of women only."

"How many are there?"

"Three hundred divided into shift coverage."

"You oversee them as well, Joyce?"

"Yes."

"I can understand why you need assistance. What do you need from me?"

"I need you to be second in command. If something happens to me or when I am not here, you take over."

"You don't have anyone else to choose from?"

"This group was just formed. I know and trust you."

"Thank you for the vote of confidence. I will do my best."

The plane landed at the former Air Force base K. I. Sawyer in Upper Michigan. It had been bought and converted because it could handle Air Force One on its long runways. President Connelly was born in nearby Marquette, Michigan, and when he could, he returned to the area to relax. The former nuclear weapons area had been converted to a site where the president could conduct official business. There were cement bunkers that went several stories underground. The offices they contained there were staffed by air force personnel. There was a war room with a digital screen on the wall. It was only activated when the president was in the building. President Connelly departed Air Force One. Despite the sunshine, cool air greeted him. He could see the huge snow piles that were at various locations on the runway and taxi area. *They will be there until June,* he thought. There wasn't any snow on the ground on this spring day.

He looked at his chief advisor as they walked to the limo. "What is the weather supposed to be like tomorrow, Charles?"

"A little warmer than today with the sunshine."

"See if you can get me on the course here."

"Okay, I will contact them."

"Thank you." President Connelly liked playing on the course that was developed for the base years ago. It was only nine holes, but there were many challenges. It remained open to the public after the base closed.

It was early in the year, so there was a good chance it would be available.

The ride to his home always made him feel like he was in another world. Thick woods on both sides of the road blocked the light to almost feel like he was in a tunnel. The log cabin mansion was something he had built. It was near a lake, and he had a dock and boat ready if he wanted to fish. He had no neighbors for at least ten miles. He stretched when he arrived, and his wife met him at the door and gave him a kiss. She had left Washington, DC, a week ago. He put his arm around her, and they went in the house and closed the door.

Violet asked Connie about her sector.

"Every group member will be out of the target areas within six hours."

"Charlotte, how about yours?"

"Violet, the sector is evacuated."

"Tessa?"

"Within three hours."

"Diana?"

"It is clear."

Violet saw the countdown was at 29:45. She was getting nervous. She may not be the one pulling the trigger on the plan, but she knew many would die no matter how careful the plan or precise the strikes were. But the strikes were necessary to have the leaders of the world realize they had no hope in defending their countries. There was a plan on what to do afterward, but the plan needed more troops. *But will it, as the Führer changed the plan by attacking now. We will adjust to whatever the result.* She considered herself second in command. Hawk seemed to be a follower and had never shown any interest to be anything else. Probably the reason he was the only one from his war regime to survive. The promotion of Joyce made her happy. She was confident she had her respect and support should anything happen to the Führer.

Joyce picked up her phone. "Megan, I have a few questions. Do you think Allison would be a good fit for the facility defense group?"

"Joyce, remember she has no idea she is a group member. I told them you were offering me a job of a lifetime and we had to move quickly to get it."

"Job of a lifetime. Very well put. You know the group members aren't suppose talk about their past. This could be one way to find out on how disciplined our group is."

"Should I give her the choice, Joyce?"

"Well, look at it this way. If the Decider is informed that she is, he will be very happy. It confirms his reason for Phase Z."

Megan sat there pondering it for a few seconds. "I will talk to her about it tonight. Just how soon do you think she is needed?"

"I think it is best to wait until after the initial attacks. Oh, we have a boiler room apprentice position available for Adam."

"Interesting, I will talk to him about that as well."

"Good, get some rest as we all will need it soon."

"Thanks, Joyce. I plan on it." She left the room and wondered how Mary and John would take the news.

John Mason listened to the Houston Rocket basketball game with his earphones as he buffed the hallway floor. This was his twenty-first year working for NASA in Houston, Texas. He worked the afternoon shift from 4:00 p.m. to midnight. He cleaned the main hallways used by the daily visitors. He took pride in his work. He liked to work hard to play hard. He never married and often said he liked Houston because he could never run out of woman. His 6'4" inch muscular frame and boyish face still attracted them after he turned forty a few years ago.

Martin Schmidt was ready. The countdown clock read 25:00. He pushed the Start button on the control console. This allowed the whole system to start activation and a gradual power increase. The other stations will contact him as they do the same. Then they will connect in series to provide the power the network will need to complete its primary mission.

Megan saw the light at the bottom of Mary's bedroom door "Mary, you awake? I need to chat with you."

Mary appeared at the door. "Come on in. Why the chat?"

Megan sat on the bed, and Mary sat next to her. "Mary, Joyce asked me if Allison would be a good fit to join the facility security group. It is all female, and they work a variety of shifts."

"You know it would be a good fit for me, but me as Allison, I am not so sure."

"That is what I told Joyce, but she didn't see any issue since the group is forbidden to talk about the past."

"Megan, if you think it could assist you. I'll do it."

"It could. Plus you know it doesn't have to be forever. Besides it will make the Decider happy when he finds out."

"Okay, what about John?"

"Joyce lined up a power plant position."

"Interesting, when we will start?"

"Soon, but after the plan is activated."

"Understood."

He watched the countdown go under twenty-four hours. He moved around it and sat at his desk. He got the report that Martin had activated his network and was in the process of powering up. He hoped the equipment to eliminate detection worked as well as it had in tests. He leaned back in the chair and shut his eyes. *Am I being impatient?* he thought. Maybe he should wait for more troops to be deployed. *But they will be at our mercy if all goes well. It will then sort itself out.* He was sure of it.

He decided to try and get some sleep. If nothing else, the countdown would seem to go faster. He called Evan and departed to his bedroom.

Cyrus Montgomery awoke early and knew it would be a long time before returned to bed. The countdown was at 13:00 He would be launching at around 2:00 p.m. his time due the time zone differences. He had wanted to sleep longer, but his mind kept going over imaginary checklists. It had been so long since they had planned for this day. The war had stopped their research. But they had prevailed, providing it is a successful mission.

His control room was active and full of his staff. It was now in twenty-four-hour coverage that will be continuous until the orders come to change that status. The other location for launches was in constant contact and ready to go. The responsibility for both location was strictly his, and he didn't want it any other way.

Joyce could feel the tension in the building rise as the countdown was less than ten hours. Violet had chatted with her, and Joyce could tell she was very nervous. *She should be*, Joyce thought. Starting a conflict that could change the outlook of the world was a major decision. Violet and the board are a factor in its pursuit. The facility was about to in high alarm, and Joyce was confident it could hold up against anything other than a nuclear attack. They had to locate them first to even consider it. Being heavy fortified underground had many advantages. She looked at the time and needed something to eat and a nap for the long night ahead. She drove to the cafeteria and was surprised to see Allison. She approached the table. "Hi, Allison, care if I join you?"

Allison looked up. "Oh, hi, Aunt Joyce. I am nearly finished, but I have nothing better to do if you want to chat."

"Thank you, Allison, I need a break."

"What is going on? It seems there an electricity in the air."

The waiter approached, and Joyce ordered.

"Allison, how much has your mother told you about this place?"

Mary knew she had to keep everything low key and not overreact. "She said it was a chance of a lifetime, Aunt Joyce."

"Has she mentioned my idea of joining the security team?"

"Yes."

"Good, I'd like to chat with you about that in the near future. As for your question, I will explain all the commotion at the same time."

"Okay, I see your food is about to arrive. Did you want to discuss anything else?"

"No, Allison, that is what I wanted to know. You have a good day."

"You too, Aunt Joyce."

The food arrived. The salmon looked delicious, and the first bite confirmed that it was. The steamed potatoes were just the way she liked it. She savored the frozen peaches, and a glass of red wine helped her relax. Just over eight hours to go. She needed a quick nap but was reluctant to move. She had another glass of wine in hopes that it would help her nap.

He awoke confused at first thinking it was morning. It was dark in his room, and it took him a while to realize it was 8:00 p.m., not 8:00 a.m. He had finally gotten a dreamless sleep. It dawned on him that there were only four hours before the countdown was over. He hadn't asked to be woken up and wondered if everyone would have let him kept sleeping. The phone rang as he sat up in bed. He picked it up. "Hello."

"Adolf, will you be in the control room soon? The power grid is nearly energized, and I am assuming you want to see it."

"Yes, Violet, I will be there soon, and you assumed correctly."

He placed his phone on his night stand and called Evan to get his uniform ready. He walked to the bathroom, and in a short time he was in the shower.

The control room was active when he arrived. He saw that it was less than three hours before Operation Wolf Bite started.

The digital screen was focused on one of the power generators in Martin's grid network. His control room staff consisted of people that had earned his trust and had been training for the positions for years. Their patience was phenomenal to him. Nearly ninety years since the end of the war, and it took a while to recruit most of them because of their family commitments. But their belief in him made him feel proud. He had earned their respect. It was soon time to share the success of the plan. He focused on the screen. It was difficult not to watch the energy expand in the tall mushroom-shaped generator. It was at least eight stories tall. The power was collecting in the mushroom-shaped level on top of the structure. He found it amazing. He pushed a button on his control panel. "Martin, that is a fascinating sight you have created. Everything going as planned."

"Yes, but I don't have much time for talk."

"That is all I wanted to hear. Talk to you later."

He sat back in his chair. His excitement was building. Less than two hours to go. He noticed Violet and the other board members arrive, and they sat in an enclosed meeting room behind him. There was a window where they could monitor everything in the control room. He went to the room. "All you ladies rested and ready for a long night?"

Diana smiled and said, "It's been a long time since I heard that from a man. What do you have in mind, Adolf?"

He laughed. "Fireworks, if you are ready."

"Probably not the fireworks I was hoping for. But I am ready," Diana responded. The group laughed.

"Less than a hundred minutes and it starts. Time for me to get my checklist out. Talk to you later."

Violet watched him leave. "Charlotte, is the control room being videotaped?"

"Yes, and every computer entry recorded as well."

"Good, it should be quite active and difficult to follow."

They all had programed the death ray targets. The death rays, once they were deployed and activated, are programed to follow the list of targets in a specific order. This should eliminate any ability for a worldwide counterattack. The large digital screen kept changing from location to location. The launch site had the rocket getting prepped as the countdown continued. The Führer returned and had a handful of dark sunglasses. "Take your pick, ladies. I have been told we will need them in less than twenty minutes."

The door opened behind them, and they turned to see Mr. Hawk. He looked at them and said, "It is done." He had set up communications to all the world leaders so they could communicate with that after the attacks. They would give those conditions for the ultimate worldwide surrender. They would continue to attack until then. Hawk had a pair of mirror sunglasses.

"Hawk, I hope you don't blind us with your sunglasses providing a flash," Tessa said.

He chuckled as he sat in a chair. The Führer had left as fast as had he came in. The countdown was down to three minutes.

Martin Schmidt watched the countdown clock hit zero and disappear from his monitor. That meant Operation Wolf Bite had commenced. He ordered full power to every station on his grid. They were all assigned specific satellites. There was a backup plan in case of failure to destroy a specific satellite. The flash from the bolt of energy nearly blinded them despite the sunglasses. It went high in in sky and was so fast you couldn't tell if it was lightning or not. There were other bolts that they could see in the darkened skies. The first fatalities on the operation occurs in the orbiting Skylab. That was the first target. Martin contacted Adolf with the news.

The world will know now, Adolf thought.

Martin continued to watch his monitor as the satellites reduced in numbers. He hoped his arsenal wouldn't be detected before the death rays were launched.

President Connelly was watching SportsCenter on ESPN when the screen suddenly went blank. He waited for a few seconds and then changed the channel. He got the same result on all the channels.

A phone call interrupted his search. It was from his chief advisor, Charles Crosby.

"Mr. President, we have a worldwide disaster in the making. I strongly suggest you get to the command center at the K. I."

"I am on my way!"

CHAPTER 8

WAYNE ANSWERED HIS CALL FROM the president, and the Secret Service agent said he would be ready in five minutes. President Connelly told his wife he was leaving, and she should be ready to leave if he contacted her. Her Secret Service was put on alert. Wayne arrived with the car. Another secret service agent sat beside him. The president got in the back.

"To the K. I. control complex, Wayne."

The ten minutes it took to arrive there felt like an hour. Wayne got out the car first, and the other agent moved to behind the wheel. Wayne opened the door, and the president exited and entered the building. The bright overhead lights caused him to shield his eyes for a moment, and he went to the control room with Wayne beside him. He was met at the door by Charles Crosby. "Charles, what is happening?"

"So far from what we know, there is an unidentified electrical force that is killing all the satellites."

"Just our satellites?"

"No, all the satellites in orbit."

"How is that happening?"

"There are reports of many lightning bolts from various unknown locations streaking from the ground to the orbiting satellites. One other thing, the space lab was attacked first and is destroyed. The occupants were killed."

"Obviously this is an act of war. Order the military to DEFCON 1. We need to find out all we can about who is behind this."

"If we have the communications to do that."

"Find a way!"

Cyrus Montgomery was trying to hold his emotions in check as the last satellites were eliminated. He contacted the control room and told them the next phase could start. Adolf gave the news to Cyrus himself. Cyrus contacted the other site, and the five-minute countdown began. The countdown was needed as the computer would go through each system check. The payload for each rocket included the death ray and an attached satellite. One was a communications satellite, and the other was a spy satellite that would be used to monitor the world's status.

Adolf watched the rocket engine fire its thrusters. This was the critical moment for the success of the operation. The world would be at his mercy if the death rays were deployed. The rocket began to move upward. The walls of the island came into view, and the rocket soon disappeared through the cloud that permanently surrounded the top of the island. Another view came into view, and the rocket streaked upward through the blue afternoon sky. The screen image then split into two views to see both rockets becoming smaller and smaller as they rose to the deep blue upper atmosphere. Cyrus contacted Adolf when the rockers reached the desired orbits and then jettisoned the payload into orbit. "Adolf, both have made it to the desired orbit. I hope to have the death rays functional very soon."

"Excellent work, Cyrus. I will start commencing the program as soon as they are ready."

Adolf rubbed his hands together in excitement. *My destiny will soon be fulfilled.*

John Mason was nearly finished with his work shift at the NASA complex in Houston, Texas when he noticed many employees returning to work. Many were running. He could see their worried looks on their faces. He went to his supervisor to see if they knew what the commotion was about. His supervisor told him to go to the roof and take a look. He hurried up the stairwell, and in the distance, he could see what looked like lightning bolts streaking up the darkened sky. But these looked different as they went in a straight line, as if they were directed at a target. Other people came up, and they started to get in groups, all giving an opinion on what it could be. The bolts suddenly stopped. John went down and clocked out. There was so much activity he waited in the cafeteria to see if he could find out more information on the phenomena he just witnessed. He sat sipping a coffee, trying to make out any information he could hear. He became restless and decided to venture back to the roof. There were still a few people on the roof. They may have stayed to enjoy the nice cool breeze coming across the roof. He looked to the north and spotted what looked to be a ray of light coming from a star. But this light came down quickly, and it seemed to expand as it approached the ground. It may have been a few miles wide, and the brightness caused him to shield his eyes. Intense heat hit him as the ray was about mile away when it hit the ground. Everything in its path turned into a fireball. He didn't have time to react as he and the building disintegrated when the ray hit. The complex was destroyed in minutes and everything nearby was engulfed in flames.

"Mr. President, the Pentagon was just destroyed by an outer space ray."

President Connelly sat down and closed his eyes. "Any word on the White House?"

"Not yet, whatever the source of this force is, it appears to be hitting military targets first. They also have hit all worldwide rocket launching sites to cripple any response."

"Hard to believe they could know of all the sites, and so far it is effective. We find out the source. Do we have all our aircraft in the air?"

"Just what is left from the bases that weren't destroyed? Same thing with the other countries. The ray has even hit moving carriers, and they were gone off the radar in seconds."

"Charles, we may be without any options soon. We can't respond if there isn't a target."

"I wonder if the other countries will feel the same way, Mr. President."

"I don't know how they couldn't."

[Following is an official OnlineBookClub.org review of "Sea of Red" by Gary A. Osborn.]

"Never think that war, no matter how necessary, nor how justified, is not a crime." This is a quote by Ernest Hemingway, and it forms the foundation for my review of *Sea of Red* by Gary A. Osborn.

After an attempted robbery at a client's house, John Dwyer can't seem to remember what happened afterward. With his newly gained physique and repeated blackouts, he can't help but wonder what's going wrong. After being present at the Anderson house when an explosion occurs, he discovers a secret organization where a different world exists. Alexander Wolf, a Führer, heads the organization. Is there war looming?

Sea of Red is a beautifully written work of fiction. The plot is unique, with unexpected twists and turns. The author made sure to infuse the element of surprise in this book, which made the narrative quite engaging and suspenseful. Connecting to John Dwyer's character at the beginning of the book made it easier to picture and grasp the author's intention. The thrills, mystery, and suspense of this book are what make it an exciting read.

What I liked most about this book was its mind-boggling content. The unexpected plot twists had me affixed to the story with an eagerness to finish it quickly. Every chapter was engaging. This book was what readers would call a page-turner.

The author's ability to paint a mental picture in the mind of the reader is commendable. It's so easy to imagine the story through his descriptions. It felt like I was watching a movie in my head. Specifically, the mental image of the last three chapters was the most thrilling.

On the flip side of the author's descriptive writing style, the description of sexual intercourse was somewhat explicit. The author narrated this scene to the minutest detail. Though this wasn't an issue for me, I felt the need to point it out in this review. I believe there are readers who would find the detailed description of sex scenes a bit disturbing. However, if you're okay with this, feel free to read this book. Frankly, the description of sexual activities didn't take the book off-track.

Again, the author's ability to combine many characters, yet executing their roles effectively, was remarkable. It made me read and understand quickly. I've read tons of novels where a large ensemble of characters became the bane of the story. The author did his due diligence to ensure that all characters came alive. This was very commendable.

With only a few errors, the book seemed professionally edited. Considering that there was nothing I disliked about this book, I rate it a **four out of four**. If you love a thrilling tale of mystery filled with suspense, this book is for you.

4 out of 4 stars

Share This Review

Cyrus Montgomery was pleased that the satellites he launched were now functioning. The communications satellite could only be contacted using his code. With the other satellites destroyed, he couldn't image how anyone else could crack it. The satellite will be used to communicate to the world. It will be only way to broadcast worldwide. He contacted the control with the news. The death ray had taken years to perfect. Its main power source was the sun. The mirrors that magnified the sun's rays took time to get it to function on a large scale. It now produced a ray that was over 3K wide and generated temperatures of over 5,000 degrees Fahrenheit. He was proud of his work.

Adolf turned toward the control room and signaled for the Hawk to come to him. Hawk exited, and Violet could see them in a close conversation. She assumed it was for the contact to the world. She watched the screen, and at first when the ray struck, it was difficult not to be excited. But the more it was used, the more the human loss created by it started to enter her thinking. Thousands had perished either by the ray directly, or of the fires that it created. But it had to happen to gain the control they wanted. The target list was growing shorter, and the world would soon see more of the advanced technology.

Martin Schmidt got the call from the Hawk. It was time to implement Phase S. He thought of it as the spiderweb. He would now direct his energy to constructing a world wide web surrounding the globe. It would be able to detect and destroy any flying object. It would slowly be built in small rainbow-shaped layers that would be connected. That process would take a few days. *The skyline will be webbed for twenty-four hours a day or until Adolf terminates it.*

President Connelly went to his private office at the facility. His Secret Service agents were always nearby. He needed a break to compose himself. It was nearly morning, and the level of this destruction by an unknown force was beyond comprehension. It had to be a force from out of this world. The level of technology was more advanced than anything they had. The world was facing its demise. The other countries looked to the US for help. There were very few options. The Pentagon was gone. The missiles were destroyed. All rocket-launching facilities were destroyed. Communications were hampered by all the satellites being destroyed. Radio could be the next target. A worldwide panic could be next. *The attack force has not made any contact so we could negotiate and see what it wants.*

There was a knock on his door. "Come in."

It was Charles. "Mr. President, I think you need to come outside and see this."

It was a quick walk to the outer door. Wayne was waiting for him at the entrance. The predawn sky was getting lighter. Charles pointed to the distant horizon, and there was a pattern developing in the lower portion. It was slowly adding pieces to its web. It looked like neon signs being connected and then illuminated. But it wasn't neon. It looked like electrical charges.

Oh God, what are we up against? was his first thought.

Violet and the board watched as the final target was eliminated. "Now the waiting time begins," Tessa said, stating the obvious.

"Let's hope they don't wait long," replied Connie.

"It will also depend on what the Führer decides," Violet said, looking at him in the control room. He happened to turn to them and waved them to come in. He was pointing at the screen when they arrived.

"Phase S has started."

Violet could see the energy take shape as it slowly climbed the sky. There wasn't a view of the horizon that it couldn't be seen. "When it is completed, we will contact the world leaders with our surrender terms," Adolf said in a boastful voice. "Everything is going as planned. Time for us to get some rest."

He won't rest anytime soon, Violet thought. *He is so charged up.* She and the rest of the board members knew they were being dismissed. Violet told the board to meet again in ten hours. They all had been up nearly twenty-four hours. She looked back and saw Adolf back at his seat in the control room. An uneasy feeling was coming over her that he wanted to do more damage, bypass the plan. She hoped that wasn't true, but it would only take a few computer entries later to find out if her feeling were correct. The excitement had ebbed out of her body, and fatigue was replacing it. The critical part was over, but now the reality of the situation was next to deal with. Just how would the countries respond? Joyce had a cart waiting for her when she entered the hallway. She sat in the passenger seat. She gave Joyce a nod, meaning that everything went according to plan. They were quiet as they drove along the green walled hallway. "You near the end of your shift, Joyce?'

"Yes, Megan will be relieving me in an hour."

"Get some rest. We all will need it."

Violet entered her darkened room and the flipped the light switch near the door. She was tired, but she knew sleep wouldn't come easily. Her bedroom felt cool to her after the heat of the conference room. She removed her clothes and got her fuzzy blue robe on. It was similar to a Snuggie, but a higher quality. She got a gin-and-tonic mix out of the refrigerator and poured it into a glass. She sat in her lounge chair and found the remote for her CD player and turned on soft listening music. The images she saw today kept coming in her mind. The drink didn't help erase those. The music became her focus, and that didn't have the effect she wanted. She knew chaos was expected the enormity of it caught her off guard. She hoped everything would continue to go according to the plan.

President Connelly felt like he was in a nightmare. How could this have happened without detection? The world as he knew it no longer existed. Every military base was destroyed. Fireballs were in many cities destroying everything it their path. Very little communications. They were at the mercy of this threat and not sure of what was to come next.

CHAPTER 9

COLIN MITCHELL COULDN'T STOP SHAKING. He had witnessed the Pentagon being destroyed on his drive to work. It had exploded into a huge fireball, and the neighboring buildings were consumed by fire. The ray from the sky that caused the damages only lasted around fifteen seconds. It could have destroyed the city in minutes. He tried not to let his fear get stronger by wondering what and who was behind this. He managed to drive to the TV station and saw the parking lot was half full. He worked the morning shift.

What should I do? went through his thought process. The urge to go back to his apartment and gather his things was strong. But then what? The city was waking up to be greeted by mass hysteria. He opened the door and looked in the distance. The fire and billowing smoke would normally get his juices flowing, and the opportunity to film it was what he worked for. He wondered if there were any remote trucks out filming the damage. He would be in one of them if the station wanted to pursue that story.

The front lobby was vacant when he entered. He heard noise coming from the conference room area and headed in that direction. The station manager, Stan Marion, was talking to a partial staff and stopped when he saw Colin open the door.

"Come in, Colin, glad to see you are still with us. So far this is all we have. I was informing the group that as of now, we have no satellite feed. There has been very little contact from any government. The police and firemen don't have any answers or directions. We can only broadcast to a select few who haven't got any cable or satellite TV. We can broadcast with our radio transmitter if enough people know about it, possibly on the internet if that is still functioning.

So, I ask you with a limited staff and broadcast options. Should we continue broadcastings?"

Colin scanned the room, and no one spoke. Then he cleared his throat and said, "Does anyone have an idea what hit us? Is the world going to end?"

They were all quiet until Stan replied, "Colin, if it is the end of the world, do you want to go home or stay and report it? That is the question for all of you. Right now, it is a minute of time. Those who want to go can leave, and I wish you the best of luck. Those who stay are welcome to stay here for as long as we have supplies. I am going into the other conference room. Those who are staying, please follow me. Those who leave, it won't be held against you. Stay home until you feel it is safe to return."

They all jumped when a blank monitor came on. There was a sixty-second countdown, and it was satellite feed. Stan pointed to two engineers and instructed them to quickly set up a recording. They followed him to a control center that had a bigger monitor. They arrived as the last seconds ticked down to zero. The screen monitor showed a podium with a plain white background. Then from the left, a masked man came out to the podium. His mask looked like a fierce bird. He turned on the microphone at the podium. Then words were heard, but no one could see his lips move.

"People of earth, the following message is being translated to every language known to man. We have made any attempt to destroy us impossible. Your weapons of war have been destroyed as well as all weapons manufacturers. We will continue to monitor any attempt to do so. We have the advanced technology to destroy the earth. That isn't our desire.

"We desire to make the earth a peaceful and desirable place to live for all its inhabitants. Now, for the immediate future, please go on with your lives. Governments will be contacted, and we will want confirmation that it was received. We will give directives to them that will need to be followed or there will be ramifications. Communications will be as you have them now, as this is the only satellite functioning and any attempt to destroy it will be punished. Any areas that go into anarchy will not be tolerated. That will be inviting instant destruction. Earth is at the crossroads, so you will decide further action by your behavior."

The screen went blank.

They started to chat with each other before Stan said, "Who thinks they are aliens? Give me a reason."

Colin scanned the room, and no one seemed to be willing to speak. He thought for a moment and said, "Why would an alien invader have a mask and say 'keep everything as it is'? I mean they could take anything they want with a superior force. I know it is advanced technology, but can you believe they could master all the languages in a short amount of time?"

"Interesting view, Colin. In a way, I hope you are correct. Well, it appears there won't be an attack in the near future. I need some to stay and see if we can get some information out for the people," Colin volunteered.

President Connelly listened to the broadcast of demands from the control room. Everyone stopped what they were doing and joined in. When it was over, their faces focused in his direction as if they tried to read his thoughts. He signaled for his chief of staff, and they entered his office. The president pointed to a chair and circled the desk to his. "Tell me some good news, Charles."

"Care if I lie?"

"At this point, no."

"Okay, for the bad news. Whoever they are, as far as we can ascertain, they have destroyed everything we have to respond with. The only potential good news is that they may have missed targets with our allies and the rest of the world. We just don't know at this time."

"I like your optimism, but I think that isn't the case. This looks like a well-thought-out attack. I am leaning more to an internal power than from a force from outer space. The force wants to maintain the status quo from that message they just sent. They want to control that and not take everything over by eliminating us."

"If that is the case, Mr. President, why would they want that?"

"So, they don't have to start over if they send the world back to the Dark Ages. The people could be more willing to follow their demands."

"So, you think we have a chance against a foe that is one of us?"

"If we have a chance at anyone, I'd rather have it from one of the human race—that is, if they don't forget they are part of it."

It was difficult for him to stop watching the monitor. The targets had been hit. Adolf continued to get satellite pictures of the damage the death rays produced. All military targets had been destroyed. He was amazed that it could take out submarines, but a pinpointed narrow ray was able to. There were just a few console controllers in the room with him. He was tempted to continue using the death rays, but the worldwide broadcast had been delivered, and they needed to give the world time to respond. He was coming down from his adrenaline rush, and he could feel fatigue affecting him. He contacted his bodyguards and waited a few minutes. He rose, and the remaining people in the room rose with him. The cart was waiting when he entered the hallway. His bodyguard at the steering wheel. They turned a corner, and in the distance, he saw Megan and Allison coming toward him. Megan had a shocked looked on her face, but he couldn't read Allison's reaction. He signaled his bodyguard to stop just before they got to their location. He walked up to them. "Hello, Megan and Allison."

He watched their reaction to his new appearance, and Megan said, "Hello, Alexander?"

"Yes, I am known as Alexander. I am also known as the Decider, the Führer, and my real name as Adolf Hitler. We had a glorious day today. So, take some time to celebrate. The work will start soon."

"We will be ready to serve anyway that is needed," responded Megan.

"I am sure you will." He looked at Allison. "You will inform Allison of the future plans?"

"Yes, she will be joining the security team."

"Excellent! What is Adam's status?"

"He is in training to work in the powerhouse."

"Excellent choice!" He gave them a quick hug and went back to the cart and disappeared down the hallway.

Megan looked at Mary. "I can't believe what just happened. It must have been a great day for him."

"I can't believe I didn't recognize him before," responded Mary.

"You and me both, and I think we can add John to that list," Mary said.

"Should we tell him, Megan?"

"I don't see why not. If he had been with us, he would also know. The Führer is out of his den."

"Yes, it appears the Wolf did bite. I need to check the status of everything with Joyce."

"I'll go back and inform John before he leaves for his post."

"Okay but contact me when you are done."

Violet didn't get much sleep, but was at the command center before the rest of the board. She was reading reports on damage caused by the death rays. They had been very effective knocking all the targets. *But now the concern is, how will the world react, and will their forces be able to keep everything it check.* With the Führer deciding to speed up the attack, the phases in the plans were altered. They had wanted more trained troops to control the world's response. Tessa entered the room. "Good morning, Violet. Did you get any sleep?"

"Good morning. My body tried, but the mind wasn't in the mood. How about you?"

"About the same as you. What does the information tell us so far?"

"Everything has gone as planned so far. What happens next will be the question we need to have a solution for."

"What is the status of the next launchings?"

"The dome is open, and they should be launched anytime. We haven't heard from Cyrus. I will contact him."

"Martin, that is quite a show you have put on. How difficult is it to open up the dome so I can launch the satellites today?"

"Cyrus, not difficult at all. I just have to reduce the power, and the web will slowly come down to wherever I set the power at."

"Martin, do you think it is possible to develop a protective force field for a spaceship?"

"I think it is possible. But I might have to accompany the ship to make it sure it functions properly."

"There will always be a spot for you, Martin. Think you could handle the weightlessness?"

"I have been a bean pole my entire life. Don't think it would be much of an adjustment."

Cyrus laughed. "Then how about the G forces?"

"If you think they are difficult, try having a lightning bolt go up your ass."

Cyrus laughed again. "Okay we better get down to business. I have two satellites to launch."

"The dome is opening now. Good luck, Cyrus."

"Thank you, Martin."

John was surprised when Mary came in their home yelling his name.

"What's up, Mary?"

"Well, I feel like a stupid idiot."

"Mary, that isn't something to brag about."

"Wait till you hear it. I think you will feel the same."

"Okay, I am curious. Why?"

"Alexander exposed himself to me."

"Oh, I hope you have a witness."

"Oh Christ, John, I am not trying to be funny. Alexander told me who he really is."

"You feel like an idiot for that?"

"Yes, you want to take a guess who he is? He visited us many times, and I sure missed it."

"Who, Mary, Adolf Hitler?"

Her jaw dropped and stared at him.

"What, Mary? It is him?"

"How long have you known?"

"I didn't. Just an off-the-wall guess."

"Not only that, John. He also said he was the Decider and now to call him the Führer. He changed his looks back to when he was. I still can't believe I didn't recognize him from before."

"Mary, I didn't as well. We weren't looking for him, although now that I think about it, many signs were there."

"Really, what do you mean?"

"The closeness of the group with the war survivors."

"Well, I think you might be a bit off the wall on that one. We didn't even think we were the only group. There are many women in power. Not something that happened during the war."

"Okay, Mary, now that you know, does that alter your thinking in any way?"

"Not really, I'll put his last ninety years as the test of what he has accomplished."

"How about what he is doing now? Is that for the benefit of mankind or himself?"

"John, please be careful expressing that line of thinking before we see the results."

"Your fear speaks volumes."

"Perhaps you are correct. Let's hope not." She came over and embraced him.

"We just got confirmation of the launching, and the satellites are functioning."

"Thank you, Tessa. Is the dome back in place?"

"It will be in about ten minutes, Violet."

"Charlotte, is the newest communication to the world prepared?"

"I am just editing it now. Then it will be sent to Hawk and the Führer."

"Excellent! Connie has the control room made contact with the new satellite?"

"Yes, the program has been activated, and it is responding to the commands. It should arrive to the targeted area in a few hours."

"You people are the best," she said, smiling at them all.

"We are the best in the world," Tessa replied. "We need to have some well-deserved time off soon."

"Don't worry, it will happen," responded Violet.

Violet took offense to Tessa's comment. *We are about to change the world, and she wants to take time off. I wonder how committed she is to the cause. If I get the chance, she will be removed if her attitude doesn't improve.*

She noticed Diana staring at her. She smiled and nodded. Diana returned the nod. Diana was the one woman she respected totally. She seemed to have a sense that she knew what was going on but rarely brought an issue to the forefront, unless it could be seen as contributing to the board.

CHAPTER 10

Colin Mitchell was exhausted. For as long as he had been in the news business, he had never known a day like today. The mass ciaos he had witnessed had drained him of his emotions. He saw families stuffed in cars exiting the city. It made him wonder what he would have done if he had a wife and kids. Where would they go? He imagined that most thought the big cities were still a target, and with Washington, DC, he understood their reasoning. Gas stations had long lines, and the stores were full of panicked people. The police force had stayed intact, and the fire departments seemed too busy to think of anything else. Smoke was still billowing in the late afternoon skyline. The heat ray had not only destroyed anything it had landed on, but the heat was so intense asphalt roads a few miles away liquefied and still bubbled. Any vehicle that came up to it soon became a fire trap, killing everyone inside. Trees as far away as two miles were ablaze, helping to cause whole neighborhoods to become engulfed in flames. So far, most of the city had electrical power. He feared that could be the next to go as the fires spread despite the efforts of the fire department. His exhaustion started to affect his judgement. He went to his car in the parking lot and put his driver's seat back as far as it would go and closed his eyes.

Mary couldn't believe the Decider was Hitler. That thought was stuck in her mind when she lay down after her work shift. She was getting more upset the more she thought about it. She lost my husband during the war and lived a life feeling his loss until she got this second chance. The fact she was forced by him to participate in Phase Z upset her even more. She had just experienced having a twin, and the closeness she felt with Adam may have been not because they

230

thought they were twins, but the love they had in their previous relationship. Now she began to understand the frequent visits Alexander made. He really didn't care about them but was more interested in the result. She was beginning to understand Megan's fear of not exposing that they had reverted back to their true identities. It was a difficult situation, and she didn't have any idea how it might end. She could be Allison for life and have to hide her relationship with John. The thought of that caused tears to run down her cheek.

Adolf didn't get much sleep despite his exhaustion. His long wait was more rewarding than he imagined. The excitement over yesterday was dulled by a glass of wine. He looked at the glass of wine and smiled. *To think I wouldn't drink for years*. A few of his mistresses were upset that it was allowed. But after ninety years and the need to distance himself from his previous habits; the wine was part of Alexander's makeup. He never got drunk as he knew he needed to stay in control. It would be so easy to move up the timetable and continue his craving for the world. His troops had to be sent to retrieve and protect the world's treasures, much like it happened during the war. Only this time, the art would be housed in the world's largest display, which he had plans to build. Those plans are about to become active after yesterday. The people will be awed to have them all in one location for eternity. He ordered troops to arrive in London and other cities. They would not be recognizable with their new dark green uniforms and helmets that covered their faces. He knew this could upset the board. It wasn't in the plans, but he would make them understand.

President Connelly awoke, and it took a few seconds to realize he fell asleep in his desk chair. He got up to stretch his legs. He walked from his office to the hallway. He could see the digital screen in the control. There wasn't any activity sighted. The loss of the satellites had rendered them useless. The room still had activity as the staff continues to use phones to communicate and get intelligence. Charles saw him and headed in his direction. "We have confirmation that the attacks appear to be over. There isn't any good news to report in regards to a possible military response. The globe is now encircled by the force field web. It is believed it can attack any flying aircraft. We have lost all the aircraft that we have launched."

"So the field has circled the earth? I need to see that." He signaled to his Secret Service and went to the outer door with their escort. They exited first and soon gave him the signal to follow. It was late in the afternoon, but the web was in full view on the horizon. He couldn't help but marvel at its creation. It looked like there was electricity flowing from web to web.

How is this possible? he thought to himself. He looked at Charles. "Looks like we are stuck here."

'That might be a good thing, Mr. President."

"If good is such a thing anymore."

Violet saw Diana in the cafeteria. "We need to talk in my office when you get time."

Diana saw Violet's worried face and said, "I will be there in five minutes."

"Good, I will contact the others."

Diana wondered what is was all about. She soon lost her appetite thinking about it and headed toward Violet's office. Charlotte was in a cart in front of her and was getting out when she got to her parking spot. "Charlotte, you have any idea what this is about?"

"No, she must have something important. Why else the emergency call."

"Not sure I would classify it as an emergency, but I can't think of what else it could be. I am sure we got all the targets."

They walked into Violet's office and were quickly directed to a small conference room next door by her secretary. Diana saw Connie seated at the round table, so she and Charlotte seated themselves. Violet got off her cell phone. "Tessa is on her way and will be here in a few minutes. She opened her briefcase and retrieved some papers. They were sorted out and bound together with paper clips. She passed out a copy to each of them and leaving one on the table for Tessa. "Go ahead and review them. I will start the details when Tessa arrives."

The shocked looks from the group as they reviewed them coincided with her feelings. Tessa walked in the room. She also saw the worried look on the others' faces. "What is going on?"

"Please sit and review the papers, Tessa. When you have, I will start the discussion."

Tessa had a shocked look and nodded to Violet.

"It appears our Führer has been doing more freelancing with the plan than we have been aware of. Troops have been sent to London, Paris, New York, Chicago, Florence, Rome, Vienna, Washington, DC, and Berlin. What do these locations all have in common?"

"Great works of art," answered Connie.

"Exactly, could it be he has plans for those works of art? The troops could be there only for securing them?"

"Do you think he could be planning on attacking those cities and wants to save the art?" asked Diana.

"There could be a number of reasons, so I feel we have to confront him."

"Violet, you want to do it now?"

"Yes, I don't like the board being bypassed. He could forget we are here in his present state of mind."

"I am with you, Violet," stated Connie.

Violet heard the others give their support. It was understood that she would be the one to do the deed.

John tried to focus on his work tasks, but the thought of the Decider being Hitler kept entering in his thoughts.

"Adam," came over his walkie-talkie. "You can slowly open the steam valve."

"Copy that, Joe." He put the walkie-talkie aside and slowly opened the valve until he heard the steam enter the pipe. It would cause damage to the pipes and system if he opened the valve too quickly. They needed to slowly heat up and to let the steam pressure slowly rise. He stayed at the valve and continued to slowly open the valve until Joe called and informed him the pressure had raised enough to allow Adam to open the valve completely. Joe was his supervisor. Adam guessed he looked about twenty-five, but he knew since he was in the group that he was much older. Joe was quiet and stayed to himself. He just went to work and had always lived underground since he became a member of the group. It was difficult to get him in a conversation. If he knew what was going on in the world, he never commented on it. John wished he didn't know.

Sleep never came easy for him, but after last night's excitement, he just lay on his bed with his eyes closed and relived the excitement of the success. It couldn't have gone any better. It took a few seconds of blinking his eyes to make out the digital alarm clock on the bed stand. It was 4:55 a.m. He reached for the phone. It took a few rings when he heard a tired-sounding Evan respond. "Yes, sir?"

"Evan, I am leaving my room soon. I won't be needing you today."

"Oh, thank you, sir. I hope you have a good day."

Adolf hung up the phone and proceeded to exit his room and entered the cart that was waiting for him. He got in the passenger side was in constant thought while one of his bodyguards drove him to the command center. He was waiting to hear from the general in charge of acquiring paintings from the museums in London. There were a number of museums in the world he sent his forces into to obtain paintings and other artworks. They were ordered to acquire them anyway possible, mostly under the guise of protecting them. In his mind that was exactly what they were doing. He would place them in a hall for everyone to see for eternity. The big screen monitor was focused on Great Britain, the one country he wanted to destroy completely. They had foiled his plans too often during the war. Not invading Britain was one of his biggest regrets of the war. If there is a country that could find a way to stop us, it would be Great Britain. That is not going to happen. He remembered saying that he would rub out Britain's cites during the war. That statement would come true soon.

The lights to the conference room behind him came on, and Violet exited to the command room.

"Adolf, can we talk in the conference room."

Her look convinced him that it was needed and followed her.

She closed the hallway door, and he closed the door he entered.

"Something amiss, Violet?"

"The board has come across some troop movements that we aware of."

"You mean that weren't in the original plans?"

"Yes."

"Weren't the original plans in regards to troop movements altered when we moved up the attack?"

"Yes, but shouldn't we be informed of any movement?"

"Violet, I am aware of and ordered the troops. If I feel the need to include you and the board, I will do so!"

The door to the control slammed as she watched him leave. "How do I explain this to the board?"

Joyce drove her cart to all the posts. None of her troops seemed aware of what was going on in command center. Most of their training focused on anyone attacking to get the product. The thought of going to her room became a strong urge. Megan had to be contacted before she gave in.

Megan was in the security headquarters office when she arrived.

"Oh God, I am glad you are here."

"A bad day, Joyce?"

"One that a good bath and a gin and tonic will cure."

Megan laughed. "Is there a man in the equation?"

Joyce shook her head no. She looked around and whispered, "Adolf ruined it for me with men. I don't mean that in a good way."

She saw Megan raise her eyebrows and nod. "Nothing new to report, Megan. I am off for the night."

"Enjoy your evening, Joyce."

I can't believe I told her that, she thought as she drove to her living quarters. *I trust her, but that was careless. Adolf could return me to his mistress if he found out. I worked hard for him, and he took me for granted. Life might not be worth living if that happened.*

The wine flowed easily after her bath. A text from Violet got her attention. She wanted to know if she could meet with her. She was tired but answered for her to come to her quarters. Violet arrived holding a bottle of wine.

Joyce noticed. "So, a bottle of wine is needed?"

"It will help my mood."

"Tell me why, Violet. You have my attention."

"I had a conversation with Adolf today. There have been troop movements that the board wasn't aware of. I asked if he was aware of them. He blew me and the board off. He said was aware of them, and the board needn't be concerned."

"Do you have any idea what the troop movements were for, Violet?"

"No, just that they were made in the big cities in Europe."

"Hmm, you think he is after the great works of art again?"

"Joyce, I didn't think of that. But if he is, I wonder if he plans on attacking the cities after they are removed. That wasn't in the original plans."

Joyce picked up the wine and opened it. She handed a glass to Violet. "Let's hope not. We don't need him going rogue after all this time."

Violet emptied her glass and went for another. "That could be the beginning of the end for all of us."

CHAPTER 11

PRESIDENT CONNELLY LOOKED AROUND HIS table of advisors. "Do we have anything left? Nukes? Stealth bombers?"

"It is hopeless, Mr. President," General Frost responded.

"Hopeless, Frosty? I refuse to believe it. Do you know something I don't?"

"Sir, we can only hope some bases are intact but unable to contact us. The reports we have manage to receive state there has been total destruction to all bases and nuclear weapons storage areas."

His fist slammed on the table. "Damn!" was his response as he left the room. They sat there quietly and waited.

Charles said, "Let's see if we can find some hope out there." They all filed out of the room. Charles was undecided on where to go. He had never seen the president in this state of mind. He decided to leave him be and departed to his office. His cell phone screen was blank, but he couldn't stop checking it. The food supply was something that was brought to his attention. Normally they kept about a month's supply on hand, but with the supply system in question, they needed to find a way to secure food and supplies. The Upper Peninsula of Michigan is isolated and hadn't been affected by the worldwide attack. Dennis Milford was in his office when Charles located him.

"I heard you are concerned about the supply chain, Dennis."

"Yes, Charles, the situation revolves around panic. Most are too scared to continue. Luckily, the president is from the area, and it is known to the suppliers that he is here. It looks like we will continue to be well stocked. Well, as long as money still has value."

"Another thing to think about. Hope that doesn't become an issue. The president doesn't need that added to the situation."

"Amen to that."

"How has the response to the message we send been received?"

"We have been contacted by nearly every country, Mr. Hawk."

"Who hasn't responded yet, Violet?"

"There are a few isolated countries in the Pacific, but the major country not to respond has been England."

"Have you double-checked England?"

"A number of times. We are sure they are able to respond."

"I will relay that information to the Führer."

Violet looked at the board members. "I think the Führer will look forward to destroying them." They nodded in agreement.

She called the meeting to an end. She thought the destruction of England would be a mistake, but knowing the Führer's hatred for the British, she knew he would welcome the chance. *Millions of people will die, and the country would be decimated for many years to come. The smoke and debris could cause changes in the weather worldwide. Plus, the attack would have to be justified to the rest of the world if we want their cooperation.*

The goal is to have one central government with the Führer leading the way for peaceful coexistence. The group's arsenal should be the deterrent to any resistance.

"What are you thinking, Violet?"

Charlotte's voice startled her, and she realized the group members were still at the table.

The looks on their faces were intense. "I was considering if the destruction of England would do more harm than good."

"Do we have any option to stop it?" asked Tessa.

"Only to convince the Führer not to," responded Diana.

"What do you think, Violet? Should there be an effort to try?"

"The Führer might respond to a written report explaining the pros and cons of destroying Great Britain. We need to create them very soon. Everyone willing?"

They looked to one another and nodded. Then left to their offices to create one.

Violet thought there was little chance of them persuading him not to. She knew he hated the British. But she went and called the Hawk in hopes there was still time for the reports.

He was leaning back in his office chair when his phone rang.

"Hawk."

"Hawk, has the Führer decided what to do with Great Britain?"

"Violet, he has been napping. The fatigue finally caught up with him, so he doesn't know. Why?"

"The board and I would like to give him our thoughts about the pros and cons of destroying it."

"I will mention it to him, but he might not be pleased because he hasn't thought on it. He might not want to discuss it."

"Understood. I am available for any discussion should he want to."

"I will make him aware of that. Anything else?"

"That is it. Thank you, Hawk."

"That is difficult to believe, Violet. Thanks for the update."

"Stupid British," Joyce said. "How could they not see the danger?"

"What are you talking about?"

"Megan, the British have failed to respond to the worldwide message that was sent. If there is a country the Adolf would want to avenge, Britain is near the top of his list."

"Oh my god, do you think he would kill millions of innocent people?"

"With his current mind-set, I wouldn't be surprised. His dream is being realized, and any chance that could be stymied, it will cause him to do everything possible to squash it."

"I hope that won't escalate the situation. The future needs the earth to be habitable."

"I couldn't agree more, Megan. We don't need to escalate global warming as a result of the death ray damage. I am not sure the board has much influence with Adolf since he returned to his Führer mind-set."

Megan sat quietly then got up to leave. "Have a good shift, Joyce. It has been very quiet in our area."

"It needs to continue. Enjoy your night off."

Getting younger has changed Joyce, Megan thought as she drove to her quarters. *She is more focused and very in charge. Hard to believe she had to be his mistress as punishment.*

The smells of a cooked meal welcomed her when she opened her door. "That sure smells good, Allison."

"Thanks, Mom." It had taken a while for John and Mary to return to the Allison and Adam personas, but after a few near mishaps, they decided it was safer to fall back into those names.

"What's the occasion for having a Turkey?"

"Just thought I would give it a try, Mom. It is my first turkey meal. I just thought, why have kitchen stove if we never use it?"

"Why indeed? Need any help?"

"No, you go relax. Adam should be here soon."

She got her book and poured a glass of wine. The recliner was next.

"What is that smell?" Adam said when he entered the quarters.

"Did someone pay off a chef to cook?"

"Okay, smart-ass. Get over here and give me a kiss."

"What is the occasion, my dear?"

"That is the same thing Mom asked. I saw this poor neglected stove and thought it needed a workout. I have never cooked a turkey before, so I got one from the cooks."

"You never cooked one in your first life?"

"No, always had someone else did it. Okay, I need to get to the potatoes."

"You are full of surprises. One reason I love you."

"Oh, you just love my cooking."

"Oh, there are other ways you cook that get my attention."

"Okay, you two. That is too much information."

"Okay, Mom," they both responded, smiling.

"The turkey is ready. You both go sit down at the table."

"Sir, the rumors are true. Newly elected prime minister George Windgate was at one of the military bases when an attack destroyed it. That area is smoldering, and there is no chance of anyone surviving."

"Thank you, Charles. Keep me posted."

"Will do. Is there anything you need?"

"No, Charles, thank you." He watched his chief of staff walk away.

Now what, Hog? he thought to himself. There were a few days left in his term. They had recently vacated the prime minister's home in London. He moved to his home near Brighton, and Charles came with him until the end of his term.

The electorate had spoken. They had enough of William Hogarth. His nickname of Hog was caused by his enormous appetite and wild parties.

He had gotten so big in size that the media started calling him Hog Girth. When his drug use was exposed, a general election was called as he refused to resign. He and the party lost in a landslide.

The attack on Great Britain left the country in a state of confusion. Who was in charge after the apparent death of William Windgate? The majority party, the King, or himself. Let them decide. He was out of the communication loop in Brighton.

"Glad it went so well, General. He will be very pleased."

Hawk knew the Führer would take this news as an omen when he heard the Great Britain hadn't responded to the message. The fact the attacks made it easy for the removal of all the artworks in Great Britain would be like lighting a fuse for the attack that was about to come. He doubted that the board would dissuade him.

"Hawk, we have the reports finished. Is the Führer awake?"

"Not yet, Violet. He will be given these."

"That was a great meal, Allison."

"Thanks, Mom."

"Yes, it was!" replied Adam.

"Before you get up from the table, I have some news for you. I trust you won't repeat it. I found out the Great Britain hadn't responded to the worldwide message that sent. That could mean it will be destroyed by the heat ray."

"Oh my god. The whole country?"

"Depends on what the Führer's decides, Allison. He has no use for the British."

"I hope that doesn't happen. Of course I will keep my opinion to myself, Mom."

"Good idea, Adam."

His door opened. "Hawk, any news while I was away?"

"Yes, Adolf, the artwork has been gathered in London and is on its way here."

"That is great news. Was there any difficulty?"

"The general said it was easy with the confusion after the attacks."

"A perk we didn't realize."

"Speaking of the attack and the aftermath, Great Britain is the one remaining major country that hasn't responded to the message we sent."

Hawk watched him smile and nod his head.

"Adolf, before you decide what to do, the board sent these reports to you regarding that."

He took them from Hawk and sat down. He glanced over the reports. "Did you ask for these, Hawk?"

"No, Violet gave them."

He looked for Hawk's waste basket and threw the reports into it.

He left without saying a word.

"He is pissed."

CHAPTER 12

"TAKE ME TO THE CONTROL room." He was too upset to have breakfast. "How could they offer a report without me requesting them first?"

Global warming caused by the heat ray? He didn't believe it. Far more fire and smoke during the war. *I am now the most powerful man in the history of the world. The board will now be an afterthought. They aren't needed.*

They all stood up when he entered the control room. He signaled for them to sit down. "How long before you can station the death rays over Britain?" he asked Stephen, the main control engineer.

"All of them in about forty minutes, Führer."

"Then do so. In the meantime, put the map of Britain on the main monitor."

The wall monitor in front of him showed the map of Great Britain. He could see the icons for the rays' approach the island. "Direct them to the London area, Stephen."

"They are on the way."

London then Dover were the first areas he targeted. Both areas were reasons the attack on Britain failed during the war.

"Sir, the rays are nearly in position."

"Okay, can they be programed to attack by starting a circle and continuing to circulate until it closes?"

"If you mean to start at the outer ring and eventually attack everything from outside in, then yes."

"Take two of them and start one on the west and the other on the east about 10K from the center. Program them to go clockwise. I will control the third ray manually. You can transfer control for all of them to me after you finish programming them."

"Yes, Führer. I am finished."

"Stephen, you can leave the control room."

"What did Hawk say, Violet?"

"He said the Führer threw the reports in his waste basket and he was pissed off. He flew out the door."

"If we haven't heard from now, you can bet he doesn't care what we think," Charlotte responded.

"I have to agree," said Connie. "I think our status in the chain of command has been lowered."

"I won't go that far, but I think we need to keep our distance and stay in the shadows to let this play out."

"I hope you are right, Violet." She was surprised to hear that from Tessa.

Stephen left the control room, leaving him alone. He wanted to feel the power without anyone observing him. The wall monitor showed it to be 5:57 p.m. in Britain. It will be the last day on earth for the majority of people in London. If there are any survivors, he would respect their resourcefulness. They hid underground during the war, but they wouldn't have much time with this attack. Besides the heat should take all the oxygen in that area. It became 6:00 p.m. in London. People looked up and saw three rays coming down from the sky—one in the western sky and another in the eastern sky. One came down in the heart of London. It took him a few seconds to realize where the ray was located, and he directed to the Thames River. The river was changed to a huge ball of steam vapor that destroyed anything near on either riverbank. He slowly directed it down the river, destroying every bridge along the way. With the ray being about 2K wide, anything on both sides of the river were destroyed or near enough to be ignited into a fireball. The other rays were circling in. It was time for him to direct his elsewhere. *London will now be a footnote in history.*

Connie texted her. "Violet, you need to come to the board conference room as soon as possible."

"I am on my way."

She grabbed a muffin off her food tray and left the cafeteria.

They were all around the computer monitor on the table.

"London is gone. Just a huge fireball is all that is left."

"Are you certain, Connie?"

"Yes, Violet. Millions of people vanished in a manner of minutes."

"Oh my god, what is happening now?"

"The rays are going to all parts of Great Britain. It appears he plans on destroying the major cities. He is taking them back to the Dark Ages. If there are anyone left when he is through."

"Truly a sad day for mankind."

"Yes, it is, Diana. For mankind. Sad that our opinions weren't considered."

"I agree, Violet. Were you aware his bodyguard wouldn't allow me in the control room when I wondered what he was doing at the entry door? He said no one was allowed until further notice."

"Well, as long as we can get reports on our computer, we will need to monitor the situation. We might need to come up with a plan."

Violet knew they all understood what that meant.

"I know you won't stop my plan this time. You will be struggling to survive." The process of eliminating Britain went easier than expected. It made him want to do more. He set the rays to go east. Stalingrad or whatever the name of the city was currently was on his target list. He needed Stephen to create a program like the one used against London.

"Stephen."

"Yes, my Führer."

"I need you to return and do some programing."

"Right, on my way."

The map of Russia was displayed on the wall monitor. "Stephen, set up the same program for the city Volgograd. It was Stalingrad at one time."

"The rays should be here in twenty minutes. Do you want me to stay, Führer?"

"No, if I have a problem, I will give you a call."

"Yes, sir."

Adolf waited for him to depart and decided this would be the last target for the day. The world would know that not cooperating with him would lead certain death to any government and its people.

Adam turned to Will. "You want to play another game?"

"Sure, you have hooked me on this shit."

Adam laughed. Adam knew better than to ask his past, but he knew he was from a different generation as they all were. They hadn't been exposed to video games. It took his mind off the information he was aware of concerning the death rays. Will never mentioned or asked if he knew what was going on in the world. He was happy to have a second chance with no stress. Everything was available to him as long as he followed the directives and worked hard. Everything included female companionship for an evening. They all were sterile, and no abuse was tolerated. It was up to each party if they wanted to connect. There were plenty of opportunities. "Think I have you this time, Adam."

Adam returned his focus to the game, but he couldn't turn the tide, and Will won. "I finally beat you!"

"It is about time. I was starting to get bored."

"Sure, asshole."

Adam laughed. "No comment."

Will laughed at his response.

"I need to get going, Will. See you at work tomorrow."

"Okay, it allows me to savor my victory longer, Adam."

Adam smiled. "Now who is being the asshole?"

He got out the door before he heard a response.

Violet looked like she had been crying when she walked into Joyce's office and closed the door behind her. "Christ, what is wrong, Violet?"

"I am not sure there is a Christ after today. Adolf murdered millions of people in a few hours. There isn't much left of Great Britain, and he repaid the former Stalingrad."

"Violet, he did it before. Why do you seem so surprised?"

"I just thought after everything went as planned, there wouldn't be a need to exterminate anyone. There isn't a country that can stop him."

"What you say could be telling. You said stop him and not us. Things have changed in the recent weeks. We have moved down in status once he got what he wanted from us, which has been typical with men from our generation. It might be time to consider where we are at in the scheme of things for the future."

"Joyce, I agree with what you are saying. What are you considering?"

"Think about it, Violet. The world is in its most vulnerable time in history. It can be led by one central government or, in this case, one man. I think what we witnessed today is a sad testament to mankind. I think this could be the perfect time to have woman-kind in charge."

CHAPTER 13

"YES, PRESIDENT CONNELLY, IT IS true. London and the other major cities are destroyed. The whole country is in flames. As far as I know, I am the only living member of what is left of the government. I am powerless with only this landline for communication."

"Oh my god, Hogarth. Do you have any idea of who attacked you?

"No more than anyone else. We were at the mercy, and they didn't show us any."

"The bastards! We could be next. Washington could be the next target. The chances of me going there are very slim. Especially with the power web scanning the sky. Good luck, Hog. We both will need it."

"I think we are beyond that, Mr. President."

"Charles, come to my office."

It was a few minutes until Charles knocked on the door and entered the office. "Do you need something, Mr. President?"

"Just something I doubt you have. A way out of this mess. I just got word that London and the rest of Great Britain was destroyed. Then heard a city in Russia suffered the same fate."

"That confirms what I just heard. It appears it was Volgograd in Russia."

The former Stalingrad."

"Just that city in Russia?"

"Yes."

"Great Britain and Volgograd. Why Volgograd? If my history is correct, it was the city where the Nazi's were stymied in World

War II. Add Britain, and both would be targets for Hitler if he was alive."

"Now to think about it, Mr. President. I believe the Nazis were trying to construct a death ray that used the sun power to create a ray to attack the earth."

"They never had the time to complete it, but it does make me wonder if some group utilized their plans."

"It would take a lot of funding and technology to accomplish that scenario, but we are witnessing a power that can't be explained."

"I'd rather deal with that scenario than one generated by an alien world."

"I agree. But both have us in a near checkmate status."

"Let's hope we can come up with a miracle move and they have a case of chess blindness, Charles."

"I think if we broadcast this, there will be a lot of panic. Any thoughts?"

"Stan, has this information been confirmed?"

"Yes, Colin. We have received a number of reports confirming it. London and the major cities in Great Britain have been destroyed. Whether we are next is frightening."

"Stan, I think there is already plenty of panic. The streets are still filled with traffic heading out of the city. I don't know how the government is reacting, but they might want to get out of town if they haven't. So I am in favor of it."

"Okay, Colin, anyone else?"

"I think we should, and I think it will be my last broadcast, Stan."

"Okay, Andrea, thank you for all you have done. That goes to all of you. If anyone else wants to leave and there isn't enough staff to keep it going, then we will sign off. You will be paid regardless. For whatever that is worth."

"Hawk, we need to alter the next message. Include video of the destruction of London. We want the message to be clear. Any resistance will not be tolerated."

"Yes, Adolf, you just want London to be shown?"

"Yes, it is a strong enough message."

"When do you want it broadcast?"

"Whenever it is prepared. You can ask the board to assist you if you desire. They are good at that type of thing."

"I will get right on it." The thought of asking the board for help didn't appeal to him. They had been shunned by the Führer before the attack.

He knew they were totally against it. Now the Führer suggested using their input to justify it and explain the policy for the future. The dread of contacting them was overtaken by the fact he needed their contribution."

"Violet, I need you to come to my office as soon as possible. I have a task for the board."

"I'm in the cafeteria having breakfast. Will it wait until I am finished?"

"Of course."

She put her phone down.

"That was the Hawk. He has a task for us. He wants me in his office as soon as I am done."

"That was nice of him to wait. I wonder what is so important."

"I would guess it has to do with our next message to earth, Charlotte."

"Oh yes, I don't know about you, but I like the idea of being considered from another world. It feels more powerful and intimidating."

"Yes, I agree, but I doubt the Führer does. He wants the world to know he finally has accomplished worldwide domination."

"Violet, you think he will include us when he announces to the world?"

"I did at one time. I am not sure anymore."

He heard a knock on his bedroom door. "Adam, we need to have a talk with you."

"Okay, be there in a second." *She said we. I wonder who "we" is.* He arrived at the dining room table. Megan and Allison were sitting and staring at him. "Okay, I have my own bathroom. I didn't leave the seat up on the other toilets.

Megan shook her head in fake disgust. "We thank you for that, but we have a serious matter to discuss. Their serious look got his attention, and he sat down next to them. "What is this about?"

"Adam, have you heard anything in your work group that has been going on with the attack you know about?"

"Not a thing. It is business as usual. Why do you ask, Mom?"

"Because there has been some serious discussions regarding what happened recently. The Führer went rogue with the death rays. He destroyed London and all the major cities in Great Britain. Then he destroyed the former Stalingrad in Russia. When I say *destroyed*, I mean down to a fireball. They are gone."

"Holy shit. That bastard."

"Careful, Adam."

"Sorry, Allison, it is difficult to control my tongue after what he did to us."

She reached over and held his hand. "This is about to get serious. Joyce told Mom that the board is considering removing the Führer before he destroys other countries and the environment."

"It doesn't get more serious than that. Is there a plan in place?"

"Not yet, Adam. Like before we don't let it go any further. I told you both because if needed, I can count on you."

"Most definitely, Mom, and count me in too."

"I love you both."

"The Führer wants an updated message to be broadcast. He wants the world to know that any resistance will be met with total destruction. He wants to use London as an example."

"Just London, Hawk?"

"Violet, that is what he requested. He wants it as soon as possible and suggested you and the board to be included in the process."

"I will call the board together, and we will try to hammer out something."

"I am confident you will as you always have."

"Thanks for the vote of confidence, Hawk."

"Are you staying, Colin?" He was surprised to see Andrea Armstrong in front of him.

"I am not sure. If the station stays open, then more than likely. I don't have the resources to move anyway, and I don't have a place to go.

"I have the resources and have a cabin in northern Maine. I don't want to go alone."

"Are you asking me to go with you?"

"I am looking for someone. Care to come to my place to discuss it? I do need help packing if nothing else."

The guys in DC always thought she was hot. He knew her to be very professional. *What the fuck*, he thought to himself. "You drive and I follow?"

She smiled. "Why don't you ride with me?"

"I live in Maryland, so it will take a while."

"Okay, I hope it is scenic after what we witnessed in DC.

"It is, but Baltimore is fairly close. Colin, you are of few guys that never hit on me. It is one reason I asked you."

"I always had a healthy respect for how serious you took your duties as an anchor. One reason I am with you."

She laughed. "Well, that is a good start. I take it you aren't gay."

He laughed. "Not in this lifetime. I hope that is okay."

She turned and gave him a very seductive look. He turned away to keep from becoming aroused. "I hope I can convince you to go to Maine with me."

I am sure you can, entered his thoughts. *If we can get there.*

"How does it read to you, Tessa?"

"I think we did what was asked."

"We all have read it, and we can deliver it to Hawk. I will do that now, and I would like a closed door meeting with all of you when I return."

"I wonder what Violet wants to discuss?"

"I think it is about a plan we mentioned before, Tessa."

She sat there a few seconds. "Oh! Do you think it is still needed?"

"Difficult to decide. We must be ready if it is."

"I agree, Diana. Time will tell."
"Yes, Charlotte. It will."

Hawk gave him a copy of the message from the board. He thought it was presented well but not as powerful and intimidating as he wanted.

The control room was vacant, but Stephen was in a room nearby if he needed help. Maybe a city destroyed on every continent would be the message that was needed. The map of Africa appeared on the wall monitor. "Lagos, Nigeria, will get the world's attention." He had mastered how to control the rays. It would take about an hour for them to arrive.

The map of India was next to appear on the wall monitor. "Mumbai will be next. I can't believe they changed the name from Bombay."

He studied the map of China while the rays moved into position for Lagos.

The rays were nearly there. He programed two to do the enclosed circle pattern surrounding the city while he freelanced with the other. Send a message and decrease the population. They won't be missed as the attack began.

"Any word from Hawk?" was the first thing Violet heard when she returned to the board conference room.

"He didn't say anything when I gave it to him. I assume he gave to the Führer. You know about as much as I do, Tessa. I found out The Führer is in the control room, with his bodyguards controlling the entry. Joyce's security group hasn't been contacted to supply protection. That could mean there will be more attacks."

Connie had her laptop and activated it. "I still have access."

Violet looked at the others. "If we do this, we need to all be on the same page. I trust that we are, and it will be a group effort. Removing him could be the easy part. What is left of the world will be our responsibility. Mankind was mentioned at our previous meeting. Joyce mentioned there will never be a better opportunity for womankind to control the future. I think we need Joyce to be included in the planning. Any objections?"

They all agreed. "Oh my god. There is another attack taking place."

"Where at, Connie?"

"Lagos, Nigeria, Violet."

"It is time to plan. I'll call Joyce."

CHAPTER 14

CHARLES KNOCKED AND OPENED THE door after he heard the president acknowledge the knock. "I can tell by your expression it is bad news."

"The cities of Lagos in Africa, Mumbai in India, and Shanghai, China, have been destroyed."

"Christ, I think we are at the end of the world. Africa, India, Russia, Europe, and China. We could be next. They are hitting where they can do the most damage. Except for Volgograd. It is obvious their first message to the world was bogus."

"Mr. President, there was some positive news."

"I am ready for it."

"We do have some weapons that weren't destroyed. We have a few warehouses that have stored the weapons that were overproduced. Mostly tank and artillery units. There are thousands."

"If we only had targets to focus on and the troops to operate them, it would be great news, Charles. Do we have any contact to what is left of the armed services?"

"There are some retired generals who know of this place and have made contact."

"That is something to focus on. See if any of them can get here."

"Okay, hope it starts something going our way."

"Hope is all we have."

"It literally has become a scorched earth campaign the he has implemented. He is the only one who knows when it stops. He has killed well over a hundred million people and any other living thing in those areas. The fires and smoke created will kill millions more."

"So, Violet, do you really think you can express that to Hawk and not have him relay it to the Führer?"

"Maybe not to Mr. Hawk, Diana, but to the others in the field."

"Then we need to take Hawk out of the loop. Any ideas?"

"Diana, I have a possible solution. I will have to make a few contacts to see if it is feasible. That okay with everyone?"

"I think we are all in agreement that any input from you, Joyce, is welcome."

"Thank you, Violet. I need to leave now, and I should know by tomorrow."

Megan was in the security office when she arrived. "We need to talk privately. Can you meet me in my quarters as soon as possible?"

"Joyce, I will get a replacement and be right there."

"I will be waiting."

"Do you want a glass of wine?" was the first thing Megan heard when she entered.

"Do you think I will need one, Joyce?" She smiled when Joyce poured her one.

Joyce pointed to the dining room table so she could sit across from her.

"Megan, the plan is to remove him. How we do it is the next step. We need to have a few people we can trust to execute whatever is decided.

"Execute? Is that part of the plan?"

"Oh, poor choice of words. What we decide to do after he is removed hasn't been discussed. Although I have some suggestions," she said with a wicked smile on her face."

"I bet you do, and I won't ask. I have a few I can trust to follow my orders. It helps that nearly all don't know who the Decider was or is."

"The Hawk, his bodyguards, and those in the control room are our main concern. Those in the field will have to be dealt with later. We can say he went in transition to put them at ease. What happens to him will be decided by the board."

"So tell me your plan?"

"Tell me if you think we can do this?"

"Great work, Martin. The mission was accomplished. We will be starting the next phase, and you will then be free to follow your plans. "But first, I will be contacting Cyrus. I want to have you both come here as soon as we can make safe arrangements. We will have something to celebrate."

"Thank you, my Führer. It feels good to call you that. It has been a very long wait to get here. I am glad it was worth it."

"It is time for the world to become one. The world will now advance to where we will take it, and that is the next realm. We have forever to accomplish the remaining goals."

Adolf ended the conversation on that. He leaned back and succumbed to an urge to have a glass of wine. It had been so many years from the days he hated the thought of drinking. But the isolation wore on him. "It is time to celebrate and relax." He could feel himself unwinding with every sip. He felt a bit of guilt deviating from the plan, but he was certain the added attacks would be beneficial in the long run. He sat the drink on the table and closed his eyes.

"The tents are set up, Prime Minister Hogarth."

"Thank you, Captain. What is the supply situation?"

"We have basic rations from our reserve warehouse. We are trying to get vehicles and drivers to distribute those. That is all we can supply. It is anarchy in Brighton and the surrounding villages, so we have no idea if they will survive. I have about fifty men under my command. We will stay and guard this area, but we will need a portion of those rations."

"Captain, use whatever is necessary to maintain your troop level. I don't need to tell you how we are in the survival of the fittest mode. Try to keep the anarchy away from this area."

"I will do my best."

"I am sure you will. I will be in my home's office if you need to report."

"Yes, sir."

"The walk to his home was a labored one. He wasn't sure he could make the five-hundred-meter distance. His vehicle was being used by Charles trying to find supplies. The bed withstood his fall on it. What to do now? The landline phone system was more miss than hit. Cell phones weren't much use with no satellites to connect to. The smoke and pollution caused by the rays were covering what was left of the country. Fires were raging without resources to stop them. He thought about killing himself, but despite his reputation of not caring about anyone but himself, he knew that wasn't the case. Besides most that criticized him are likely dead or wishing they were.

Allison and Adam would be returning from their work shift soon. Megan felt confident they would want to participate in the plan. Much of its success depended on the people wanting to continue the longevity. Is there anyone worth jeopardizing it?

"Mary, I need to talk to you. When you get settled."

"Mary and not Allison? This must be serious. I'll be right there."

"Take your time. I need to talk with John as well. He should be here shortly."

Mary changed out of her uniform and put it in the washer. She heard Megan talking to John. He appeared in the hallway. "Do you have any idea what this is about, Mary?"

"It has to be very serious to want John and Mary?"

They walked to the table. "Yes, I want to discuss this with John and Mary. For if it doesn't turn out the way we hope, you will no longer be Allison and Adam. We have a plan to remove Adolf and you could be major players in the plan."

"I am so in."

"You sure, John? What about you, Mary?"

"Just tell me how I can help?"

"Well, here is the plan."

"John, we need you to put a gas in his ventilation system to make the Führer and his servant unconscious. Mary, you and I will go to Hawk's office and detain him. Joyce and her guard will subdue the bodyguards. Any questions?"

"Megan, you do know I work on the boilers and not on the steam/ventilation systems? I am not sure I can deliver."

"Do some research and let me know as soon as possible."

"I will this evening."

"Won't someone be there? Just Otto, Mary."

"Otto? Yes, automatic?"

He tried to avoid her punch on the arm, but she got it good.

"Okay, you two. Stop acting like teenagers. Any other questions?"

"What happens to them after we get them?"

"Mary, Joyce's groups will move them to a secure location. I think it best that we don't know. I also think you know what happens to us if this doesn't work."

"Oh joy, Phase Z again."

"John, you might wish that was the case if we don't."

"Megan, is there a plan B if I can't deliver?"

"John, make sure Adam delivers."

"What gas do I use?"

"The board will supply it and instruct you how to use it."

"Is that all they need me for?"

"John, there is another task if you care to try and pull it off. We need someone to take Mr. Hawk's place for a short time. We don't have very many men we can trust to do it, and you are about his size."

"Wow, anything else. Does the board know I'm the guy to lead the way?"

"Not yet, I will relay your willingness to Joyce. She will inform the board."

"If I say I will and the board agrees, how soon will the plan start?"

"As soon as you can deliver."

"Or Adam," Mary said and a smiled.

"Yeah, maybe Adam can do that, and I will be the Hawk."

"You joke, but you and Mary have lived two different lives. You may be the only two in the history. Okay, okay, let's stay serious. So is it a go, John?'

"I will do my best."

"Mary, still with me?"

"You have to ask? Of course."

"I will contact Joyce."

"I will go to the plant. I do have work there that needs to be done and then do some research."

"Okay, Adam."

He came over and gave her and Mary hug.

"What do you think, Mary? We asking too much of him?"

"If there is a way, he will get it done."

CHAPTER 15

Martin Schmidt was pleased to hear about the successful completion of the attack phase. His concern, which he didn't mention to Adolf, was how much longer the web was needed. It took a significant amount of power to maintain. His equipment was starting to wear down and was in need of maintenance. The plan was for the web to circle the earth until the phase was completed. The future after that was uncertain. He would like to focus his efforts on making the world self-sufficient energywise. The thought of going in space and using his talents did interest him, but whatever the Führer wants comes first.

"Can you trust him, Joyce?"

"Yes, I knew him in Reese. He worked with us and proved his worth. I now know him as Adam because he was one of the two that were in Phase Z. He will do whatever his 'mother' Megan asks of him. Same with daughter, Allison."

"Oh, I remember the incident now, Joyce. So they never retained their memories of their previous lives?"

"No, Connie, they haven't. They were visited often by Adolf. He monitored them closely."

"Megan vouches for him, and I vouch for her. She is aware of the consequences."

"Joyce, we will get the items needed for the operation."

The door opened. "Am I interrupting anything?"

"Come in, Mr. Hawk. Nothing that can't be interrupted. Did you need something?"

"Violet, the Führer informed me that he thinks it is time for a victory celebration. He wants Cyrus and Martin to be part of it. They will be coming as soon as we can retrieve them. He thinks it is time to tell the world they are under our control and what the future will look like."

"How soon is this celebration expected to happen?"

"Violet, as soon as it can be arranged."

"Do you know if travel can be safe?"

"The Führer said everything will be cleared very soon."

It was if he can read my mind. He does amaze me sometimes. Martin contacted the other power plants, and the process the powering down the worldwide web was started. *I wonder how the Führer looks like now.* The last time he saw him was as Alexander. It was quite the transformation. He even drank some wine. Time to arrange his plans for the trip and make sure the safeguards were in place for his base and equipment.

Wayne radioed him. "Mr. President, the sky web is subsiding."

"I'll be right there." He knocked on Charles's door. "Come outside!"

I still can't helped be amazed, he thought to himself as each circle in the web slowly retracted into the next layer below it.

"I sure hope someone destroyed that power source."

"We can hope, Charles. Hopefully the communications will improve without that electrical interference."

"We may not want to hear any news. At least getting airborne could be an option."

"That won't happen until they allow it, whoever they are. I am worried what they will do next."

The door closed when Hawk left the conference room. "That was too close. We can't be that careless again. We need a video camera for the entryway and have the images on one of our laptops."

"I will take care of it, Violet."

"Thanks, Diana. I think it best to alter our plan with the sudden celebration put in our laps. Any comments?"

"Martin and Cyrus are returning to be part of it. I think he is going to announce his and their return to the world, what is left of it."

"I agree, Charlotte, would that be a good thing?"

"Tessa, I think that could open the door to disaster. I think because of our technology the world leaders think we are some unseen force that can destroy their country. Exposing our identity could give them hope on how to respond. Add the fact they will know we have a way to regenerate ourselves could invite an effort to obtain it."

"You make a good case, Violet. So we need to make a plan for the celebration and one to stop it?"

"Yes, Connie, I think we need to get to work soon. Violet, when you get the video camera set up, we will start."

"Violet, it will be done as soon as I get the equipment."

"Great, I will contact Joyce to see when she is available."

Damn, I need to finish packing that valve, Adam thought.

He tried to find the air handler that supplied air to Adolf's quarters on the air controlling computer but hadn't been able to. Maybe it wasn't in the computer program and controlled elsewhere. That was a question he couldn't ask. It wasn't part of his job to know. He returned to the valve and finished packing it. The drive back to their quarters was a blur as he racked his brain for another method to do what was needed. The thought of entering Adolf's quarters and putting something in the air vent didn't seem possible. He was extremely well protected. Joyce, Megan, and Allison were at the table when he arrived. "Hate to tell you this, Adam. There has been a change in plans."

"Well, I hate to tell you, but so far the other plan may not have worked. I could find any listing for the air handler for the Führer's quarters."

"Did you happen to notice one for the hall?"

"If you mean the gathering hall, yes, I did, Joyce."

"The board was informed that the Führer wants a victory celebration. He is having the main players in the attack returning to be part of it. It is possible that he will broadcast this to the world. The board thinks that is asking for disaster and wants to stop it."

"Joyce, does the board have any details on the celebration?"

"Not yet, Megan. They have to make arrangements to get everyone here. After that there hasn't been any directions on what will be the on the agenda."

"So this is on hold until you do? Still want me to look into the first option?"

"Yes, Adam, we might need all the options that are available to get this done."

The United States was on the wall monitor. Washington, DC, was tempting, but he decided on St. Louis. Then on to Canada. He didn't want not to avoid it since he was in the northern part. Quebec City would be the target. These will be the last targets prior to the celebration. It will keep them dealing with the aftermath. The attacks took nearly four hours.

When they were done, he called Evan. "Evan, I would like a salmon dinner with the usual vegetables served in my quarters."

"What would you like to drink?

"I am in the mood for some lemonade."

"Yes, my Führer, anything else?"

"Contact Hawk, tell him I need him."

"Right away, sir."

The salmon was done to his liking. He was finishing his meal when Hawk arrived.

"Yes, Adolf, what do you need?"

"I need some female companionship tonight. Do you have any that can fill my need?"

"You know I do. Do you want me to bring you some portfolios?"

"No, why don't you surprise me?"

"Okay, I will see what I can do."

Adolf watched Hawk about to exit the room. "But a redhead would be a good surprise."

Hawk chuckled and left the room.

The shower felt good to his fatigued body. He planned on a long session with the woman Hawk supplied. The power of youth was on his side, but she had to respond to his requests. But it was easier now. The women had many years of experience to make their desires known. He had his that got him off. The fake mustache was removed. There was no need to grow a real one. The blond wig was used as he transformed into Alexander. He wanted to forget everything that happened during the week. It was time to celebrate and then address the task of ruling the world. The bed was round. It made it easier to use every angle. The pillows were used to prompt him up as he read. The tank top he had on was loose and easy to take off. He wore a pair of shorts he liked to work out in.

Hawk buzzed him on his cell phone. It was the signal that meant the woman was about to enter. The book shielded his view and her view of him. She gradually came into view when he started lowering the book. He was taken aback by her beauty. The long auburn-colored hair highlighted her beautiful face. Her waist was narrow, and her breasts were straining against the pink nightgown. Just looking at her caused him to feel aroused. He hoped her personally matched her appearance, but that would wait until later.

"What are you reading?" she asked with a voice that he was surprised how it made him feel like it was only meant for him. Her hand settled on his chest when she crawled into bed next to him.

"*Breaking Cages.*"

"Never heard of it."

"It is written by Charlotte Horlock. This is her first published work. It is about an alien who escapes his planet and eventually has an affair with a married woman. Give me a minute to finish the sex part."

"Oh, want to read it to me."

"Well, my dear, the sex is rough but only because of the alien nature. But she enjoys it."

"Define *rough*."

"He pounds her so hard she has bruises on her legs."

"Does the alien have a long tongue?"

He laughed. "Do you like a good tongue lashing?"

"Of course, if a man can do it right."

The book was put down, and he turned to her. Her beauty had him rock hard. His tongue danced across her nipples, and she moaned. The trip down to her belly button caused an increase in the moans. His fingers entered her, and the slow stoking had her ready for his tongue. She screamed in ecstasy when he started. In a short time, she moaned, "I am about to come," and instantly wrapped her legs around his head. He escaped her headlock.

"Pound me hard, pound me hard," she begged.

It was the wildest ride he ever had. He had trouble staying on. He released into her and fell back onto the bed. She found a towel and slowly toweled him off. Then she started stroking him, and when he revived, she was on top and rode him.

Exhaustion grabbed him after various positions.

They both lay across the bed, looking at the mirror on the ceiling. He turned to her. "That was a great time. What is your name?"

"Yes, it was. It is Rhonda. What is yours?"

He hesitated for a moment. "Alexander."

CHAPTER 16

"St. Louis was destroyed, Mr. President. The surrounding areas are ablaze. We were able to contact the governor. She has sent all the resources they have to the area."

"Contact the governors in the surrounding states and see if they can provide assistance. Charles, any other attacks?"

"Yes, Quebec City was destroyed."

"So far the attacks have been circling the world. Have you heard of attacks in Central American or South America?"

"Nothing to report. Think they are next?"

"I'd be leaving any major city in those areas, Charles. But I'd have no idea where to go. That is what too many are facing. Is the web still visible?"

"Yes, but it is much lower than it was."

"I wish we had a way to communicate with this unknown entity."

"Think that would be helpful?"

"Better than dealing with the unknown, Charles."

"I am not so sure, sir. They could pinpoint your location."

"Charles, I would be surprised if they don't know it now."

Joyce listened to the new plan and nodded in agreement. Hawk had informed them that the celebration would be in the grand hall. A big meal would be served, and then they would exit to the auditorium to broadcast to the world. Adam needed to be contacted to see if their plan was feasible. They only had a few days to get their plan ready. The plan was hampered by the requirements the Führer demanded. He wanted to look over the message the board created for this occasion. The world's reaction to his being the most powerful man in its history was what he wanted acknowledged. She gestured to Violet that she was leaving, and Violet nodded in acknowledgment.

Adam listened to the plan and said, "It could be done, but his coworkers might be an issue."

"How so?"

"Like I mentioned before, the air handlers aren't my responsibility, Joyce. It would look suspicious."

"Yes, they could report it to our security force. I might have to remove you from that department. That work for you, Adam?"

"Only if the plan works. I am willing to risk it if you all are."

"It is now or never, as far as I am concerned," added Allison.

"You know where I stand, Joyce," Megan replied.

"Fuck it." She signaled them to follow her.

Violet was nervous. She knew what happened to anyone who tried and failed to remove the Führer during the war. Her life would end if the plan failed. But millions of others had met their death by this man she used to worship. Cyrus and Martin would arrive soon, and what was left of the world would know who was responsible for the massive destruction. It was difficult to imagine the world wouldn't attempt to destroy them knowing they were humans. The plan they had to stop him was extremely risky. She had lost sleep going over every detail. The bed was cool when she got between the sheets. A glass of wine and a book was her routine before trying to call it a night. But it was difficult to focus on the book. The storyline hadn't taken her mind away from her thoughts of the plan. The buzzing of the phone startled her.

"Hello."

"Violet, I need to talk to you. It is urgent."

"Joyce, can you come here?"

"Yes, I am actually at your door."

Joyce rushed in when the door opened. Violet could tell she was excited.

"What's the matter, Joyce?"

"We got him."

"We got who?"

"We got the Führer and Hawk."

"I am a bit confused. You got the Führer and Hawk? What have you done with them?"

"Violet, the four of us. Adam, Allison, Megan, and I have that under control. I think it best you don't know. We all want you to replace him. You will need to address their absence."

"Thanks for the vote of confidence, but you really don't think I have a need to know?"

"Violet, yes, you should, but the others and I have a personal vendetta with him. I hope you will let us take care of him. He won't be involved anymore, and neither will be Mr. Hawk."

Joyce waited for a response, and she saw Violet smile. "I will leave the task of dealing with those two with you."

"I was hoping you would say that."

"The board will be informed. We have much to plan.

She gazed at the hairless body on the table. The rhythm of his breathing was almost hypnotic. She jumped when someone lightly touched her shoulders. "What are you thinking, Mary?"

"I am thinking of killing you for scaring me, Adam."

"Oh, you can kill Adam as long as John survives."

"I think it is too soon to mention it, Adam."

"Why, Allison, he is on the table and in the drug-induced coma, remember those?"

"You know I don't. I wonder what Joyce has in store for him. Let's wait until she deals with him before we do."

"Yeah, after what he put her through, I can imagine. Okay, you win. I still can't believe how easy it was to subdue him. I am not sure the other plan would have worked."

"Yes, John, it was a surprise."

The sound of his laughter echoed in the room.

"What's so funny?"

"You called me, John."

She hesitated. "Did I?"

He raised his eyebrows and a smirk was on his face made her realize she had.

He didn't smirk for long as Megan and Joyce arrived. Two orderlies followed, and Joyce gave then directions. She nodded to Megan. Megan left, and Adam and Allison followed. Not a word was said until they arrived at their quarters. When they entered and closed the door, Megan signaled for a group hug.

"I need some wine," Megan said as she went to find some.

"Bring two more glasses."

"Ah, you both will have to get your own wine."

"I'll get some. Meet you at the table."

"Thanks, Adam."

"Cheers!" Megan lifted her glass. The clinking of the other two glasses followed.

"I can't believe we did it."

"I agree, Allison. Joyce was in beast mode."

"Beast mode, Adam?"

'It is a term that I heard watching football, Megan. It means someone is extremely determined."

"Well, it does describe her tonight."

"I was shocked the way she took out his bodyguards."

"Yeah, Allison, I didn't expect her to use deadly force, let alone a handgun with a silencer."

"I think she had planned this for quite some time."

"Probably from the time he forced her to be his mistress, Adam. She has insisted that she deal with his elimination."

"Do you have any idea how she will, Megan?"

"No, and I am not going to ask. It is better we don't know, and the less mentioned about tonight, the better."

"I can understand that reasoning. Now what happens?"

"That will be left to the board to decide."

"I wonder what is up."

"Good question, Charlotte. Not often do we get the Code 1 meeting."

"It has been a while, Connie."

"I think that 'been a while' has been at least fifteen years, Diana."

"Tessa is correct," they heard as Violet walked in.

"But this Code 1 will be the top reason to activate it. I have been informed our plan for the Führer's removal is no longer needed. He has been removed, as has Mr. Hawk."

The group looked stunned. Diana was the first to respond. "How did that happen without us knowing?"

"Joyce went rogue on us but does not want to bypass us for leadership. She just wants to deal with him. I think you can all imagine why. I think we can allow that."

"Will we find out what happens to him?"

"I think Joyce will share the news, Tessa. Now we have some very serious issues we need to deal with. The situation is now on us. We have Cyrus and Martin arriving soon. The world is in limbo waiting on us and trying to survive. There are some troops that have been doing tasks, and they only answered Adolf. Did I miss anything?"

"Yes, how long do you think we can pull this off before he and Hawk are missed?"

"I think since I have been shown in the chain of command, we can do this. Remember, only a few of the complex know who the Decider was. Mr. Hawk never shown his face. The troops who Adolf addressed know I was the presenter, and I believe will accept any version of his being absent. They also don't have the resources to interfere with what we need to do. We can deploy them anywhere under his name. Now what do we tell the world?"

"I think we demand the world to make changes. One unified government."

"I think that is a good start, Diana. Let's make it a world led by women. The men sure have fucked it up."

"I agree, Charlotte, there is so much work to do to regain the world's trust."

"I don't know if that is a good thing at this time. We need the world to fear us to get things done."

"Good point, Connie, I think you all make good points. I think it is time to send another message. Do you agree?"

The group nodded in agreement.

"Okay then," Violet said. "Let's do it the way we completed the first one."

Joyce watched as they started the Phase Z process on Adolf. He was to remain unconscious during the complete process. It would take a few weeks to complete. She had complete confidence it would be. The staff didn't recognize him, and she would closely monitor the procedure. Plus, with Hawk paired in the process, the identity of Adolf is less likely to be discovered.

"Mr., President, we could be getting a message. The blank white screen has changed."

"Thanks, Charles," he said as he went to the main monitor.

"People of earth!" caused them all to react with a nervous jump due to sudden and loud message. The voice was computer generated.

"The time for you to regroup and survive is now. If you don't accept our demands, you will be destroyed. We demand that you develop one central government. That government will be led by women, and it needs to be formed by six months so we can communicate. We won't interfere unless there is chaos in parts of the world. Those areas will be removed. Air flights will be reinstated but closely monitored. Any attempt to create military action will cause a deadly response. The future of the planet is uncertain. It depends on your response."

The room was quiet when the monitor returned to the blank screen. The president looked toward Charles. "Any comments?"

"We are doomed."

Joyce felt the eyes of the baby staring at her. *Could he know what was going on?* That thought rolled about in her mind. Maybe she should have killed him like she decided to do with Hawk. She hoped a new environment and loving family would mold him into a man whose potential would be realized for good endeavors. She had a couple lined up who wanted a child and had the means to provide in this troubled time. The hallway she was on ended, and she parked her cart. She entered the group home and waited in the living room waiting for the couple to arrive. Adolf let out a cry, and she reached and got a bottle out of the baby bag. He started to devour the milk. "I see your table manners haven't improved, Adolf."

She laughed at her statement. A car enter the driveway, and she opened the door. "Is this the baby, Joyce?"

"Of course, he is waiting for you to name him, Judy."

"Look, Carl. What do you want to name your son?"

Joyce looked at them. "I hate to rush you off, but I must get back to my work. He is your son. His parents are deceased. We need no further contact. I hope you both have a great experience."

They thanked her, and she watched them leave. "I finally got the bastard, Eva."

The End

ABOUT THE AUTHOR

LINDA AND GARY ARE MARRIED and raised a family. He has worked in the maintenance field, but he was primarily a boiler operator. This is his first published book. He has written another unpublished book. The idea for this came to him as he drove by a group of wind turbines. The rest of the book was written by the seat of his pants, so to speak. He didn't follow any plan.